Pemberley Beach

by Elizabeth Famous

"Follies and nonsense, whims and inconsistencies do divert me, I own, and I laugh at them whenever I can."

Jane Austen

Dedication

For my oh so lovable kids, who have challenged me in every imaginable way: physically, emotionally, morally, intellectually, artistically... Please actively take care of each other and keep it in the forefront of your minds how charming and fascinating you are. Don't be like me and miss your mom every single day; you need to be strong to follow your dreams.

Chapter One

Looking back, it was all her mom's fault. If not for her plotting and scheming, Elizabeth would not have run into Will Darcy at Netherfield that night. And her sister Jane might never have fallen for his friend Bingley.

From the balcony, party guests could see all the way to the boardwalk of downtown Derby, a whirl of spiraling lights and movement like a bright pink Barbie beach club. The boxy modern behemoths of Ocean Drive gracefully intermixed with the town's stately Victorians from this far-off point of view. Derby's most famous landmark, the striped Netherfield

Lighthouse, was just next door, on the eastern tip of Netherfield Island. So close you could run a clothes line over.

Elizabeth skimmed her fingers along the scalloped shingles of the exterior wall of Netherfield House. As she reached the corner, she rounded the bend to the other arm of the mansion's fourth-floor wraparound balcony. She had remained outside for most of the town's weekly fireworks display, watching Bingley and Jane as they stood as close as possible without touching.

She'd done a bang-up job as wingwoman, but she didn't want to push her luck at not tipping over the spiked iron railing. So during a pause in booms, she waved goodbye to Jane, not calling her a little minx in front of Bingley; that would have to wait 'til later.

To get out on the balcony for the fireworks, Elizabeth had used a propped-open stained glass window at the gable end of the L-shaped balcony — doors were blocked by renovations. Returning to the same spot, she reached her leg over the window's sill, gingerly put her weight on the top rung of a step ladder set up inside the house, then turned, grabbing the side rails, and stepped down one rung.

Glancing behind her, she prepared to dismount onto the scuffed parquet of the fourth-floor hall when Will Darcy came out of a hidden doorway and walked right into her path.

He halted and she froze, clinging to the ladder, about one

foot off the ground.

She said nothing.

"After you," he said, with an unhurried wave of his arm.

You've got to be kidding me. The last time she'd seen him was a glimpse years ago at the town carnival, but she'd never spoken to him or even come face-to-face with him before.

Her foot slipped, and her ankle came down hard on the floor just as Darcy reached to grab her under her left arm, softening her landing.

Feeling like a klutz, she rushed to move out of his grasp, straightening her thrift-shop dress.

His arm fell to his side, but he didn't recoil otherwise, despite brushing the shaved skin of her underarm.

She turned away, her eyes falling on dark velvet drapes. They were standing together in an oval alcove at the end of the hall. Netherfield had more bump outs and odd shaped rooms than staircases, and it had seven staircases.

"Are you alright?" His sedate drawl was distant yet polite.

"Uh. I'm fine," she mumbled. "I shouldn't have skipped that ladder safety course."

The impression left on her arm by his steely grip stung a bit, but oh my god, his defined features read so handsome up close.

She knew Will Darcy by sight, as any born and raised Derby resident did. But she also knew him by reputation. He was a total snob who had nothing to do with her family, the Bennets, or anyone he perceived as wannabes.

Behind Darcy, a young man with pavé diamond earrings materialized, striding up to Elizabeth. "Hey kid, hang with me and you won't have to climb ladders anymore. I'm Cornel. You?"

What the hell? Common sense required avoiding Darcys and this was another one.

Cornel was Will's cousin, a member of the slightly less rich but showier branch of the Darcy family. Cornel dug his hands into the pockets of his pressed cargo shorts. "Wait a minute. You're Jane Bennet's sister, aren't you?"

"Yes," she chuckled. "I'm Elizabeth, but you can call me Jane's sister if you like."

Forcing a smile, she groaned internally at being identified, but Will Darcy did not betray any symptom of surprise at the news he was among unsavory company. Had she already been pointed out to him as a Bennet?

"Have you been over to see the lighthouse?" asked Cornel with a friendly accent. "Bingley carried your sister over. She was worried about her shoes. I can offer you my carrying services if you like." With a wolfish grin, he added, "Or any other services."

Will Darcy turned on his cousin, frowning.

"I might walk over," said Elizabeth, studying Cornel's expression in search of any of the condescension present in Will's. "But I haven't been carried in years and I don't want to relapse tonight."

Cornel smiled sloppily. Perhaps he thought Bingley was going to get lucky that night so he'd go for leftovers in the form of Jane's sister. No one would fault him. Her extended family's reputation as romantic mercenaries who slept with rich men to pay the bills had been the work of many generations — her aunt Phyllis Bennet hitting a high note with her successful pursuit of a Darcy, but that was another story.

"I'm heading downstairs for a glass of water," said Elizabeth, wanting to duck out before there could be any crass mention of her family. "Can I get you two something?" she offered with a chirp, hoping they'd say no. "A cup of coffee maybe?" she asked Cornel, who looked three sheets to the wind.

"Let me find a waiter," Cornel insisted, referring to the staff Bingley had hired but who were probably partying themselves by now given their good-natured employer. "We can find you something stronger than water."

Yes, encouraging Cornel Darcy might be a tiny bit tempting. She wasn't immune to the glamour of his life. She could imagine what it would be like to be welcomed at the door of the Derby Yacht Club. She would never know unless she hooked up with some guy like Cornel.

Nope. Wasn't going to happen. She'd come too far to go down that road. "I'm perfectly fine with a glass of tap water from the kitchen. I'm heading down there now, so..."

"Or there's a stocked wine fridge one flight below in the china room," Will said in a flat, nearly robotic voice, supplying information like a computerized voice over the telephone.

Will Darcy was known for speaking to only those with whom he was socially aligned. Interacting with her must be a punishment for him.

Elizabeth smiled and said, "Thanks, I'll take a bottle of juice or whatever's alcohol free."

His striking grey eyes went wide with skepticism.

She stared back at him. The idea of sending Mr. Imperious off on an errand made her flush all over, but she told herself not to laugh openly at him.

Cornel had no such scruples and laughed as Will made a slight bow and plodded down the hallway toward the grand central staircase.

While Will was off fetching her a drink, Cornel seemed eager to chat and talked about the nuisance of owning a house situated on an island like Bingley.

"Of course, Will's place is in a class of its own," said Cornel, "but unlike his oceanfront property at Pemberley, I'm safe from storms inland at Rosings."

"I take the road bordering Rosings Park on my way to work," said Elizabeth. "I teach nearby at West Derby Elementary."

"Really?" said Cornel. "I never would have guessed you're

a teacher." He sounded a bit turned off.

"Don't worry. I'm off duty."

Earlier that evening, when she picked through the pink storage boxes in her closet in search of summer clothes, she envisioned going to the party at Netherfield Mansion and meeting a guy but certainly hadn't imagined hanging with Derby's version of landed gentry.

Will Darcy returned the way he came, giving Elizabeth a chance to check out the front of his long-limbed body in motion.

With outstretched arm, he delivered a bottle of lemon-flavored Perrier.

"Thank you," she said. "You're so kind."

"You're welcome," he said softly, his shoulders back.

Unscrewing the cap, Elizabeth took a sip, watching and waiting for them to excuse themselves.

Cornel leaned in, the smell of beer on his breath. "You don't exactly look like your sister. Are you two really sisters?"

She was, in fact, all around darker than Jane, so he wasn't the first to suspect they weren't full-blooded siblings. He was probably referring to how Bennet women were known for having children by three or four different men. "Uh, what about you two ... are you certain you're cousins ... I mean, have you done a DNA test?"

Cornel barked a laugh.

Darcy huffed. "Maybe you should go see if Bingley needs

any assistance, Cornel."

"I'm pretty sure he doesn't need assistance with the ladies," Cornel answered with a smirk.

Elizabeth laughed self-consciously. The absurdity of her hobnobbing with two Darcy men struck her. Imagine if it were real and not the result of an accidental near-miss collision.

Will looked down at her from his fine, tall, perfectly proportioned person. "Miss Bennet, with your permission, I'd like to have your Vespa moved. I just got a text from the valet saying he mistakenly directed you to park it in an inconvenient location."

How abrupt ... was he hinting that she and Jane had stayed too long? True, the fireworks had ended, and partiers were starting to file back inside through various tall windows, so maybe she should be going. "Oh, sure, I'll move it right away. It's probably time I get going." She was willing to accede to his request and atone if she and her sister were lollygagging.

"I didn't mean to hasten your departure," said Darcy, sounding less sluggish, "but your bike is blocked by Caroline's Benz. I can reverse the two, so this won't become an issue when you're ready to leave."

Caroline was the sister of Bingley, the new Netherfield owner. Elizabeth and Jane had just met both Bingley and Caroline Townsend earlier that night. Will Darcy must be a close friend of theirs.

"Oh, I see," said Elizabeth. "Well, in any case, I should probably find Jane. It's getting late."

His only response was a stare.

He was confusing as hell. His words were polite but his manners cold, with flashes of lukewarm.

Elizabeth shrugged. "The last time I saw Jane she was outside on the terrace, so I'll climb back outside—"

"I believe your sister and Bingley were heading down to look over the basements," Will interrupted, "But Cornel and I can have your vehicle moved for you if you give me the keys."

Elizabeth hesitated. "Uh..."

"Shucks," said Cornel with a leer. "I was hoping you'd climb up and down the ladder again."

She rolled her eyes at him. Cornel had no sincere interest in her beyond buzzed lust, and in any case, she wasn't attracted to overt cheesiness.

Will Darcy looked at her expectantly.

She snapped back to reality, digging her key ring out of her deep dress pocket. "Be careful, okay? No joyriding."

He didn't smile, but he didn't look nettled either.

She depended on her vehicle to carry musical instruments to and from work and normally wouldn't hand over her keys to anyone. But Darcy wasn't the kind of guy who'd scratch curse words into a paint job. He was more of a reluctant sommelier moonlighting as an anal-retentive parking attendant.

"It's time to bounce," Elizabeth whispered in her sister's ear after finding her in the basement watching Bingley play pool.

"Oh, Lizzy, tell me you had fun," said Jane. "I feel like I abandoned you."

"It's okay, you can make it up to me with a play-by-play rundown of your evening." Elizabeth glanced at Bingley who was chalking a pool cue.

"Oh my gosh, he's so charming," Jane whispered with a blush. "Don't you think?"

"That's to be determined," said Elizabeth with a head bobble. "Does he keep his hands to himself?"

"He's a perfect gentleman."

Jane told Bingley they had to go, refusing to give in to his pleas to stay longer.

Conceding, he smiled at both of them without the slightest artificiality. "Elizabeth, it was so nice to meet you. Thank you for coming. I'm sorry if I monopolized Jane!"

Bingley's sister Caroline was as phony as her brother was sincere but made the effort to say goodbye personally, chatting with Jane about where to get her nails done and side-eying Elizabeth.

The boat ferrying them from Netherfield Island back to the mainland was captained by a bearded elderly man in a gold-buttoned uniform. He told them about the famous 1817 shipwreck near Netherfield Lighthouse as he intentionally rocked the boat for the entire three-minute journey.

The boat's padded fenders hit the dock with a thud, and Elizabeth spotted her Vespa parked by the side of the overlong driveway and jumped off the pontoon. Jane lagged behind, assisted off the boat by the captain.

Will Darcy sat on a bench at the land end of the gangway, and, as Elizabeth approached, he stood up as if he'd been waiting for her.

She ought to go overboard with thanks but instead said, "I worried you'd sold my bike to a chop shop. You've been gone for almost half an hour."

He didn't seem taken aback. "It's safe and sound," he said flatly.

"Thank you," she answered with a smile.

In a low voice only she could hear, he added, "Excuse my cousin if he was a bit out of line earlier. He didn't mean to be inappropriate, I promise you. I took him home to sleep off the drink." Darcy had a naval officer's posture. Stiff and commanding.

"Oh, it was nothing," said Elizabeth, having already forgotten Cornel's innuendos.

She wondered if Darcy was congratulating himself on getting his cousin away from her. "But now that you've gotten

Cornel home safely, who's going to babysit *you* for the remainder of the evening, Darcy?"

His mouth fell open as he was momentarily knocked out of his preternatural calm. "What?" he sputtered.

She laughed, telling herself to cut it out before she caused a scene.

Jane, who was standing ten feet away next to the Vespa, gave her a questioning look.

Darcy stood motionless, a slight luster to his skin. "Everyone calls me Will. Not 'Darcy.'"

"Oh, it's no problem at all, Darcy." She chuckled at her own joke.

He reached into his shirt pocket, his grim expression back on. "Here are your keys, Miss Bennet."

At school she tried to get her students to call her Miss Elizabeth instead of using her notorious last name, but out of his mouth "Miss Bennet" sounded quaint, his mild Southern drawl so old school.

"Thanks again," she said, ducking out.

After skipping over to Jane, to whom she gave the extra helmet, she hopped onto her bike, kick-started the engine, and they headed home to their family's sunny yellow trailer parked along dribbling Longbourn Creek.

#

Pulling her hair into a ponytail, Elizabeth walked into the

kitchen, morning sun streaming through the small sliding windows at the back of the mobile home. She poured a glass of orangeade, and her bare feet stuck to the linoleum floor where beer spilled the night before.

"Not even a text!" Lydia, her younger sister, plopped on the sofa eating a Pop-Tart. "How was I supposed to know there'd be so many guys there?"

Jane sat next to Lydia. Her lips were nude and her hair unbrushed but she still looked like a snowy Christmas tree angel ready for deification. "Oh dear Lydia. Mom told us all to go. Don't you remember?"

Ever since news spread of a recent Duke Law School grad named Bingley Townsend purchasing the whole of Netherfield Island, their mother had been giddy with plans to snatch him up. So when they heard Bingley was going around town inviting every twenty-something he met to a house party at Netherfield, their mom proclaimed that her daughters "absolutely must attend, particularly Jane."

"If I knew Will Darcy would be there," exclaimed Lydia, "I would have come with you. I definitely wouldn't have stayed so late at Foxy's."

Foxy's was a roadside bar which, along with a one-pump gas station, made up the main drag of the Longbourn section of Derby. The only other landmark in the area was a giant neon sign announcing "Longbourn Creek Estates." Longbourn trailer park had no access to the ocean and was separated from the affluent parts of Derby by a four-lane divided freeway. Locals made jokes about not running over "trailer park girls crossing the road."

Charlotte Lucas and her sister Mariah appeared at the screen door, knocking on the aluminum trim.

Elizabeth rushed to greet them. "Hey, you're just in time to discuss Bingley's party."

"But of course," said Charlotte, who lived with her family a few doors down from the Bennets in a modern, extra-long mobile home.

Elizabeth hugged her friend. "Where were you last night? I looked for you all over. I thought you wouldn't want to face the crowd alone."

"Sorry. I had to leave early. My dad couldn't get the cable TV to work, and the game was on. But Mariah stayed."

"I have so much to tell. And you won't believe it," said Mariah, who'd recently turned twenty-one and celebrated with a BBQ of cheese dogs and iced wine.

"Well, unless you fucked Bingley," said Lydia, "you ain't got nuthin' on Jane."

"Oh Jane," said Charlotte, standing on a worn patch of shag carpet. "What an eventful evening you had! Everyone's talking about you and Bingley."

Jane got up to water an English ivy hanging by a suction

hook over the kitchen sink. She didn't like to be the center of attention, although she usually was.

"We were the first from Longbourn to arrive at the party," said Mariah, loud enough for everyone in the low-ceilinged room to hear.

"Who was there?" asked Lydia.

"Will Darcy and his country club crowd," Mariah replied. "I texted you about it."

This brought on a heated argument from Lydia, who insisted she'd never received the text.

"Anyway," said Charlotte, trying to get her sister back on track, "it wasn't just Will Darcy at the party but his cousin Cornel and old friends he's been hanging out with at the yacht club since returning to Derby."

"Returning to Derby? Has he been away?" Elizabeth just realized that perhaps the reason she hadn't seen or heard of Will Darcy in the past year or so wasn't only that she'd been busy wrangling eight dozen elementary school students.

"He was working on some project in Europe for almost two years," said Charlotte. "Did Bingley tell you about it, Jane?"

"Yes, he said he and Will met in a calculus class at MIT undergrad, and he was glad Will had come back home to Derby because he needed help with Netherfield construction permits." Her voice trailed off as she looked like she was trying to remember something.

"I didn't realize," said Elizabeth. Her family normally did not spend time with the affluent Derby crowd.

"That's because you have no life, Lizzy," said Lydia. "All you do is work."

"I could work less if I didn't have to pay your cell phone bill." Elizabeth was the only one in the family with a good salary, so she paid for all their phones on a family plan.

"He was in France, I believe," said Mariah. "Before this month, he hadn't been in Derby for over a year except for a short visit when his sister Georgiana was ill this past April."

The Lucas sisters were amazingly helpful with facts and specifics.

"What was wrong with his sister?" asked Elizabeth.

"Nobody knows," said Charlotte. "She was away for her first year at college and came home for two weeks in April. All we heard was that she was sick and recovering at Pemberley."

"Oh, fuck Georgiana Darcy," Lydia exclaimed, "tell us about the party."

Mariah leaned against the back of an overstuffed rocking recliner. "Well, after Jane and Lizzy arrived, I was standing in the kitchen, and I overheard Cornel Darcy mentioned to Will that some *Bennet girls* were in attendance. He was all cool about it. *'Jane is looking well. I haven't seen her in years.'*"

When Jane and Darcy were in high school together, she once saw him at a football game and he nodded to her, followed by an awkward silence during which they were left alone together for five minutes. However, Jane insisted he'd been friendly to her at Netherfield and conversed with her about horses and sailing.

"He *must* have noticed how much Bingley liked you," said Elizabeth, who'd been getting tidbits from Jane ever since they arrived home the night before.

"Bingley was very kind," said Jane. "But you shouldn't overstate—"

"He spoke to you half the evening, ignoring people who were hoping to talk to him about his restoration plans for Netherfield," said Elizabeth.

Jane blushed. "Lizzy, you won't convince me to see it as more than one nice evening with a pleasant man."

Mariah bounced onto the couch next to Lydia. "I have much more to tell if you two will let me talk."

"Spit it out," said Lydia, "We don't have all day." Her hand hung over the side of the armrest as if she might collapse from boredom listening to stories about a party she didn't attend.

"Well, I overheard someone talking about how Jane was 'the hottest Bennet girl,'" said Mariah. "I couldn't tell for sure who was speaking."

"That's nothing new," said Elizabeth impishly. "Anyone could have told you that." She studied Jane's placid face, trying to gauge her sister's feelings for Bingley even as Jane refused to acknowledge the extent of his interest in her.

"What about me?" Lydia pouted. "What did they say about me?"

"Foster asked if you were around," said Mariah, "and seemed disappointed when I said you weren't."

Lydia cheered up. "Oh, he's such a flirt. He does like me a lot. But I hate his truck. That awful beat-up thing. It's worse than Mama's pickup."

Their mother, who had already congratulated Jane on her progress with Bingley, was at a church pancake breakfast.

"I'm not sure if I should mention it," said Mariah hesitantly, "but there was one more thing I overheard before they noticed me."

"What is it?" exclaimed Lydia. "Go on!"

Mariah looked at Elizabeth. "Do you recall when you were in the conservatory talking to that girl from your college?"

"Yes," said Elizabeth. "Right after we arrived." This was well before her run-in with Darcy by the ladder. She had not noticed him in the crowded rooms downstairs.

Mariah twisted her mouth. "Well, Cornel pointed you out as one of the Bennets, and you won't believe what Will said."

Even Jane wanted to know. "Please, do tell us, Mariah. Unless, well, if you don't have something nice to say…"

Elizabeth prepared herself.

Mariah put on a ridiculous *Gone with the Wind* accent, "*I didn't realize there was a plain Bennet girl. That one won't tempt anyone to ruin."*

Mariah's face turned bright red as she watched Elizabeth slump into a chair. "Sorry," she mumbled.

Wincing, Jane asked, "Mariah, are you sure you heard ...?"

"Oh, yes, it was clear as day," said Mariah.

Charlotte frowned at her younger sister. "Maybe you ought to have kept that bit to yourself."

After getting past the momentary shock, Elizabeth forced a laugh. "I had thought I looked good last night — and even thought I'd made some progress establishing peace with Will Darcy. How presumptuous of him! The reason for my existence is to tempt him?" She shrugged her shoulders, her heartbeat accelerating.

It's not like she had thought Will was attracted to her when they spoke while standing by the ladder, or on the dock when he handed over her keys. But at the same time, she definitely hadn't thought that he'd found her particularly unappealing either. Sure, there was an awkwardness, but did that mean he was repulsed by her?

"He wouldn't be worth listening to if he wasn't the greatest catch in town," said Charlotte. "I'm lucky. No one would ever ask Will Darcy what he thinks of me. He's never even noticed me."

Elizabeth looked up at Charlotte, happy to bathe in her

friend's satirical countenance. "Ah Mr. Darcy, so great and yet so out of reach. It must be lonely at the top. I feel for him."

Jane stifled a laugh.

Elizabeth straightened her faded "Woodstock Music Festival" tee as if it were a designer top. "It would seem my plan to hook him is doomed to failure."

"That was unkind of him," said Jane, "but you know it has more to do with his bitterness toward our family than anything else."

"He has a legitimate gripe, you know," said Elizabeth, feeling hyper like a one-liner comedian. "Someone as good-looking as him shouldn't be forced to mingle with those of inferior cheekbones."

For a moment she thought about how her aunt had damaged Darcy's parents' marriage and perhaps Will's happy home life as a kid. Aunt Phyllis, who could have been Jane's double except for the age difference distinguishing them, had a one-night stand years ago with Darcy's father, and everyone in these parts still felt the consequences of it.

Elizabeth pushed that thought aside. Whatever legitimate complaints Will Darcy had about her aunt's machinations, insulting her looks wasn't going to make her sympathetic.

"Don't let him get under your skin, Lizzy," said Charlotte, clearly eager to rally her. "If it weren't for all the things his money can buy, anyone who ended up with him would be miserable."

"Seriously," said Elizabeth, not allowing her voice to drop to a somber bass-clef range. "I don't see what all the obsession with him is about. So he's rich." She shrugged. "There are hundreds of rich men in Derby and not all of them are egotistical jerks. Am I right? And personally, all I'm looking for is a plain old normal sort of nice guy."

"Poor Lizzy," said Lydia, shaking her head as she reached for the TV remote. "I've never heard anyone call you ugly before. I promise to make Pratt dance with you at Foxy's Friday night."

"One thing is for sure," said Elizabeth. "I'll never dance with Will Darcy."

Chapter Two

One week prior to the party at Netherfield, as Will sat with a group of friends in the yacht club's Osprey dining room, a stunning all-American blonde glanced across the room and beamed at him. After an introduction and a minute's conversation about mutual acquaintances, he knew she was his for the taking. He could, whenever he liked, reap the benefits of his name and place in the world, even if both were given at birth and unearned.

Following cocktails and three courses, he led his lithe admirer outside, escorting her on a midnight stroll along the boardwalk. Taking her hand, he ate up the view of her soft symmetrical features. He was going to taste her later — nothing too theatrical, but it would last satisfactorily long.

Stopping across from the Prince Albert Hotel on the corner of Charleston Street, he stretched and felt a pulling ache in his bicep. "I was thrown from my horse yesterday," he admitted with a slight frown.

"Oh, poor baby, are you injured?" she exclaimed. "Maybe something's broken!"

He averted his face, amused by the idea of a broken bone going undetected for thirty-six hours.

She brushed her hand against the outside of his hip bone, pressing her breast against his upper arm. "You must be done in."

"No, not at all," he assured her. "I could stay up all night. I've been resting at home most of the day."

She sprang to her toes excitedly. "At Pemberley?"

"The main Pemberley house is occupied by my parents," he said flatly, not elaborating.

Ever since his teens, his dates had asked questions about Pemberley, such as whether he'd inherit the entire estate when his parents passed away, primogenitor style, or have to split it with his sister Georgiana. He rarely indulged them with more than a monosyllabic answer. Remaining mute on the subject might be brusque, but it was better than saying what was actually on the tip of his tongue when asked such morbid questions.

"So you live in town?" she asked.

"No, on Pemberley grounds. I have a small ranch of my own near the horse paddock."

She nodded thoughtfully, frowning, then suddenly rebounded, "Your parents' house is magnificent, like Tara come to life! How did you drag yourself away from it?"

"Do *you* live with your parents? It would be awkward at my age, don't you think?"

"I live with my parents, but I'm never home," she replied.

"When have you seen Pemberley?" he asked distractedly, imagining her naked on her hands and knees in front of him, a small fire in the hearth, for light, as they assumed the position on the rug in his den.

"Last summer," she answered. "We vacation in Derby every year, and last July I was invited to the Darcy Family Reunion by your cousin Wickham." She looked proud.

"Wickham George?" He'd known Wickham since they were boys, but they were no longer on speaking terms.

She nodded.

He frowned, slowing his step.

"I was so disappointed to learn you were overseas," she said, "but everyone said you were building houses in Tuscany, France. How exciting!"

He wondered if she could find Tuscany on a map — not if

she looked in France.

"Wickham's your cousin, isn't he?" she asked.

"No. He's perhaps a very distant relative by marriage. I'm related in some way to almost every longstanding family in Derby if you go back far enough, but I definitely wouldn't call him family."

She looked undeterred. "Yes, your family is so huge. I've never seen so many people at a party before and still half the rooms were empty. And no one but Wickham and me went upstairs! I couldn't believe how gigantic Pemberley was when I was there."

"It's still the same size," he said coolly. Generally, Will avoided dating women who had been previously involved with other men of his acquaintance. An old-fashioned hang up to be sure. In the specific case of Wickham George, there was additional cause for concern.

But as long as she didn't start commenting on Wickham's physiognomy, and he used a condom, he might possibly overlook her past relations with Wickham for the sake of the stirring in his loins.

She looked far ahead, up the coast, the continuity of which was broken by inlets visible in the low light of a crescent moon.

"So, are we walking toward Jekyll Island?" she asked. "My sister-in-law has a house there."

"No, Georgia is south of here. Since the ocean is on our right, we're walking north, toward Pemberley. If the ocean were on our left, we'd be walking south."

They reached a portion of the boardwalk skirting the main Derby Beach. During daytime hours, the now deserted dark gray expanse was alive with families crowded under umbrellas, sunbathers on towels, and scaffold-like lifeguard chairs positioned thirty feet apart. A patchwork of noise, fried food, and gaudy color combinations Will assiduously avoided.

Directly to their right stood a stack of lounge chairs behind a sign that read "Tags required from 8 am to 5 pm" and a tented cabana with "Old Pemberley Hotel" fashioned on the side in curly font.

"So this is *your* beach?" She coquettishly smiled up at him — he was a foot taller than she was in heels.

"No, this land hasn't been ours for many years," he said. "It's the public beach, as I'm sure you know. The extent of our current property doesn't start for three-quarters of a mile."

Pointing northeast, he added, "But a good friend of mine from college just purchased that Victorian up the way on Netherfield Island."

The island sat only a few hundred feet offshore. On its eastern-most tip was the striped blue and white lighthouse with a pulsing yellow light on top.

"Oh." She looked confused. "That's his house ... with the

light on top?"

"The Netherfield Lighthouse? No, he's renovating the Queen Anne style home on the other side of the island."

"Doesn't anyone live in the lighthouse?"

"Not that I know of," said Will.

"Isn't it strange that they call it a house but no one lives there?"

Will began to feel the late hour. "A keep once lived there, but, thanks to automation, that's no longer necessary."

"Can we sneak over and climb up to the top of it?" she asked. "We could look out at the ocean and try to spot dolphins!"

He frowned and tried not to let his voice betray his boredom. "Sneaking over would require a boat because it's on an island, and there's not much to see at night, unless you want to look inland at the town."

She frowned then pointed out to sea. "But look! I see something."

He saw only a dark blue expanse.

"Isn't that a boat?" she pointed again, in a slight southerly direction.

"No, I believe that's a buoy," he said. "A floating marker."

"But there's a cute little light on top," she exclaimed, absurdly eager to be pleased with what she saw. "I wonder how they plug it in way out there."

He just stared at her, chin down. They had stopped

walking.

"And what's that? Look! That's definitely a boat!" She pointed at a tiny craft bobbing in the waves near a rock jetty.

"That's a lifeguard's dinghy," he answered coolly.

"It's so cute! If we went up to the top of your friend's lighthouse, I'm sure we'd have a better view of it." She smiled at him triumphantly.

He gave her a perplexed look.

Her interest in climbing the lighthouse hopefully indicated a desire to be alone with him, but perhaps it was more an attempt to counter the know-it-all twang of his voice, a fault he was well aware of and which had caused him trouble before.

His shoulders sank, his eyelids feeling heavy.

Back at the restaurant where they had commenced their stroll sat a luxury marina with yachts from all over the world, and this woman was impressed by a dinghy.

He offered to drive her home.

During the ride she put her hand on his thigh, and when he walked her to the pink tiled doorstep of her family's rental she initiated a kiss that went on and on. He exhaled through his nose as her warm body pressed against him, his hand immodestly sliding down to the curve of her backside. Breaking away from her embrace, he thanked her for the privilege of her company and dragged himself back to his Aston Martin parked at the curb and drove himself home.

It wasn't going to happen. He could not pretend that he wanted her for anything more than sex. If they dated, she'd annoy him with her dimwitted, uninformed comments. Eventually, she'd catch on and notice as he turned away in disgust. He was hopeless at guile. Even if he could hold back on making snide remarks for a few weeks and enjoy her, it would be excruciating to break things off when the time came. To be a gentleman and do it properly required sensibility he couldn't vouch for, and the thought of trying to comfort her through lamentations was not only draining but demeaning.

"Considering she slept with Wickham, I shouldn't be surprised she's into dinghies," he said to his collies, Shire and Felix, as they lapped at his hand, wanting to be let out the side door of his house.

He opened the tempered glass slider, following the dogs out into the cool night air.

All he wanted was to gratify his libido, but instead he spent another evening resenting his own scruples.

There was no reason that a man, even one such as himself, couldn't be satisfied with the company of a pleasant, nice-looking young woman from a decent family. He ought not waste time with women in whom he saw only alluring beauty and not a modicum of long-term potential. It was beneath him.

After sniffing the grass, his dogs roamed far, chasing branches that rustled in the breeze. The dogs had the advantage of open space, untouched woods, rocky terrain abutting the ocean, and a solitary beach only a hundred yards off. Not once had a Darcy of Pemberley put a dog on a leash and paraded it down the flagstone sidewalks of downtown Derby.

Will's animals were blessed with the opportunity to run at top speed, jump into streams, and tussle recklessly in the sand. Just as Will himself had done as a child.

A map of Pemberley's five miles of undeveloped seaside property was imprinted on his brain, and at twenty-eight, Will was for all intents and purposes the hands-on overseer in charge of the estate's upkeep as his father settled into undeclared retirement.

He glanced back at the brass lanterns that marked the front walk of his small modern home set among pecan trees, breathing in the smell of sweetbay magnolias. The Pemberley fan he had wanted to have sex with that evening was more of an ornamental hothouse flower than a local bloom.

Flings and dalliances with women like her no longer made sense. Once his erection was satisfied, regret took the place of pleasure. When his date from Saturday night contacted him Wednesday afternoon expecting more, he was ashamed of his struggle to muster up the enthusiasm required to meet for coffee. He must only date women who could hold his interest, or at the very least, toward whom he was not baldly disdainful.

The town of Derby, despite all its favorable attributes, had a reputation for being inhabited by two sorts of women. On the one hand, there were wealthy tourists, like his dinghy-loving date, who came for the luxury spa services, designer shops, and posh boutique hotels that booked for $1,000 a night. On the other hand, there were native-born gold diggers who considered being on the prowl a full-time occupation and did not bother with employment involving hourly wages.

Of course the gold digger trope was both sexist and outdated. Notorious local families like the Bennets of Longbourn Creek were remnants of the past, of the days when Southern men of a certain background went out on their wives as sport. Unlike so-called Longbourn trailer park trash, most local girls came from respectable families and didn't swim topless whenever the urge took hold, or sneak into hotel bars to pray upon men who overindulged. There were women Will's age who volunteered at the senior center and looked nice if not knock-out gorgeous like his companion that evening at the yacht club. It was possible to find someone to date regularly, not just hook up with.

Inside for the night, the doors locked and the dogs sprawled out on the bedroom floor, Will collapsed on bleached white sheets. Not bothering to undress, he only removed his shoes. Taking off his clothes would remind him of his unfulfilled carnal desires.

Lying face down, his belt buckle cut into his abs and his

shirt untucked as he turned in bed, cool air tickling his back, his pants-waist sliding down his pelvic bone.

Tomorrow, after the investors meeting at the credit union, he'd return a call from Anne de Bourgh, a longstanding friend of the family who'd recently graduated from Bryn Mawr and left a message for him with his father's secretary. She was the type of woman he should be dating.

He was back home in Derby, employed in real estate development ventures -- one of which was just about to break ground -- and acting as steward of Pemberley. If an eligible woman presented herself, he was going to do as every other male heir in his family had done and set down roots. A girlfriend would not only be preferable to being tormented by lust, but a relationship, as opposed to a pointless sex romp with a stunning woman who gratified his ego, was the rational choice. He would not be spending his nights with a young woman who didn't know the Atlantic Ocean was east of the Eastern seaboard.

Chapter Three

Elizabeth's first year teaching instrumental music at West Derby Elementary had wrapped with a rousing rendition of "Hot Cross Buns" performed before a discriminating audience of parents and grandparents who jumped to their feet in a standing ovation as she cut off the last note. After the concert, she was approached by the music director of Wintergreen School of Music and offered a summer job on the spot.

On Monday after the party at Netherfield, she started her part-time position teaching small group music lessons to junior high school students on woodwind and brass instruments. A great job except for the squeaking of beginner sax.

If Mariah Lucas hadn't overheard Will Darcy casting aspersions on her looks, Elizabeth would have thought she looked good when she caught her reflection in the glass door on her way into the studio. As it was, she felt bleh.

Pulling a bag of M&Ms out of her super-sized tote bag loaded with drumsticks, reeds, dampers, and turkey feathers, she placed the candy on a heavy black music stand, which she dragged front and center.

She dangled a carrot, bribing her students to practice. It was an effective technique so she was sticking with it until a parent complained, then no candy for that kid.

As she grabbed a handful of M&Ms and munched on them one at a time, she thought that it probably wasn't her body Darcy was dissing but her face. Hers was kind of distinctive, a mix of Eastern and Western features with disproportionately large, dark eyes. Darcy's preference was probably blondes.

During lunch break in the music building's courtyard decorated with boxed hydrangea, she was desperate to feel like she could get herself on the right track with men, so she struck up a conversation with a guitar teacher who had a side hustle as a DJ and offered to share a juice box. Later that evening he texted to ask if she wanted to go out for dinner the following night.

Going on a date with a not rich, not super-hot guy was a good way to stop subjecting herself to the scrutiny of guys like Will Darcy. Accepting Darcy was occupied with serious matters like preserving bloodlines and didn't have time for her nonsense, she could avoid cold-cocks to her self-esteem.

Tuesday afternoon, Jane got a call from Bingley asking her to join him for a last minute dinner at the Derby Country Club.

Elizabeth wished her sister luck on her first official date with Bingley and was off to meet the guitar-playing DJ at a seafood place built on an old pier where you ate soft shelled crabs served in plastic baskets.

When the check arrived, DJ, as his friends called him, told her, "Not only are deli sandwiches much cheaper; they don't look like insects."

Hopefully Bingley wasn't similarly commenting on the seafood tower at the country club with Jane.

As Elizabeth and DJ walked out into the parking lot, he started popping peppermint Tic Tacs.

She twisted, swinging her arms. "I have to get home for a good night's sleep."

He stopped crunching mints and frowned.

Hopping on her Vespa, she was off, waving with a smile.

He was alright, definitely harmless, which she didn't take for granted given guys she'd met in the past, but there wasn't much of a spark and she wasn't taking things any further that night.

Jane didn't get home till 3 am, although her clothes were exactly as they'd been when she left the house.

Bingley had been a dream, and Jane had spoken to Will Darcy again without incident. She and Bingley already had plans to get together again and watch *North by Northwest* at Outdoor Movie Night in the park.

At Foxy's with Charlotte on Wednesday night, Elizabeth danced with anyone who'd have her and hung out with the folks without water views, obstructed or otherwise. No fuss or inducements to mortify herself like she'd done with Will Darcy at Netherfield.

Thursday, Elizabeth received an invitation via the US Postal Service for a dress-to-impress dance party at the main Derby beach.

The honor of your presence is requested at a

Beach Ball

On Saturday, July 20, 2019

At 9 pm

Sponsored by Derby Town Council's Recreation

Committee

The town website, www.DerbyCentral.org, was humming with everyone desperate to be someone's plus one. Elizabeth knew why she was among the lucky few who received two free tickets; she was the volunteer conductor for the Derby High School Marching Band, which performed at all the town's parades.

"It's going to be like an elite singles night," Charlotte said, turning her laptop screen to show Elizabeth a write-up in the online version of the local newspaper.

"Not sure about the elite part, but I know where there are singles events every night ... *any bar in town*," said Elizabeth, who was visiting Charlotte's trailer.

"But guys like Bingley and Darcy don't hang out at bars," Charlotte smirked.

"That's the point," said Elizabeth wryly.

"Don't get mad at me," said Charlotte, moving to the one-wall kitchen to make tea, "but I think Darcy has a right to act all proud."

"Uh, is this a freedom of speech thing?"

"No," said Charlotte with a grin, "but just think of all the women he has buzzing around him, most of whom don't impress him much; it makes sense that he's guarded and unapproachable."

Elizabeth twisted her face. "Because he's popular he gets to diss people?"

"Well, if I were him and I could have anyone or anything I wanted, I'd be full of myself too," said Charlotte.

"Uh, my sister is dating a guy with a membership to the country club and the yacht club who is civil and polite to all the world."

"Bingley is a different personality."

"And...?"

"Seriously, Lizzy, I know you can't stand him but if Will Darcy asked you out, you wouldn't go out with him ... just for a chance at a sliver of that lifestyle?"

Elizabeth laughed, "Oh come on, Charlotte. I know you'd never act so materialistic, or advise *me* to."

\#

A week later, Elizabeth's second date with DJ started with hard cider and ended with miniature golf, in which he claimed to be a junior champion although he mostly hit the ball so hard it ricocheted off the green.

"Do you ever play on the big course at the country club?" asked Elizabeth.

"Not for $150 a round," he said, returning to his favorite subject of how things cost too much. "I only play mini golf unless my cousin gets me a comp. He works for the chamber of commerce and gets all kinds of free vouchers for stuff."

As Elizabeth lined up a shot, DJ touched her hair. "You're perfect. As pretty as a picture. Flawless."

Laughing, she thanked him. "I upgrade from my usual messy ponytail when playing mini golf."

"Don't joke! I'm serious," he insisted, his speech slightly slurred, his beer goggles on. "I just want to look at you all night. But you never act serious."

"Hey, I just got an idea," Elizabeth said excitedly. "Why don't you DJ a 70's disco party at Longbourn in the outdoor pavilion? We could do a Saturday Night Fever theme. Everyone would come."

"Really?" he exclaimed, sobering up in an instant. "I book weddings and corporate events. I'm not interested in going small time at Longbourn. You know, most people who live there try to avoid mentioning it."

This attitude was a letdown, no matter how hot he thought she was. He would need to find another flawless woman to appreciate his flattery and his championship golf swing.

A third date was not likely, but they could be friends.

#

Bingley mentioned to Jane during one of their phone calls that he'd be out and about in Derby on Sunday afternoon. Buying flower pots. Returning an ottoman. Looking for doorknobs at the antique shops on Market Street. So, Elizabeth came up with a plan. After Sunday brunch of chicken and biscuits at Aunt Phyllis's doublewide, they'd set out for some window shopping and accidentally run into Bingley. If all went well, Elizabeth would make an excuse about having to do some lesson planning for her summer school classes and return home solo.

After checking out tchotchkes at the artsy gift shop, including a tiny bottle of perfume with a 20's flapper charm attached, they made their way to their favorite stop, Derby's family-owned designer shoe store with brands from Milan and Paris.

Jane took a seat by the window where a pitcher of ice water with lemon was set up on a marble table.

Elizabeth stretched a display pair of plastic sandals onto her feet. "I think these look better without feet in them."

"You should have got that perfume bottle," said Jane.

"Yeah, I need to treat myself ... to help make up for my plainness," she joshed.

"Oh, Lizzy," said Jane dolefully.

A ding-a-ling from the chimes hanging at the door made her look up.

Caroline Townsend glided across the terra-cotta floor tiles to where Jane sat sipping lemon water.

"Jane, where have you been?" Caroline exclaimed. "I was just telling Bingley how I longed to see you again."

Caroline's skin was peeling a little on her chest. Her arms looked tan against her jewel-tone crop top. Her face was pretty like a contestant on a reality show before having her makeup done.

After complaining about sweltering heat, Caroline selected some shiny peep toes for Jane to try on.

"I like them," said Jane softly, "but I don't think I can afford them."

Elizabeth distrusted Caroline, suspecting she was trying to embarrass Jane because of her relative poverty, but, if so, Caroline would find she was no match for Jane's poise.

Elizabeth looked down at the orange flowery sandals she'd tried on. Yes, they'd add a spring in her step at work tomorrow, but she decided to save up for a bigger splurge like a used clarinet.

Someone like Caroline, whose parents owned thousands of acres in Texas, didn't know what it was like to enter a shop knowing there was no way you'd be able to purchase anything inside.

Elizabeth and her sisters knew the feeling well. Sure, it was unsettling but it could be invigorating too. Thanks to living in such a moneyed town, Elizabeth could handle treasures, examine them up close, for a moment feel what it would be like to possess them. Like a student living along Broadway who couldn't afford to go to the shows but still felt the excitement in the air. Last week Elizabeth had been able to tickle the ivories of a Steinway grand piano at an antique shop.

Clearly Jane wanted the gorgeous, well-made satin shoes Caroline was coaxing her to try on.

Their mom's answer was Jane must snag a rich husband. She encouraged her — and Elizabeth and Lydia — to throw themselves in the way of rich men. But Jane was sworn to a life of denial if the only alternative was prostituting herself to rich Derby men like her female progenitors. If she fell in love with someone well off or made a fortune herself opening a club called the *Roaring 2020s*, that was fine, but she would not contrive

46

something as she'd been encouraged to do by family members.

Grinning and bearing their mother's advice about how to reel in Bingley, Jane lived by her own higher standards and followed her heart. She hadn't even slept with Bingley, despite Mrs. Bennet repeatedly telling her, "Even people from Texas know about the three date rule."

A tapping on the shop window caught their attention and Jane and Elizabeth saw Reverend Collins, a minister of a local church.

Walking in he proclaimed in a booming sermon voice, "My dear Elizabeth, I missed you at church this morning."

Elizabeth never attended his church. For Easter and christenings, she went to the same church as her Bennet relatives, the Methodist church by the old baseball fields.

Vaguely, she remembered seeing Reverend Collins staking out the town square a few weeks back and urging people to attend his megachurch in the Rosings Park section of Derby, or at least watch his TV show on Derby Central Television.

"I was hoping, well, I do consider an invitation to Sunday service the greatest gift a man can give a woman," said Reverend Collins. "Far be it for me to say that I have the purest intentions of any man you've encountered, Miss Elizabeth, but—"

"Thank you," Elizabeth squinted at him, having trouble meeting his oozing, supplicating eyes. "But I hope you'll excuse me. I'm shopping with my sister."

With a violent burst of jingles, Will Darcy shoved opened the door to the shop, then halted, staring at Elizabeth, before releasing the door and allowing it to fall closed behind him.

She had known there was a risk of running into him when she proposed this excursion but had been willing to take the chance for Jane's sake.

"Hello," he said to Elizabeth, just as Caroline appeared at his side and pulled him over to a mirror where she posed for him in platforms like a model at the end of a runway.

He looked unimpressed until Caroline reached up to kiss his mouth, which definitely woke him up a bit. Elizabeth studied his long hands as they skimmed Caroline's tiny waist. Perhaps those two had made more progress than Jane and Bingley, who'd only kissed goodnight so far.

Elizabeth imagined Will and Caroline in bed, their hard bodies intertwined, and it was somehow much more entertaining an idea than she would have guessed.

There was even some comedy in conjuring their expressions of pleasure during the act, especially in comparison to Bingley and Jane's real smiles if they ever made it that far.

Collins hadn't stopped talking for any of this, although Elizabeth ignored him successfully for a minute. "... I have great hopes for you, Elizabeth, after I saw the photo of you in the newspaper graduating *cum laude* last year. I assure you your recent personal improvements have not gone unnoticed."

What in the world? Elizabeth had known Reverend Collins since grade school when he was plain old Bobby Collins, but he'd never before acted so attentive. "I, uh—"

"You needn't worry about those unfortunate instances from your past, when you were, say, living more, uh, loosely." Collins smiled, his skin shiny and red. "You were quite young then and seem to have gotten over that trying stage."

Huh? What the fuck was wrong with him? Implying that she used to be a slut! Because he was ordained it was his place to give her a gold star for good behavior? "Uh, I suppose congratulations are in order for you too at having edged out all the competition to become a minister on local TV."

A determined talker, Collins went on as if he didn't believe it necessary to attend to what she said. "...and Elizabeth, I should mention that I've recently established a very fortunate connection with Catherine Darcy of Rosings Park. Of course you know the Darcys have endowed the new wing at West Derby Elementary. And so—"

An idea occurred to her and she loudly interrupted, "Oh, yes, you and she might want to support the school music program's purchase of new risers." Catherine Darcy was an important member of the town council's education committee.

Collins took a deep breath, clearly revving up for another loquacious soliloquy, and Elizabeth looked around the shop for an escape but saw only Darcy and Caroline talking to each other as Jane waited patiently nearby.

A woman, with heels clicking on the floor, stepped between Elizabeth and her view of Darcy.

It was Bridget King, whose name tag said "assistant sales associate," and who must have just entered the sales floor from the storeroom in the back because she certainly hadn't come through the front door. "Look, the desperate Bennet girls, *Eliza and Jane.*"

Back in high school, Bridget had been well off and put together, with non-costume jewelry and a new Volkswagen, so Elizabeth used to make fun of her taste in bubblegum pop music.

Elizabeth had been vain. A freshman in high school she scored her first boyfriend, a popular upper-class lacrosse player who teared up when she broke up with him. Back then she was all about getting attention, a bit like Lydia was now. She had used the Bennet reputation to her advantage, which had been great for her fragile teenager's ego. Not so much anymore.

Bridget King must have been a recent hire at the shoe store because Elizabeth had never seen her there before. Bridget was probably making good money on commissions, but, unfortunately, at that moment, there was smoke coming out of her ears as she glared at Elizabeth.

Collins had not stopped talking and was now onto the topic of women's shoes, loud enough for Darcy and Caroline to hear him, the latter rolling her eyes. "I have no problem with a one-inch heel but four-inches says something about a lady's character."

Four inches might say something about a man's character too, Elizabeth thought.

Looking tranquil, with a soft, easy smile, Jane chatted with Darcy and Caroline, but the way her neck muscles strained as if she were trying to swallow air, made Elizabeth realize she was anxious to avoid any embarrassment in front of her new friends.

Bridget, who was out of earshot of any co-workers, pointed to a pair of spiked heels and said to Elizabeth, "You should try on these stilettos, Eliza. They might help you pick up those bad boys you like to date. Although, I have to say, I haven't seen you out much lately. We had hoped you moved away."

"Okay, Bridget, I get it. I was awful to you in high school. I'm sorry. But that was years ago. I'm just here with my sister. We're leaving soon."

Bridget looked at Darcy and Caroline, suddenly perking up. The Bennets weren't buying anything but these two might be a sale, and Bridget was on it. "Oh, hello, I didn't see you. How may I help y'all?"

Elizabeth could think of a few sassy things to holler-back at Bridget, but she'd been in the wrong when she teased Bridget mercilessly about the boy bands she loved, and she couldn't atone for the past by coming up with cleverer put-downs today.

"We should get going, but I'm glad we ran into you, Will,"

Jane said, detangling herself from the strappy shoes she was trying on at Caroline's request.

Elizabeth exhaled. Jane was so sincere, with a smile so naturally warm that it melted even someone like Will Darcy. He returned Jane's compliment, "Nice to see you again," and glancing at Elizabeth, gave her just the slightest nod.

Just a nod was an acceptable greeting for the less attractive sister, Elizabeth thought as she clownishly glared at him, accidentally catching his eye.

He stared right back at her.

Elizabeth felt words coming out of her mouth before she realized there was no need to speak to him. "So lucky I was able to run into an old friend from high school," she said, tilting her head in Bridget's direction. "Everywhere you go in Derby, you run into someone you know. Small town life, I guess."

Bobby Collins was now asking Bridget some unheard question as Darcy redirected his whole body toward Elizabeth.

She knew he hadn't completely missed her other conversations, even if Caroline was talking in a louder voice than anyone else. Elizabeth had seen him watching her.

After an awkward pause, during which Elizabeth thought he might decide to just turn away, he said, "Seems more like a, how do you say? ... a frenemy?"

"Ha! Yes, well, that was way back in high school, when I had nothing to do on Sunday evenings but plan my next mean girl move." Why was she talking to him? *Shut up and leave with Jane.*

He grinned slightly, but there was something so scrutinizing about the way he looked at both her and Jane, like they were being evaluated by him constantly.

"I don't remember ever meeting you in high school," he said.

"That's no mystery. We weren't there at the same time. I'm younger *and cooler* than you."

He almost smiled outright, hardening his expression at the last. "Yes, of course," he said in a low voice, "but didn't you attend pep rallies when Jane and I were at Derby High?"

"I don't think so. You would have remembered me; I wore fishnets and purple go-go boots back then."

One side of his lips flicked up a little.

Caroline had her back to them. She was looking over a display of furry slippers.

Loudly clearing his throat, Collins interrupted, "As I was saying, Elizabeth, I can understand why someone in your position would be somewhat bothered by the effects of your unfortunate family connections." He straightened his black collared shirt. "But I think the best advice for you would be to focus on respectability now and relinquish the name Bennet as soon as you might find it in your power to do so. Hint, hint." His squinty eyes twitched.

Was this his idea of a come-on? Elizabeth and her sisters all had their mother's maiden name of Bennet. Not one of Mrs. Bennet's lovers impressed her enough to name a child after him, although Jane's dad was so gracious as to pay for their trailer. It was the greatest disappointment of Mrs. Bennet's life that she never got hitched to a truly well-heeled gentleman. She planned to wring victory from the jaws of defeat by getting one of her daughters married to someone with a ton of money who'd buy her a house with a porch and a front lawn.

"Not that I'm suggesting you take your father's name," said Collins with a toothy grin. "Double hint, hint. If you know his name, that is."

Elizabeth's stomach churned and she felt bile in her throat. She couldn't trust herself with a reply because she wanted to clobber him.

Jane rushed to Elizabeth's side, moving uncharacteristically fast. "Bobby, uh, Reverend Collins, we really must be going."

"Oh, yes, you're Elizabeth's older sister, aren't you? Janet is your name, I believe. I was just telling Eliza—"

Darcy took a step in Collins's direction, almost getting in his face as he towered over him. "It's my understanding you recently hosted a Bible study group at Rosings Park, my aunt Catherine's home."

Reverend Collins looked up at Will, aghast. "My apologies,

sir!" With a sweeping bow, he exclaimed, "I didn't recognize you, sir. You must be, uh, Fitzwilliam Darcy."

"Just William."

"Of course. William, sir. The illustrious Fitzwilliam Darcy was your grandfather." With an officious sweep of his hand, he said, "Your aunt is the most exceptional lady I've ever known. It is impossible to praise her too highly. She allows me to host my humble Bible study group at her magnificent home every Thursday evening. I'm sure you are honored to be so fortunate as to be her nephew. Yours is a family name to be proud of. Many times, I've told your aunt, *Catherine D'Arcy* is probably the most noble-sounding name ever heard in the Americas.'"

Bingley appeared outside the glass door and waved to Jane with a quick come hither hand motion.

Jane glanced worriedly at Elizabeth, who whispered "Go ahead," and Jane rushed out to answer his call, wearing only the stockings she'd put on while trying on shoes.

Collins said in a feigned whisper, directed at Darcy, "I'm afraid some of our friends here are not so fortunate as to even know the identities of both their parents. But I shouldn't speak of it. Hush, hush."

"Excuse me?" Elizabeth no longer cared that she was being studied by Will Darcy or that she gave away too much by assuming Collins was referring to her. "What did you say, Bobby?" She was ready to fight.

Bridget King ran to the front store window, pointing at Jane, who was outside and out of earshot, "Elizabeth Bennet, your sister is ruining those silk stockings!"

Elizabeth tried to adjust to the jarring change in subject. "What?" she exclaimed, tasting remnants of bitter lemon pulp from the store's complimentary fruit water.

Bridget scowled. "She's walking on that filthy jagged sidewalk in silk stockings. I'll lose my job for destroying merchandise. Your aunt has already scammed us with bounced checks more than once. And everyone knows your little sister tries to return shoes in the wrong boxes. I'm going to have to call the police if your sister doesn't pay for that hosiery this minute!"

"Wait," said Elizabeth. "Jane thought they were peds for trying on shoes. They were lying on the table. It's an honest mistake."

Darcy was questioning Collins about his aunt Catherine's activities at church, continuing to absorb the reverend in conversation.

"An honest mistake? That's lingerie she's ruining!" Bridget exclaimed.

Elizabeth took out her credit card. "Jane didn't realize that, and you don't have to mention it to her. Thank you."

Jane would hate to waste money on expensive ripped hosiery.

Elizabeth glanced at Darcy. Not again! Not in front of Will

Darcy and Caroline Townsend. Many times, she had watched her mom get yelled at by shop owners for returning used clothing or asking for more than her share of free samples. She knew Aunt Phyllis had been in trouble with the police for stealing lace and served probation. Given Jane's connections, this accident might seem like something intentional.

Elizabeth watched in astonishment as Darcy asked Bobby Collins an absurd question about what sort of shoes his younger sister Georgiana might like, and Bobby was happy to oblige with a long-winded answer.

Will was redirecting Collins's ridiculousness.

He's engaging Collins to keep him away from me!

Caroline didn't look pleased as she watched her brother and Jane through the front window of the shop and heckled Darcy's conversation with Collins. "This is so tiresome. Should we be going?"

"I'm at your command," Darcy answered.

Bingley and Darcy's cars were called for and brought around by a valet. Mr. Collins pointed out his Cadillac parked across the street, offering Elizabeth a ride, but Jane and Elizabeth said their goodbyes to all and walked off on foot, old sandals on their feet and torn stockings tossed in a gray trash can.

When they got to the end of the block, Elizabeth rested her head on her sister's shoulder.

Jane decided not to go off with Bingley that afternoon, but

the two did make a date for the next day.

#

It wasn't until Elizabeth stepped into a steaming bath
back home in the trailer's narrow acrylic bathtub that she fell
apart.

Jane gets Bingley while I'm stuck with Bobby Collins.

At that moment, Reverend Collins was probably sitting in
the front parlor of his rectory, looking out at the view of Rosings
Park, applauding his charity in attempting to court Elizabeth
Bennet despite the fact she was an illegitimate slut.

With none of her usual buoyancy, she sunk low in the
bathwater, soap suds tingling her lips. Stretching her legs, she
pointed her toes, her hand running over her tummy and thigh
where a stray hair annoyed her. Over on the rusty towel bar
hung yellowing towels her mom had decorated with patches of
faux cowhide fabric.

Every look that passed between her and Darcy at the shoe
store made her sigh—or cringe. He wasn't befriending her, that
would require that he speak to her directly and without a
conceited look on his face, but he had diverted Collins's
prodigious conversation to spare her.

Had he decided to atone for some sin, say forgetting to tip
the maitre d', by offering his services to plain women that day?

His chivalrous conduct, if it was that, didn't give her much
pleasure. Would that Darcy had exited the store without

witnessing her humiliation. Having him there to see her called out by Bridget and courted by Collins made her think he would look down on her even more than he had when only his family, money and looks set him above her. Having Bingley's friends hear Jane be accused of stealing was excruciating.

Will Darcy was baffling. Outside the shoe store, as she and Jane were getting ready to be off, she had tried to thank him for distracting Collins on her behalf, but he cut her off, barely looking at her, and was as curt as ever.

"I appreciate how you tried to help me avoid Bobby Collins—"

"Oh. It's nothing," Darcy had said flatly. "Please don't mention it." He turned to Bingley. "Am I driving Caroline to the club or are you?"

He saved her from an awkward conversation only to awkwardly converse with her himself. It didn't make sense. She didn't believe in Will Darcy's random acts of kindness.

And whatever Darcy was up to, she hoped it wasn't going to come back to bite her or her sister.

Elizabeth sat up to wash her hair, scratching her scalp with her fingernails, causing shivers of pleasure to tingle the skin at the back of her neck. As she looked down at her naked body, more tanned than usual from a bit of swimming at the beach the day before, the idea of Will Darcy and her in a hate sex tryst popped into her head.

Impossible. Conventionally attractive women like Caroline Bingley were hanging all over him, *and he publicly declared I'm not up to his standards.*

His behavior at the shoe store might have something to do with Bingley and Jane. Elizabeth didn't trust his good intentions toward Jane, despite the fact he seemed friendly with her. Maybe he stuck around as a reconnaissance operation to get sharable dirt on Jane's family.

Her sister's situation was perilous. She truly liked Bingley, far more than any other guy she'd met in a long time. Elizabeth could see it and Jane had all but admitted it to her — although she never acted overly attached or inappropriately desperate for his attention.

Jane and Bingley were from such different backgrounds and the drama at the shoe store only reinforced the impression that Jane came from a family of white trash and was trying to play up.

Bingley's friendship with Will Darcy said something important about him. He was more than a gracious, affable guy who liked everyone he met. He was a multi-millionaire by birth who unapologetically enjoyed enormous privilege. He and Darcy were set apart from 99% of the people Jane knew in terms of their expectations and tastes. How could Bingley not see himself as someone Jane was fortunate to know?

Whatever could be done to help Jane minimize their

disparity was worth it. There was a chance something real was developing between her and Bingley, and true love deserved the greatest of efforts. Jane had a temperament and goodness that made her deserving. It wasn't fair for her to be brought down by her family. For Jane's sake Elizabeth would put up with Will Darcy and swallow her pride.

When she was honest with herself, Elizabeth wanted what Jane seemed to be in range of. She wanted to feel more than the tepid emotions that had been part of her relationships with guys thus far. She wanted to be an impressive woman whom an amazing man would fall in love with.

Her demons stood in the way. Her feelings of inferiority when faced with guys like Darcy and Bingley were only part of the problem. There was also her dating history which ranged from lackluster to terrible and the nonexistent role models for good relationships provided by her parents.

The bathwater was now cold and had turned a soapy opaqueness. A sad soup she was stewing in.

Contrary to Bobby Collins's insinuation, Elizabeth knew who her father was. She knew his full name: first, middle and last. Knew he was born in Kentucky. Knew he was half Portuguese ethnic Gypsy. Knew he was a guitarist in a Tom Petty cover band that traveled the country but never recorded an album. And she knew he had died all alone in a Los Angeles hotel room when she was in high school.

The coroner's report said it was an accidental overdose of pain meds mixed with sleeping pills. Her aunt in Kentucky sent Elizabeth a box of vinyl Eagles albums to remember him by. So much for an inheritance.

Not that she ever saw her dad much when he was alive. A card once in a while. A couple visits a year.

But in the fall of her third year in high school, when she was dressing like a sex kitten and deciding which among a long list of boys she would go out with next, the news of her father's death was icing on the cake of her low life.

People who knew her back then thought she would probably end up knocked up in high school like her mother before her. They thought she'd pursue men who bought her stuff like Aunt Phyllis had. She'd have a baby with some musician who'd leave her to go on tour with his band like her dad had done.

Not long after her dad's death, Elizabeth made the mistake of dating a twenty-something guy who pushed her around when she "talked back." Their disastrous coupling, which ended with him slapping her in the face, was rock bottom.

From there, she turned things around, gave up on guys, and applied to college where she thrived. No love life to speak of, she focused on keeping her scholarship and staying on the dean's list.

Now, after a great first year teaching, after receiving

praise from the school principal for her rapport with students, she believed she could find happiness, even with the stigma of being a Bennet. She was not giving up on herself.

Chapter Four

Slipping into the high-ceilinged school gym, Will found testimony before the town council was already underway, just as he had contrived.

He grabbed an empty chair, attracting the attention of only a few people, all of whom frowned at him.

A man standing at the podium looked down as he read from a prepared statement. "Mr. Darcy of Pemberley may own half of Derby, but he don't own the town council. Y'all work for us! And we don't want any part of Pemberley touched." He looked up and, spotting Will, pointed at him. "Well, there he be. The gentleman's gracing us with his presence."

All eyes turned on Will.

Twisting, he unbuttoned the jacket of his wool-cashmere suit and leaned back in his chair. He and an elderly gentleman were the only two in the hot gym wearing ties.

After several more residents argued against his plan to build French country-style homes with pergolas on the Pemberley side of Lambton Canal, Will was called to speak on behalf of his development project.

"First of all, as owner of the swath of property in question, I'm happy to sell it to anyone in this room at below market price, provided they agree to leave the land fallow, but seeing as I have already donated oceanfront property for the public park in the area, I believe I have a right to develop a small portion of Pemberley's woods, assuming I do so in accordance with the style of the neighborhood."

After an hour of deliberation, the fairness of the council when faced with the merits of his reasonable proposal won out, and the announcement of the two vote margin of victory was met with only a spattering of boos.

Will didn't jump for joy as he strode across the gym floor to shake hands with the council members.

It had all turned out as expected.

He had prepared for contingencies and accomplished his goal. And given his resources, how could he expect anything less of himself?

But now, after a jam packed first Saturday of July, Will would be heading home to an empty house with only dogs waiting to be fed, no one to share his success with. A lonely thought.

Halfway home, Will turned onto winding Carriage Road, the sound of bullfrogs and crickets overpowering. All four windows were down and he could smell the mossy swamp grasses that overgrew in the summer.

A Dodge Charger came roaring out of the evening mist, driving down the center yellow line.

It was followed closely behind by a Mustang, also speeding.

The second car's fender scraped Will's, even as he turned the wheel to avoid it. Cursing under his breath, he pumped his breaks, bringing his car to a screeching halt.

After stepping into the breezy night air, Will ran his fingers along the indentation on the front driver's side of his car.

The damaged Mustang, like its companion vehicle, made a U-turn and pulled over.

Doors opened and at least six young men got out, including a tall guy, all bones, who, kicking at the dirt, turned to look at Will and called out, "Ain't nobody gonna call the cops, right?"

Will shook his head, glaring at him with undisguised

annoyance, yet agreeing not to call the police.

A girl, laughing with a cackle, straggled out of the back of the dark blue Charger with a can of something in her hand.

She seemed very young to be hanging out with so many guys. There were no other females he could see.

Something about her was familiar to Will, but he couldn't place her.

The young blonde woman wobbled around the hood of the car, holding onto the vehicle for balance. When she reached a side window, she banged on it like she was trying to get someone's attention.

With a wide swing of the car door, Wickham George exited the circus car, animatedly talking to the girl.

Will felt blood drain from his face and his adrenaline surge.

It would be better to drive off, leave the scene of an accident, than be tempted to confront Wickham. Will hadn't seen him in many months and it was still too soon.

Two young men, one tall and one short, shuffled their feet as they crossed the road toward Will, mumbling apologies.

Wickham stayed behind, turning his back, seeming to want to hide himself in the darkness.

Lucky for both of us he doesn't have the guts to face me.

For an instant, the idea that the accident was on purpose, that Wickham was now homicidal, occurred to Will, but, no, the young men standing in front of him with keys dangling from their fingers were the only drivers.

"Yeah, real sorry about that, Mister," said the taller of the two who was at the wheel of the Mustang when it collided with Will's vehicle.

Will smelled alcohol on his breath.

He ought to call the authorities, but it would take them a quarter of an hour to arrive at this desolate spot, and the perpetrators would be long gone by then.

What about photographing their license plates? If there were a serious penalty afforded these kids, one which might serve as a deterrent, one that outweighed the risk of bodily harm to himself, he ought to take photos of the accident with his phone. But they looked panic-struck so this was a risk. The group could jump him. Maybe he should feel lucky they stopped at all.

Will tossed his linen business card, embossed with "Pemberley" and a horse head logo, to the tall kid with keys. "If you decide to call your insurance company tomorrow, my information is on that card."

The Mustang driver stepped backward toward the waiting group of his friends and nodded emphatically, looking happy to be getting off easy and most likely resolving to make zero phone calls and lay low for a few days.

Will was ready to leave. This hassle was already not worth the trouble it had caused him and he hadn't begun to deal with repairs to his car.

Turning to go, he glanced over his shoulder and saw the girl who had spoken with Wickham looking at him.

"Do you need a ride?" Darcy called to her.

She quickly strode across the street, halting before him with a drunken stagger. "Oh lord, I know who you are." She bent her head to the side with a silly smile. "I'm Lydia."

Two more cars appeared out of the darkness. Driving very slowly, they pulled over and parked along the side of the road.

Young men with wide-eyed looks got out, probably hoping to see blood and gore. They must have been called by their friends who'd been drag racing.

Darcy asked Lydia if she lived nearby and noticed Wickham in the background pantomiming whiplash to another guy. He wasn't paying much attention to Will's interaction with Lydia.

If this girl weren't in danger from Wickham, she certainly was from the number of men present, and she was too young to be hanging out with drunk drag racers.

"May I drive you home?" he asked her.

She nodded enthusiastically.

As Will ducked into his car, he pretended not to hear Wickham holler, "I didn't know he was into young ones."

Will assisted Lydia in locating her seatbelt as she giggled, clumsily fumbling with the shoulder strap.

Sitting back, she let him buckle her in. "Nice car!"

He didn't answer.

"What sort of car is this? Not a Bentley, right?" She guffawed so loud the sound bounced off the interior acoustics. "I can't believe I'm riding in Will Darcy's car."

"How do you know my name?" he asked, as he turned a corner leading to the highway.

"Everyone knows your name. The guys back there were like, *Oh my god, it's Will Darcy. We're dead. His dad is justice of the peace. We'll be locked up in solitary. He's gonna sue us.*"

Will frowned, feeling he might have been played by their humble-sounding apologies. But what was he to do? Act according to their false estimation of him and call his dad for help?

If he ranted and raved and threatened those kids, they'd be more likely to take the information he'd given them and make up a story.

"Were your friends drag racing?" he asked Lydia.

"Oh, la dee da, we were only having a little fun! Don't be a spoil sport."

"Tell me how old you are, Lydia?"

"Old enough." Her voice lowered to a hissing chuckle. "Do you wanna tea bag me? Isn't that what your cousin Cornel did with those two girls from Longbourn at the beach? I know about

70

you Darcys. Jane thinks you're so refined, but nobody but Jane is so naive."

"Jane? You mean, Jane Bennet?" said Will, not feeling surprised by the connection; although this girl's affect was unlike Jane's, he could see the resemblance as soon as Jane's name was mentioned. "You're Jane Bennet's sister."

"Mm, yeah."

Each and every one of his male relatives had been propositioned by a Bennet at one point or another. Now it was his turn apparently. And he was being propositioned by a teenager.

To be fair, Jane was much more polite and infinitely more mellow than this girl and didn't seem like a floozy, which Bingley had confirmed with a story about his night with Jane being so amazing and yet only PG-13 rated.

"How would you like it if I quoted what you just said to me to your mother?" he asked Lydia. Whether or not her mother was once a notorious Bennet girl herself, she must have matured enough with age to see the folly of Lydia's conduct.

Breaking into a cackle of hysterics, Lydia cried, "You sound like our vice principal!"

He waited several minutes before she quieted down enough for him to speak again.

"If you go out with those guys again, you may very well get arrested," he said grimly. "Just for being a passenger in a car that's drag racing you could get put on some sort of juvenile probation. I assume you are old enough to drive. You could lose your license, if you're caught drinking underage." He knew these were mostly idle threats as they weren't likely to be carried out unless the police caught her in the act.

"Oh, my god, you're so funny. I'm almost eighteen! But I don't actually have my license yet. I don't have a car." She grinned coyly. "Will you buy me one?"

"Please, listen. What I'm trying to tell you is no joke. Those delinquents you were hanging out with wouldn't hesitate to take advantage of you. There was a girl from Derby who was assaulted while trying to hitch a ride on that very same road."

Lydia laughed. "Oh, I've heard it all. They left her wearing nothing but her underwear. Did you know those guys?"

He didn't answer although he had known them. They'd been classmates at Derby High with whom he never associated.

In minutes, they were exiting the highway.

It was no challenge to find the turn off for Longbourn Creek Estates. The illuminated sign was bigger than most of the trailers on the "estates."

He couldn't recall the last time he was at Longbourn. Maybe tagging along with his dad to check out police activity when a block party had gotten out of hand.

He rolled down his window under a whining light

mounted on a telephone pole, and Lydia pointed to a yellow mobile home with rounded corners and exposed axels.

It was just as you would imagine. The name "Bennet" was painted on the mailbox in white lettering, and a fake red-roofed wishing well sat out front. White shutters with heart cut outs decorated the miniature windows, and plastic turf covered a postage-stamp-sized front patio under an awning.

Lydia leaned on him as he helped her out the passenger-side door. He tried to tune out her ramblings and ignore her hands moving around his waist as they made their way up the cracked concrete front walk, but he didn't miss hearing himself called "Darcy" several times over — just like her sister Elizabeth had done at Netherfield. Luckily few people in town had the nerve to insolently referred to him by his last name alone as if he were the backup shortstop on a minor league baseball team.

Lydia's arms felt boney and her clothing seemed damp with chilled perfume and perspiration. This might be repulsive if she were a grown woman but she was absolutely childish. She reminded him of his date hanging on him after junior prom.

Jane answered his knock at the door with alarm. "Oh my gosh. Is she okay?"

"Yes—" he began.

"Look who brought me home!" interrupted Lydia, partly successful in achieving an upright position. "Will Darcy offered me a ride! Can you believe it? Beat that, Jane."

"Oh, Lydia, here, come with me," said Jane. She detached her sister's hands from Will's body, which Lydia still reached for.

"Why didn't you tell me Darcy's car is cooler than Bingley's?" Lydia demanded, face to face with Jane. "I know you've seen both up close; although, you've only been *inside* Bingley's — Oo la la."

Lydia's laughing fit made it impossible to speak as Jane moved her into the house.

Out of nowhere, Elizabeth sprang into Jane's place in the doorway.

Will stiffened, his ears still ringing from Lydia's tittering.

"We weren't expecting, uh, ..." said Elizabeth with a forced smile.

He stared at her a moment longer than necessary.

She bopped from hip to hip, strands from the sloppy bun on top of her head coming undone. "What a surprise to see you ... with Lydia. It's very kind of you to ... uh."

He nodded, not certain whether to bring up the fact her underage sister made a pass at him. Lowering his voice, he took a half step forward. "I—"

Elizabeth's arms shot out wide, gripping both sides of the door frame.

He felt a rush of indignation. Did she actually think he'd push his way into her home without an explicit invitation?

He considered turning around and walking off as a silent

rebuff.

But the opportunity to communicate one-on-one with her was too much for his curiosity to forgo, so, instead, he glared at her.

She dropped her arms, looking surprisingly contrite and seeming to have received the message about the offensiveness of her intimation.

Perhaps she wasn't calling into question his manners so much as trying to hide something inside of the house from his view.

"Is your mother home?" he asked coolly.

"Uh, yes," Elizabeth replied. "But, uh, she's getting ready for bed. I'm sure she'd want me to thank you for bringing Lydia home safe."

"You're welcome," he said evenly.

"I didn't realize you ran a car service." She looked like she hoped to elicit a laugh.

He didn't bother. Was it wrong to expect a more profuse or at least sincerer expression of gratitude for the aid he'd rendered her sister?

Elizabeth's eyes were huge. She was waiting for him to speak. *And say what? Make polite conversation?*

He looked her up and down, not bothering to hide that he was checking her out. Why should he worry about protecting delicate female sensibilities she probably didn't have? For all he knew she made passes at men she knew for four seconds like her younger sister.

Elizabeth wore no makeup he could detect. It didn't seem like she'd been out that night. Her cream-colored camisole wasn't see-through, but it was distracting to see her braless, her nipples pointy under the shimmery fabric. And above the tied waist of her pink pajama pants was a glimpse of her bronzed abdomen.

She pulled at the hem of her top, eliminating the midriff. "I'm not sure what Lydia was up to, but ..."

"She was with *older men* who were driving recklessly." His stomach grumbled in complaint. He was wearing down. He'd had only a peach since lunch.

"Oh." Elizabeth nodded, cringing. "She told us she was going to the movies with Pratt, a friend of hers. I'm not sure what happened."

"Pratt, you say?" He stretched his shoulder, gripping his elbow. "I don't believe I recognized many local boys in the group she was with."

Lydia hollered from inside the house, just beyond his view, "We ditched Pratt, Lizzy!"

Elizabeth took a step toward him and pulled the trailer door closed behind her with a creak and a thud.

Will couldn't make out the rest of what Lydia said.

The lightheartedness he'd seen in Elizabeth at Bingley's

party was gone. Some of the confusion he'd seen in her at the shoe store was evident. In all honesty, she was just plain pathetic stuck in this god awful place, the whole neighborhood smelling of cheap beer and bad taste.

Lydia pushed open a tiny window to the left of the front door, her face sticking out the opening for a second before she disappeared back inside and Jane's disembodied voice wafted out. "Lydia, please tell me you haven't been drinking. Swear you weren't drinking."

Ear splitting laughter from Lydia was interrupted by a shrill female voice, almost as loud. "Oh, Lydia, dear, you're finally home. I'm so happy you're okay. Jane, stop fussing with her. Oh, Pratt is a dear boy, isn't he? He wouldn't let her get into any trouble."

This must be the mother, but Will couldn't see her. The little window Lydia had opened provided no view inside the house.

From inside, Mrs. Bennet screamed, "*Will Darcy?* Will Darcy drove you home, and he's outside?"

Elizabeth leaned against the front door as if holding back a flood, but the opened window acted like a speaker broadcasting what was being said inside.

"Mother, please, not so loudly" was Jane's muffled reply. "Let's take Lydia back to your bedroom. We'll talk about it there."

Jane clearly had to work overtime providing discretion for her family.

The mother's voice came again. "Well, I'm certainly not going to get dressed just to see Will Darcy, not after how nasty he was to Lizzy. That odious young man."

Will blanched. He was so stunned he could barely meet Elizabeth's eyes. They both distinctly heard what her mother said.

He shook his head. "I honestly have not the slightest idea ...."

Elizabeth blushed from her cheeks down to her upper chest, her eyes watering. "Oh, it's nothing. My mother can be a little, uh, ... she often feels slighted by things people say, so well, um." Her speech rambled. "I'm sure she's only talking about some overheard offhand comment. You know what I mean. Don't you?" She forced a laugh.

What in the world? As far as he knew, he'd never been in the same room with the mother. How could she have overheard something he'd said about Elizabeth?

He'd spoken to Bingley about Elizabeth more than he wished to admit, even called her impertinent once while out to dinner with friends, but he could recall nothing nasty.

Had he said something thoughtless in front of Jane?

Only recently he'd try to *help* Elizabeth by getting smarmy Reverend Collins out of her hair. He'd been the opposite of nasty.

"I'm sorry if Lydia inconvenienced you," said Elizabeth, interrupting his thoughts with a strained voice.

"It was nothing," he replied, deciding not to mention the damage to his car. "Well, I ought to say goodnight ..."

She nodded rapidly.

She was eager for him to go and he could not blame her. She didn't want her family life exposed, and not wanting anyone to hear from her mother or Lydia was to her credit and meant she had some proper feelings.

Lydia peeked out the nearby open window. "Lizzy, you won't believe it, but Will Darcy tried to kiss me!"

"That's false," he snapped stupidly, without thinking. In a whisper, he added, "Why am I not surprised she's a liar?"

"Lydia, go to bed," Elizabeth hollered at her sister.

Lydia's head ducked back inside.

"You have to excuse her," said Elizabeth, her lips squeezing shut for a moment as if she didn't trust herself to open them. "She's very young."

"So therefore you excuse her antics?"

She blushed, shaking a little although the night was warm. "As taxing as she is at times, it's not for you to judge her. You don't know what her life is like; you haven't had her experiences."

He shook his head. "But you *have* had her experiences?"

"You never did anything sketchy as a teenager?" she asked.

"Your sister could have been in a car accident, could have been seriously hurt." He spoke with more feeling than he intended.

"Yes, Lydia is wild and she's reckless, but we're not quite ready to call in the sheriff to lock her up, so we have to keep trying to cajole her into being more responsible."

"I hope you and Jane are not enabling her."

Elizabeth leaned forward, her shoulders rising, her eyes so alive, almost wild. "I won't speak for myself, but Jane always gives people the benefit of the doubt. For example, she thinks highly of you and says you're clever. Very odd, huh?"

His jaw clenched at her sarcasm. "How kind."

Her eyes turned sharp. "I'm more cynical myself, but Jane's approach is much better than looking down on everyone." Her lopsided grin was almost enough to soften the meaning of her words.

"Forgive me, I don't understand. You're accusing me of something. What I'm not sure."

"Disgust is written all over your face, Darcy."

Breathing in the scent of long dead pine branches, he tilted his head back, looking up at the sky. "If so, that's..." He looked at her. "... unintentional, I assure you."

It occurred to him that he was lying – a white lie, but still.

Her shoulders sank, her stance slackening a little, and she said, almost plaintively, "Thank you again for bringing Lydia home safe, but we'll take care of things from here."

He could imagine how he'd react if his sister acted like Lydia. He'd do more than just try to coax her out of her misconduct.

A thought suddenly popped into his head. "I assume you would prefer if I didn't mention this to Bingley."

Elizabeth's eyes went dark. "Is that a threat?"

His chest burned. Turning away, he told himself to calm down so as not to say the angry, indignant things he wanted to say to her. "Not in the least," he said with clenched teeth.

She looked shaken, almost to the point of tears.

"I wouldn't dream of threatening you," he added. "I will not mention this incident to anyone if that's what you wish."

She nodded, twitching a little, swallowing hard.

"I've intruded on you overlong," he said, exhaling, then after a slight bow, he stepped back and away.

"Goodnight," she said, her voice cracking.

Starting the engine, he looked in the rearview mirror.

Elizabeth was sitting on the stoop, her elbows resting on her knees and her head in her hands.

No.

He shook off the urge to go back and try to smooth things

81

over.

That might give the wrong impression, if he hadn't already.

He'd openly checked her out. He'd been overly concerned with her affairs.

For a man who had women throwing themselves at him, one thoughtless turn could lead down a road to disaster. But Will would never be a fool like his father.

Lifting his foot off the brake, he rolled down the lane to the makeshift bridge. His car bumped and swayed over the cement cylinders through which anemic Longbourn Creek flowed.

He must leave immediately and squash any idea of his being desirous of her good opinion. There was something about her way of speaking that attracted him. A lightness mixed with strength behind her words made even her barbs seem somehow captivating. It was hard to look away from her.

He would never have imagined going to Longbourn and coming face to face with Elizabeth Bennet, then having her challenge him the way she did. Even if embarrassment was at the root of Elizabeth's accusations, he deserved better for bringing home her insufferable sister. Her mother couldn't bother getting dressed to thank him but could shout from inside the house that he'd been "nasty" to Elizabeth in some unspecified way.

At home and sitting by the fire, he reflected on every

word of their conversation. He could feel sympathy for her despondence at her situation, but why didn't she take the opportunity to offer a fulsome thank you instead of suggesting he looked down on people? Yes, of course he looked down on immoral characters.

If he weren't a gentleman, the sort of person with whom she had little contact at Longbourn, he might not have shown her as much deference as he had.

He not only aimed to always treat women with respect but was accustomed to women treating him likewise. He could not remember the last time a woman had spoken to him with as much chagrin as Elizabeth Bennet had that evening.

By the time he crawled into bed, he was riled up. Reputation was of great importance to him. To pursue his real estate development projects, he could not lose the trust and confidence of the upstanding citizens of Derby. This was reason enough not to associate with what clearly went on in the Bennet household.

Who wouldn't be disgusted? In what sort of family did the teenaged daughter, who had clearly been out drinking late at night, offer strangers oral sex? The mother had sounded very off and definitely ridiculous. The two older sisters were in collusion to sweep their younger sister's conduct under the carpet, at least avoid public exposure.

Jane and Elizabeth's attempts to suppress the awful truth

about their family would be in vain. There was little chance of either of them dating prosperous men on more than a casual basis. Sure, Bingley was easy going and, as such, would enjoy himself with Jane, but no man who had grown up around people who were not derelicts would burden himself by making permanent connections with the Bennets of Longbourn Creek.

Chapter Five

The club had a stone pier that jutted out into the ocean forming a harbor that sheltered yacht club vessels including Will's sailboat swaying at anchor.

There was a fine breeze that day and not too many white caps, but to sail up the coast and back before dark they needed to get going.

Will's phone vibrated. A text from the captain read: The ship is stocked and ready.

In half an hour they were all aboard.

Elizabeth offered to "stay out of the way," and Bingley escorted her and Jane to seats at the engineered-wood table under the Bimini.

Will noticed Elizabeth staring at him as he helped the crew with the rigging, maneuvering the ship around obstacles to clear the harbor.

She wore a light summer dress over what appeared to be a boring black bathing suit.

No risqué wardrobe like when opening the front door to unexpected nighttime guests.

As they hit the open ocean, a text from Caroline popped up on Will's phone, and a salty mist sprayed the screen as he read: Eliza Bennet is surely going to use this opportunity to throw herself at you. Prepare yourself. I wish you luck.

Holding onto the mast, he set his phone to vibrate and buried it in his back pocket.

A beach bag in hand, Jane called to Bingley about going to change and disappeared below deck.

Elizabeth stayed put, her legs curled up beneath her on a cushioned bench as she watched Will and Bingley help the crew unfurl the two tall sails.

Passing Elizabeth on his way to tie off lines, Will turned and met her eyes. "Are you comfortable?"

"Yes, thank you." She sounded self-conscious.

He thought of the last time they saw each other when he'd dropped off Lydia. Barely a week ago. Whose insane idea was it to invite her sailing? Bingley's, of course. He wanted Jane to be relaxed so she'd hook up with him in one of the berths later on.

When Jane returned, wearing a white bikini, Elizabeth perked up, and the ship picked up speed, skimming the surface of the water as the sisters chatted. As they spoke, Elizabeth's expression morphed from elation to mocking disapproval in an instant and then back again. They were probably talking about guys, maybe the crew of sailors in white uniforms.

Will let the crew take over as the ship zigzagged its way up the coast, and he and Bingley went over to sit with the girls.

"We're about to pass Pemberley," Bingley said as he sat down next to Jane.

She looked out in anticipation, but Elizabeth glanced the other way, out to sea, even as Bingley tried to get her attention.

Will pretended not to notice.

Along with a pitcher of mojitos, the chef served a light lunch for four on the dining table midship, and they ate, talking of Bingley's plans for Netherfield renovations, laughing at the inauthenticity of a kitchen island with bar stools in a Victorian restoration.

With a wink, Bingley coaxed Jane to take a stroll. They made their way to the front of the ship with Jane holding onto the railings with both hands, saying, "I've never been on a sailboat before." When they reached the teak deck where thick towels were set out, they laid down together.

Left alone with Elizabeth, Darcy kept his eyes on the

coastline off the port side, which alternated between sandy beach and rocky cliffs.

Neither broke the silence.

She hadn't said much to him at lunch, just genial comments about how the fish was prepared and the color of the sea.

When the stewardess approached to ask if she could get them anything else, he answered, "No … unless Miss Bennet …?"

"I'm fine," she answered with a chirp. "Thank you."

He got up to do a once round the ship avoiding Bingley and Jane so as not to intrude and then had a word about the size of the waves with the captain at the helm.

When he returned, Elizabeth was still planted by the polished wood dining table. He pulled back the awning, letting in more sky as the sun was not directly overhead, then took a seat opposite her.

He looked at her.

She returned his gaze steadily.

He still didn't speak.

"Do you think maybe we should say something to each other, Darcy. It might be odd to sit together and say nothing."

He bowed his head. From where he sat, with the ship tilting, he got a view of her décolletage. "What would you like to talk about?"

"Hmm. Perhaps you should say something about the

weather. I'll compliment your boat. Then we can be silent again for a while."

He studied her face, evaluating its shape and features, the expression of her eyes. She was one of those women who looked better outdoors. Her brown hair had highlights of gold and her eyes shone even more than usual in the daylight.

"We speak by rule then?" he asked.

She nodded. "The two of us are both of a reserved disposition, not willing to speak unless we have something to say that's so impressive it will amaze the room." She sputtered a cough, or maybe it was a chuckle. "Therefore, we benefit from exacting guidelines that allow us to say as little as possible to each other."

He smiled despite himself. "I'm not sure that's an accurate description of you. Whether it describes me, I cannot say. You perhaps think so."

She shrugged, adjusting the strap of her sundress, which had slipped off her shoulder. "That's a sufficient reply for now." She reached for a glass of ice water, swirling the liquid in it, her lips twitching. "We can go back to ignoring each other."

"As you wish," he said, wishing he was not so drawn to her. "Please feel free to continue giving me instructions on how to behave."

She laughed out loud, then lean back in her seat with her hand on her stomach. Her flushed cheeks suddenly concerned him. He didn't want to give her the wrong idea. He would not now, or in the future, be offering to act as her date just because her sister was socializing with Bingley.

"I was wondering, or, eh, I'm not clear," he began. "Did I hear Jane say something about working at a bar downtown?"

The area where they sat was open on all sides, and a wet breeze tossed Elizabeth's hair about her face as she opened her mouth but no words came out.

Just as he'd suspected. Jane didn't have a job. The Bennets were known for leeching off of men, so how could Jane's employment status not be fishy?

Elizabeth blushed. "She's, uh, between jobs right now." Turning away, she looked at Jane and Bingley, who were now sharing a towel, their arms around each other.

Will took a deep breath. *Yes,* he thought, *I will be keeping an eye on your sister. With me around, Bingley will not fall prey to Bennet gold-digging, no matter how pleasantly disguised.*

He had seen Bingley "in love" dozens of times and not once had the relationship made it anywhere near the commitment stage. It would not go anywhere near that this time either. There was no chance of it. Jane was nice and all, but she would be sadly disappointed if that were her expectation.

Elizabeth sat up a little. "Jane saved up from her last gig, bartending at the beach, and is taking some time off."

Someone as intelligent as Elizabeth must realize that Jane,

who may be pretty and sweet, was not in the same league as Bingley, who graduated from MIT with a degree in industrial engineering and just finished law school.

"And you?" Darcy asked. "What do you do? I believe Jane said you're a musician."

She nodded. "I teach instrumental music at West Derby Elementary School."

"I see."

"It's hard on the ears sometimes," said Elizabeth, "but the kids are so enthusiastic and funny ... It's the job I always said I wanted." She smiled but it wasn't a full smile.

He scrutinized her face and considered asking what was the job she actually wanted. "And what is your degree?"

"Uh. I have a bachelor of arts." She sounded resigned to reading off her CV for him.

"In music education? Not music performance, correct?" The university near Derby wasn't bad, but it definitely didn't produce graduates who went on to join symphony orchestras. Was she one of those aspiring musicians not good enough for a career playing in an orchestra?

"Yes, music education."

"You graduated last year and got a full-time teaching job right away?" he asked.

"Yes," she said with a smirk. "I guess they had trouble filling the position."

"Hm," he mumbled.

He knew he sounded like his father questioning one of his cousins on their career path. But he was okay with patronizing Elizabeth, driving her away even. In addition to warning her with respect to Bingley being out of her sister's reach, he wanted to squash any hopes she might have about him. He was doing her a favor by giving her a clear message on that score.

"Hey, you two! There are dolphins off the bow!" Bingley called to them.

Elizabeth leapt up to see.

Will happily watched her go. He was again paying more attention to her than he intended.

Not that he was taken. He had no exclusive arrangement worked out with Bingley's sister Caroline or Anne de Bourgh, both of whom he was dating. But he was not going to have Elizabeth Bennet thinking he was a prospect.

When she returned, smiling and excited about seeing dolphins launching themselves out of the water, her cheeks were in bloom as she slid into her seat. He couldn't help but think of what he was passing up. If he sent the waitstaff below, and Bingley and Jane found their way to the guest berth, she might use her pert little mouth on him.

The thought caused him enough discomfort he had to adjust his pants, but his desire would be in vain. Even if at that moment she looked at him with a smile –"Hey , does this boat have bedrooms?" — he wouldn't bite.

Approximately twenty miles north of Derby as the crow flies, they were forced to abandon ship.

Elizabeth had been standing by the mast, the wind whipping her dress against her legs ... Will was wondering whether he ought to warn her against swaying and twisting on the open deck when Bingley came running up from below. "Elizabeth! Quick! Jane needs you. She's asking for you."

Will jumped from his seat.

Elizabeth rushed past him.

Jane was vomiting in the lavatory by the guest berth.

They took her to lie down in the owner's suite, but the way she didn't even sit up in bed to answer their inquiries meant her seasickness was not the mild or passing kind.

Will made the decision to lay down anchor and take the inflatable ashore.

Once on solid ground, the greenish hue around Jane's eyes disappeared, and Will knew he had made the right decision.

Bingley, talking nonstop out of a desire to be attentive, found Jane a seat on the crumbling dock where they had disembarked from the ship-to-shore motorboat.

"I hope you're more comfortable now," Will said, standing in front of Jane.

"Yes, but I feel terrible about being so much trouble," she

replied.

"No trouble at all," said Bingley, putting his arm around her, and pulling a backpack with drinks and protein bars onto his lap. "But we need to wait and make sure you're completely recovered before moving you."

Elizabeth, who hadn't taken a seat on the rickety dock, nodded in agreement, smiling at Bingley.

She looked relieved but was bouncing from foot to foot, as if ready to move.

On her feet were sandals, but unlike Jane's flimsy-looking slip-ons, Elizabeth's were flats with a strap in the back, suitable for walking. The back of her legs had noticeably toned muscles.

"I believe there's a tiny village nearby," said Will, drawing Elizabeth's eyes to him and preventing himself from continuing to check out her tanned body. "Would you accompany me for a walkabout? We can see what's nearby and decide how to proceed."

"Absolutely," said Elizabeth, looking a little surprised by his proposal but enthusiastic. "We'll look for a coffee shop, so Jane can rest a bit, or maybe there's a bus stop where we can catch a ride home."

"We'll be lucky to find any stores open Sunday afternoon," Will replied.

Bingley downed half a bottle of water and handed a second bottle to Elizabeth. "Okay, but remember, you're in charge. Don't let Will talk you into renting jet skis or something."

Elizabeth laughed, and Will noticed her watching for his reaction with a side-eyed glance.

"No boats of any kind," said Elizabeth, smiling unaffectedly at Bingley and Jane. "I promise."

"We'll be able to follow you in a few minutes, Lizzy," said Jane. There was tension between her dove-like eyes as if she worried about her sister walking off alone with him.

But for what possible reason?

Elizabeth moved swiftly, jumping over puddles, scaling rocky steps with ease, and splashing mud on the back of her cottony dress.

Will quietly followed her, a half a step behind as she led the way.

When they came to a paved road, she looked right, then left, then right again. "I think it's this way."

"And on what do you base your assessment?" he asked, suppressing an urge to belittle her with a grin.

"Pure instinct," she said, looking pleased with herself.

"Well, I believe you're correct," he said. "The town should be north of here."

They set off and, round the second bend in the road, they found the village. The main street contained a real estate office, a dentist, and a gas station. All of which had 'closed' signs.

Elizabeth spun around, wide-eyed. "It's like a ghost town."

"I believe it used to be a fishing village until the fisheries left the area," he said.

"Too bad they didn't rebrand themselves with a spiffy name like *Ocean Breakers* and build 4 bath condos with sea views."

"Right," he said, checking the sun's position in the sky and not considering whether her comment was directed at him.

She dug a thick phone out of the pocket of her dress. "Bummer. I still don't have cell service."

"Me either," he said, checking his phone. "I'll walk west toward the highway and call a car service from there."

"Look!" Pointing, she set off jogging across the street where a gas station attendant sat in the shade by the side of a cement building painted with a teal wave.

Without getting up, the attendant shrugged in response to her questions. "My boss locked the office. These days no one stops here asking to use the telephone. Why do ya'll need a ride to Derby if you've got a boat over yonder?"

Her hand on her hip, and her head tilted to the side, she looked like someone persistent enough to tell him to get off his ass and go find her a telephone.

Will thought of his sister, who would have taken a seat out front and waited for service, expecting to be asked if she needed anything.

"But I saw a sign for a bed and breakfast," Elizabeth said to the attendant, who reclined in his lawn chair in order to look up at her. "Do you know if it has a restaurant?"

"They shut down years ago," he answered.

"And there's no other place that might have a phone we could use?" she asked.

"None open today."

"There must be a hotel by the interstate," she said.

"There's one about twenty miles north."

Elizabeth shook her head. "Do you know if there's any place in town where we might have better luck with cell phone reception?"

The attendant squinted with open mouth, showing his front two teeth. "All I know is what I told ya."

Elizabeth said goodbye and turned to Will. "Let's look around town a bit more."

"What for?" As fun as it was to watch her nimble body scurry about, it was time for him to take charge.

"Maybe we could bang on someone's door and ask for help." Her face was glowing.

"This is not a place where residents are accustomed to tourists stopping by."

She looked undeterred. "But I saw a cottage with a cow flag out front that seemed welcoming."

"I don't believe we can infer from a cow flag that the occupant will hand over his phone. This is a backwoods area. Locals don't look favorably on unfamiliar persons setting foot on their property."

She twisted her lips. "There could be someplace up the road, closer to the highway. I saw a billboard with a Harley Davidson advertisement. Maybe that means there's a dealership nearby."

"A motorcycle dealer around here?" he asked. "In my experience, few people share your strong preference for bikes." Since the night of the party at Netherfield, he'd spotted her several times on her Vespa riding around town.

Watching the gears in her head turning amused him. Her determination to find a solution to their problem without relying on him was commendable and unexpected. But they would be running out of daylight in not too many hours. "If we're done with the wild goose chase, I'll walk you back to Jane and Bingley and then head west until I get cell service."

She huffed at the words "wild goose chase," then pinned him with squinting eyes. "I wouldn't want to be rash and send you off on your own. You might get lost. And, I'm guessing you don't like to ask for directions."

He gave her a slanted grin. "I need to get going so I can contact a car service to pick us up."

She frowned, shuffling her feet, the hem of her dress

splashed with dirt. "To get a cab to come get us in the middle of nowhere would cost as much as tickets to go see the Rockettes in New York. Couldn't we call and ask someone for a ride?"

"I suppose, but I wouldn't want to trouble anyone to drive across the county for us when I can just as well hire a car."

"You know, I think we can walk home no problem. As soon as Jane is better. All we have to do is follow the coast then turn west at the Derby Freeway, and friends could pick us up there."

He just stared, wondering what she was about. Was her refusal about the cost of a cab as she implied? She'd just been sailing and dining on a 90-foot yacht. She had a bona fide job. She lived in the most inexpensive housing in the area, probably rent free. "I will take care of the expense," he said.

Her brows pinched together as if he'd offered to pluck out a half dozen of her extra-long dark eyelashes. "Come on, Darcy. What's the matter with a little walking?"

He stared again, wordlessly, feeling his rudeness but not bothering to be subtle. Where was she coming from?

"I'm sure you can handle a nice long walk," she repeated archly.

He shrugged. "If you insist."

If he and Elizabeth spent a few extra hours together, he could honestly say he didn't mind.

Was it such a disaster?

He could control himself around Elizabeth Bennet. Real men can resist even if they feel a bit of a strange attraction.

#

They started out slow, Elizabeth offering to give in and let Darcy call a high-priced taxi if Jane felt sick again.

But Jane was enthusiastic. "This is a great idea. I love a walk. It's just what I need."

Soon they found their way to North Oceanside Drive with its roomy sidewalks and set a leisurely pace as Bingley entertained them with anecdotes about growing up in Texas — mostly stories about animals biting people in strange places. A story from college days followed about Darcy losing his on-campus parking permit and giving flowers to administrative staff to get a replacement. Then onto recent summertime adventures getting dress coded at the country club for wearing a school ring — no jewelry allowed on men except wedding rings.

Elizabeth was determined to dislike Darcy, so it was a bit disconcerting to get such a kick out of laughing at him.

Bingley's gleeful demeanor was so at variance with his friend's upper-crust languor that the contrast was inspiring to wit. Elizabeth felt an urge to let loose and help Bingley rib his friend, but she warned herself not to go too far and embarrass Jane.

Jane was at her best, less placid and more animated under the influence of Bingley's cheerfulness.

Bingley told a story about how Will was trying to keep it under wraps that he'd been thrown by his prized Arabian horse. "Even his beloved border collies left him in the dust, running home without him."

Darcy shook his head in the face of his friend's laughter but didn't seem angry.

Elizabeth couldn't resist. "I always thought of you as the kind of guy who'd have a pack of French poodles, not collies."

Darcy gave her a withering look. "I didn't choose sheep dogs. My dog chose me."

The burnt red color at his cheekbones was noticeable as he walked with long strides. He was so handsome, like a JFK Jr. of the South who'd inherited not just his ancestor's money but all their good genes. "He found me when he was a puppy," said Darcy.

"Where did he *find* you? At an animal shelter?" Elizabeth asked. "Not a puppy mill, I hope. You seem like too much of an animal lover for that."

"No, oddly enough we were out at sea, no land in sight, and I spotted him swimming hard straight toward the catamaran we were sailing. There were no other vessels around for miles. The only thing I could think of is that he fell off a cruise ship. There was one passing by earlier."

Bingley affirmed this was not a tall tale. "Right, and Will decides then and there that he must find the little rascal a mate, so he can pass on his scrappy survival instincts. Before we're even at port, he's making plans to contact reputable breeders and acquire a young female border collie."

"Lucky her," said Elizabeth. "So you're grandpapa to lots of puppies now? I'm trying to imagine you holding a nursing bottle."

"No," said Darcy. "That was years ago. Felix and Shire are like an old married couple now."

Elizabeth felt giggles rising inside her. "I understand that your dog is a great swimmer and resourceful, to be sure, but if he fell off a cruise ship, he might have some worrisome carelessness, which ought not be passed down to the next generation. Don't you think?"

"Your suspicion is correct; he's incautious about threats like snakes," said Darcy, turning to look directly at Elizabeth.

Her arms swung high as she walked. "Also, you didn't mention whether you checked to see if the original owners were desperately searching for their lost puppy."

"As for that, I did call all the cruise lines, but he must have been presumed dead because the representatives I spoke to had been given no information about a lost dog."

His deadpan calmness as he answered her inquiries had her itching to ask more pot-stirring questions, but she paused to allow Jane to make some more normal inquiries.

At a lull in the conversation, Elizabeth let it all out. How many opportunities would she have to poke the great Will Darcy? "One thing I always wanted to know, Darcy, is how you manage to keep people off your private beach. The public beach in Derby is so crowded. Some people must be tempted to trespass. It must be such a headache. Do you have security?"

"I can't tell you what sort of security I have." He smiled drolly, meeting her eye. "But, yes, often I find a family picnicking on the beach. It's not a big deal. They think they've discovered a wildlife preserve. I tell them I'm the owner; that they have my permission to stay for a few hours; but they must take away all their trash when they leave."

"How gracious of you! I'll be over next week."

"You're certainly welcome," he said without a hitch and actually laughing out loud for the first time she could remember.

His automatic sense of politeness must have kicked in and made him speak without thinking.

Elizabeth blushed all over at the thought of going to Pemberley. It was, in her mind, like a distant and impossible place.

A few hours later, after a turn in the road, Bingley called Elizabeth's name and motioned for her to follow a footpath leading through some trees to a smaller gravel lane.

Was this a shortcut to the Derby Freeway? They should be there soon.

Elizabeth did a 360, trying to figure out what was up, but in the gloaming she didn't recognize anything.

Darcy and Bingley must know something she didn't because they immediately started down the new narrower road.

Elizabeth followed, expecting to soon recognize her surroundings as they made their way up a hill and around a corner to a clearing.

Instead, off in the distance, she saw a palatial white house she'd never seen before except in photographs.

The building, which appeared on half the post cards in the Derby Gift Shop, was about a mile off, set by the ocean on a deep rocky beach. In the twilight, tall verandas were clearly visible on two sides of the house.

Love-struck Jane followed Bingley along a meandering, crushed seashell lane heading in the direction of Pemberley.

Elizabeth spun around and turned back.

Chapter Six

Darcy cleared his throat and called to her in a cutting voice, "You are, of course, invited back to my house."

Oh the indignity. Elizabeth craned her neck to look back at him without retracing even one step.

His tense features said it all. He'd been trapped by circumstances beyond his control. Poor Darcy had to watch as a Bennet approached Pemberley House for the first time ever -- his only comfort being it was benevolent Jane.

"I can walk home by myself," Elizabeth said as she began a quickstep retreat.

Darcy came after her, his step causing a loud crunching

sound. "You have to let me take you home, Elizabeth." His expression was that of a doctor trying to wrangle a patient into submitting to necessary treatment.

She turned on him, curling her lip. "*Have to*?"

He walked up to her, face to face. Bingley and Jane were forgotten. "Yes, we're at Pemberley now, so your safety is my responsibility, no more scurrying about in search of alternate transportation. You have to allow me to get you home safe."

She shook her head, hands springing to her hips.

It could have been a thoughtful offer of a ride or a place to rest before she was picked up by local friends, but he botched it with his autocratic ways.

"I know you've been living abroad," she said, "which must be your excuse, but your English has gotten rusty. I don't *have to* do anything."

He let out a huff, which was almost impressive as a measure of his temerity, but then seemed to think better of it and took on a more relaxed affect. "I apologize for my ... word choice. But my home is up ahead, down a lane on the left, behind those trees." He pointed in a northeastern direction and not toward grand Pemberley House. "It's less than a half mile off."

She wrapped her arms around her waist defensively. "Yes, I understand that." In truth, she was only just now realizing he had his own home near his parents. "But I'm going to walk to Longbourn. I'll find the way."

Not a muscle in his arms or legs moved, his mouth set like stone.

The pause was horrible to her nerves, but she couldn't back down.

"I can't let you walk home by yourself in the dark," he said with piercing eyes, seeming to hold something back. Maybe some harsher language. "It would be irresponsible of me. We can get my car and I'll drive you."

"Your car is back at the yacht club, silly," she said, studying him.

Why did he suddenly look apprehensive, and why was such an obvious fact lost on typically staid, know-it-all Darcy? They'd started their journey at the Derby Yacht Club where all their vehicles were parked.

"That's, eh, yes." His voice took on an odd warble. "I can borrow my, uh, father's car," he said, pausing on the word father.

She blushed.

He was thinking of his dad, Fredrick Darcy, Esq.. He was mentioning his father to *her* of all people.

Which meant he was thinking of his dad's affair with her aunt Phyllis way back when Will was in kindergarten and Elizabeth was unborn.

This was why no Bennet would ever be welcome at Pemberley. Not her aunt Phyllis, who, in her heyday, was said to be as beautiful as Grace Kelly. Not her mother or sisters. Not any of her Bennet cousins who lived on Copacabana Street in Longbourn trailer park.

Indeed, it had been far from Pemberley, at some rest-stop motel, where her aunt Phyllis, with the light green eyes and respect for Rolexes that epitomized the classic Bennet girl, had become intimately involved with Darcy's dad for at least one night, despite the fact he was married. Phyllis Bennet had prepared a pin pricked condom just for her date with a Darcy. A grifter move if there ever was one.

Maybe Darcy was thinking that he or Bingley were in danger from just such a Bennet family trick.

"No, don't worry about it," said Elizabeth, not wanting to look at his face another moment and wishing she could stop speculating about his most intimate thoughts. "I've been walking home by myself since 6th grade. I'll be fine."

Rising on her tippy toes, she was ready to sprint out of there.

Emotion spread over his normally stoic features. "I don't understand," he said. "First, I can't pay for a cab and now I can't drive you home. There is an issue with you and four-wheel motor vehicles? Or you and *me*?"

Her cheeks burned. When she'd made a big deal about not wasting money on a cab, he had given in. When they'd stopped for a quick bite in the middle of their long walk, she'd insisted on paying for her own dinner, over Bingley's objection as he settled the remainder of the bill while Will just shrugged. Now Will was asking questions that got too close for comfort to the seven figure paternity suit filed by her aunt over the unwanted kid she created with Darcy's father.

Elizabeth would never take cash from a Darcy. On principle. The principle that she was not like her aunt. Or her mom. Or a woman who'd want to get knocked up by, or be kept by, a rich guy.

"Okay, I give in. Call me a cab," she said, desperate to come up with a plan, any plan to get out of there. "It's only a short ride home."

It wouldn't cost too much to be picked up on the road just outside Pemberley — she would pay maybe $20 for a ride home to Longbourn, and he wouldn't feel like he was leaving her in the lurch. They'd both escape. No harm, no foul.

It was almost dark in the lane where they were standing, except for flickering lights inside antique lamp posts leading the way to Pemberley House. But she could see Darcy's facial expression.

His eyes were strained with worry. Worry about her safety? It had to be more than that.

"I really wish you would allow *me* to take you home," he said, glancing south in the direction of downtown Derby. He sounded chastened and almost pleading. "I'm responsible for you."

She stuttered. "Uh, I..." It was suddenly harder to shoot him down. She felt something in her stomach, a little pinch, like she was attracted to him. This softer Darcy was more handsome than arrogant Darcy, although he wore the same classically styled shirt and khakis.

"I think perhaps you're a little ... not yourself," he said in a low voice. "I assume you don't often have two glasses of champagne with dinner?"

"Uh, true, but—"

"Only ten minutes ago you were stumbling down the side of the road singing country western songs. It might not be safe to go off with a stranger in your condition. A strange driver, I mean."

Okay, technically this was correct. Her students had been practicing "This Land is Your Land" all week, and she'd heard it played in slow squeaky succession at least one hundred times, so she'd done a bit of marching and singing during their walk.

She was not drunk, maybe a little tipsy but the alcohol was being counteracted by shots of adrenaline.

Why wouldn't he let it go? He knew the reason she and Jane shouldn't be at Pemberley as well as she did.

Why didn't he back off gracefully given the chance? She was presenting him with an out and he wasn't taking it.

She would *not* be following Jane onto his property, and Will Darcy would be better off for it. Only imagine if his dad saw not one but two of Phyllis Bennet's nieces at Pemberley. A blond one, who looked like Phyllis, with Bingley and a mousy brown haired one walking with Will.

"Please. Just forget about it. Okay?" she whined, feeling bubbles in her stomach after the mention of champagne. "Let the subject drop. It's best for both of us."

"What do you mean ... best for both of us?"

"Because of the awkward history between my aunt and your dad, I avoid your property and your money scrupulously." She said it.

His eyes bulged. "I do *not* want to talk about that."

"Me either," she snapped. "But you won't let me walk away!"

She turned to leave, trying not to seem like she was storming off but ready to run when she was out of sight.

"Miss Bennet!"

She spun around again, feeling a cramp in her stomach that made her bend over. Just breathing was strenuous. If he didn't want to discuss this subject with her, he should let her go.

"I'm not exactly sure what any of that has to do with getting you home tonight, but—"

"You're right," she interrupted. "There's nothing to say about it. Richard was shipped off, so to speak. Good riddance, to be honest. He was awful. Nothing to talk about except *I* will never take money from your family."

His face went ghostlike.

She watched his chest expanding and contracting.

"I know nothing of that," said Darcy. "I never met him. I can never ask my parents about the situation without causing pain. I can't believe I'm discussing it ... with you. But, I can say the whole tragic topic is beyond my sphere of influence."

"I grew up next door to him," said Elizabeth. "He was a complete ass actually. You're lucky you never had to put up with him."

His mouth dropped open. "I don't know what to say to that."

Elizabeth was fifteen, which meant Will would have been around twenty-one, when Richard, age sixteen, crashed a Porsche while showing off after a night of partying in Miami and, worst of all, injured several innocent bystanders.

A portion of the paternity settlement won by Aunt Phyllis went to settle lawsuits, but she was left with at least $500,000, which meant she was set for life financially, living high on the hog as the wealthiest person in Longbourn trailer park, and given endless opportunities to garner sympathy by weeping for "Poor Richard" while he sat in jail and later joined the Navy as part of a parole agreement.

Will interrupted her thoughts. "It's a sad business but please don't imply that I had any part in 'shipping him off.' I do feel pity for whatever your cousin may have gone through with regard to his, uh, difficulties."

"You were away at college when he had his accident, so what could you do?" she said slowly.

He seemed to ponder this, almost shaking his head no but not distinctly.

"My father and I handle our own concerns. We're both adults." He exhaled loudly. "Can we return to the issue at hand, Elizabeth?"

She nodded, feeling drained.

He crept closer to her, tilting his head to the side.

She held her breath.

He stared at her, a raw emotive tinge in his striking grey eyes.

What would she do if he touched her? The idea nearly made her faint. What was happening? If he reached for her hand, she'd break. "Fine. You win," she said. All he ever had to do was ask nicely and she was putty in his hands.

He exhaled audibly. "Good."

Reaching for her, his hand hovered near her lower back as he slowly guided her toward a bench built around a maple tree.

The amount of dry heat radiating from his body as she fell into step at his side seemed biologically impossible.

She sat down and he pulled out his cell phone and quickly typed a message, presumably to Bingley.

With an unintended squeak in her voice, she said, "The last thing I wanted to do is press myself on you. But you wouldn't let me get away."

His shoulders stiffened. "You don't need to *get away* from me." He sounded genuinely offended.

She looked up at him, unable to smile but feeling pleased by his words.

He was certainly big boned in comparison to Bingley, with long limbs, a broad build, and large proportions.

What could be more ludicrous to someone like him than arguing with her about transportation? To him she had made a big deal about a pittance. Yet it was so attractive the way he now spoke to her like he took her seriously.

She gazed at him as if she were seeing him for the first time.

Understanding was so much harder than laughing at him.

"Given my family, you can see why I might be wary of you?" she said, trying to put a bit of lightness in her voice, wanting to shake off her lingering feelings of embarrassment.

"Actually...from my point of view, *I* might be the one with a reason to be cautious."

She grimaced, not wanting to believe that what he said was fair. She challenged, "Because of my family, you're allowed to assume the worst of me?"

"No," he said, never before sounding so authentic. "And I

do not. I have no reason to believe anything ill of you."

The sound of a car engine made them both turn.

Headlights blinded her.

Car windows rolled down and Bingley pulled up alongside them. "What's up, stragglers? I borrowed Georgiana's car."

#

Elizabeth and Jane finally made it home, although not unscathed.

Despite the late hour and despite having been walking for half the day, Elizabeth grabbed a couple chocolate Swiss roll snacks and went out to be by herself, treading along Longbourn Creek on the near bank, her normal walking path.

At night the wooded area lined with colorful beach chairs set next to prized "riverfront" trailers was lit by year-round Christmas lights.

The smoky smell of vinegar barbecue permeated the cool night air as Elizabeth thought of her childhood, riding her bike along the crisscrossing dirt lanes of Longbourn trailer park until she got lost and had to scout her way home.

She knew most of the longtime residents of Longbourn. She felt safe here. Unlike at Pemberley, where she was in danger of humiliation on a primal level.

She wasn't sure if she *feared* Will Darcy's gallant side more than she preferred it to his domineering side.

She ought not like anything about him.

As tempting as it might be, she could not respond to any of his seeming concern for her wellbeing with vulnerability.

Never forget Netherfield. Back away quickly.

Someone like Will Darcy would crush her fragile sensibilities just as she was ready to rise above and stop feeling like she was doomed to be just another Bennet.

Not so many years ago, she'd been weak enough to date an abusive ass because she'd just lost her dad and needed to feel wanted. Because Will Darcy said some suave things to her, spoke to her in a certain sensitive tone of voice that was so evocative, didn't mean she could allow herself to be flattered.

He would never be interested in someone like her.

She would only get hurt.

How had it happened? Why had it happened? The two of them standing in the middle of the road at Pemberley quarreling like emo teens.

Her cousin Richard, the rejected bastard child, was not allowed to set foot on Pemberley property or use the name Darcy, but there she was, taking up his case to Will Darcy, and doing all she could to rile Will's distrust.

According to a legal settlement drawn up by the elder Mr. Darcy's lawyers, Aunt Phyllis couldn't mention the name of Richard's father or put it in writing. Nonetheless, when Will Darcy was about ten years old, the secret of Richard Bennet's paternity got out. Copies of blood test results ordered in the paternity case were disseminated anonymously.

As Richard's existence became widely known, the Darcys closed ranks, refusing to answer questions about the five-year-old boy. Anyone who wanted to do business with the Darcys, which was everyone in town, knew not to mention the name Richard Bennet.

Will's mother, Ladybird Darcy, seemed to forgive her husband's certified infidelity, or convince herself Phyllis was a contemptuous temptress, because Will's sister, Georgiana Darcy, was born about a year after.

Elizabeth remembered Richard as a kid who stole dollar coins from her and her sisters and bullied other boys into handing over their electronics. Gangly, he was usually either cursing at his mother or throwing cans at cars.

Will Darcy's reaction to her allusion to Richard made it clear it was a sore subject for him. Despite his family's seeming ability to ignore Richard's existence, there was probably some drama behind closed doors. His parents perhaps had struggled to stay together right after his mom learned about Richard. Maybe Will was ashamed of his dad. Maybe Will didn't want to face the unfairness of his family's complete dismissal of Richard.

In any case, Elizabeth didn't want to keep discovering new ways to mortify herself in front of Will Darcy. There was some squishy portion of her self-esteem pummeled by his very presence. Her insecurities about her fledgling financial independence, her pathetic dating history including going off with guys to make her feel better about herself, her family's grabby exploits, and the questionable conduct of her mom and Lydia weighed on her. She needed to take care of herself, not drag herself along on Jane's dates and force Will Darcy to socialize with her.

Jane could handle herself with Bingley now; he was clearly smitten with her. Elizabeth would have to enjoy the sight of Jane's good fortune at a safe distance.

#

"So how was it?" Elizabeth asked, as she leaned back in the overstuffed recliner covered in mildew-resistant vinyl and sipped strong-brewed English Breakfast tea meant to wake her up for work.

Last night Bingley had convinced Jane to wait around with him for a late night delivery of reclaimed walnut planks at the Netherfield construction site, and Jane had stayed with him all night. She had gotten home at 5:30 in the morning, with serious bedhead.

"Oh, Lizzy! Don't ask me that," Jane laughed self-consciously as she massaged her face with creamy white cleanser.

The old stuffed chair Elizabeth sat in had been dragged into the trailer's only bathroom years ago so the sisters could hang out while getting ready in the morning. Their bedroom was crammed with bunk beds, an overflowing dresser and a second-hand stair master while the bathroom was spacious in proportion to the rest of the rooms in the trailer.

There was of course a no food in the bathroom rule to make things less whiskey tango, but Elizabeth was flouting this with her hot beverage.

"Did you do it by candlelight?" Elizabeth smiled, reclining in her cushiony chair.

Jane's cheeks bloomed as she nodded faintly and turned away.

"Come on, don't be stingy. I live through you vicariously."

"I wish you would give some guy a call," Jane said as she rifled through a drawer, "and join Bingley and me for dinner."

"Sure, I'll ring Mr. Collins." She ought to get dressed and stop procrastinating, but she'd rather quiz Jane.

"Maybe not Bobby Collins," said Jane, twisting her lips as she traced her face with toner. "Although I really believe that he may be a good sort of man despite his, uh, oddities."

"I'll stay home and finish off the ketchup meatloaf Mom plans to foist on your male callers," said Elizabeth.

Jane shook her head, smiling as she opened a jar of green mud and carefully slathered it on her slim neck.

Elizabeth leaned over the padded armrest of her chair, making a crinkling sound as she grabbed a hairbrush lying on

119

the floor. She pulled long blond hairs out of the brush before taking a crack at detangling her own brown waves. She was the only one in her family with any curl or pigment in their hair.

"All I'm asking for is a few nuggets about you and Bingley on his king-sized four poster bed. Is that too much to ask?" said Elizabeth, a twinkle in her eye.

Jane shook her head. "Did I tell you? The other night at the club they were discussing the new dress code. The board of directors is changing it next season to prohibit see-through fabric. I'm not sure if there was some sort of problem with overly adventurous outfits."

"Only *opaque* imported silk is acceptable at a yacht club," Elizabeth laughed. "And yet think of the poor women who have been trying for the appearance of nudity to capture Darcy's attention. Thwarted again."

"Come on, he's not so bad," Jane said as she wiped her face with a brown washcloth.

"What are you talking about? He's the second worst thing about this town, right behind the mini Chardonnay bottles they sell at the beach." Elizabeth prodded a scab on her knee. "Forget about Darcy. Let's talk about his friend. Was he cool about you-know-what?"

Jane's first serious boyfriend had refused to use condoms, and she had been terrified of pregnancy for months. It turned her off to guys for a while, and she became an advocate of group get-togethers, like playing arcade games at the boardwalk, as alternatives to one-on-one dates.

Jane sighed as she applied tinted moisturizer in a shade close to pearl. "He was cool. It was very nice."

Getting up to stand behind Jane, Elizabeth looked at herself in the mirror. *Who's that Gypsy bumpkin making pouty faces?* Her arms and legs were marked with various beauty marks and scars. Jane's skin, in contrast, was immaculate.

"You're big time now," Elizabeth whispered. "First sailing on the Darcy yacht, and now spending the night at Netherfield. Soon you'll be riding horses on the beach at Pemberley. But I have to ask, did Bingley say anything about Darcy complaining about me after our conversation outside Pemberley?"

"Oh no, not at all. Bingley was thrilled with how the day went, overall, I mean, except for when I got sick. He thought you and Darcy were great together. He thinks you're very funny. And Will told him he was quite pleased with how it all went off on the whole."

"Okey-doke." Elizabeth felt a strange tingle of elation, maybe at hearing Bingley enjoyed both her and Jane's company. She pulled on jeans and a sleeveless tee, then wiped an eyelash off her cheek and shrugged. Good enough for work. Her students didn't care if she wore make up.

Jane dusted her face with powder using a giant make up brush that seemed half the size of her face and exhaled softly.

"Could you ever have imagined it when everyone called us Bend-over Bennets in high school? Being at Pemberley and having them drive us home in that car."

Jane rarely talked about the cruel things kids said to them in high school, the rhymes they made up using their last name and the times some guy yelled, "You're a whore like your aunt." It was too painful for Jane. She must be in the best mood after fucking Bingley to bring it up.

"I guess there's no way I'm going to get information about his penis," said Elizabeth, quickly swiping her underarms with deodorant.

"Lizzy!" Jane exclaimed with laughing disapproval.

Elizabeth collected towels from the floor and hung them on hooks. "Just take care, Jane. You never know how much Bingley's influenced by the Darcys, and to some degree they still hate our family, despite any outward niceties from Will."

"I've made no assumptions about the degree of Bingley's fondness for me. I like him a lot but there's nothing serious at this point." Jane colored her eyelids with honey shadow.

"You're every man's dream. *Oh, it's not serious — we're just sleeping together.*"

Jane smiled. "I told you about that time he said he'd never really been in love before."

Elizabeth felt a chill. She was excited but worried. "Oh Jane, please promise me you won't let him buy you *anything*."

Jane dropped her makeup brush in the sink. "Of course not. Don't think I'd be so weak, Lizzy. I know how that would look."

"Yes. Yes. Of course you do. I'm sorry."

Jane picked up the brush.

"Remember Tim, my first boyfriend, the jock," said Elizabeth. "I was so excited to be dating a senior, thinking we were having the most amazing sex. He'd finish in thirty seconds, hollering about how I was so sexy that he couldn't hold out any longer." Back then Elizabeth had thought she was hot stuff. No self-esteem issues with her. Her dad hadn't overdosed yet. She was popular with guys. Little did she know, both she and her beefcake boyfriend were totally lame. "Please assure me that your night was nothing like that, Jane."

"Not at all. He was just cute. Bouncing around. Like he couldn't keep still."

"What?" Elizabeth yelled, feeling dubious of his prowess. "Like the way he talks when he's excited, switching from topic to topic, talking about three things at once."

"No, he was just enthusiastic and so sweet."

"He had condoms?" asked Elizabeth.

"He went out to buy them."

"I can picture it. Him telling you how beautiful you are as he kisses you," said Elizabeth dreamily, thinking she'd never have happiness like Jane's.

#

The pink Tiffany roses Bingley sent Jane were set out in a
red glass vase on the coffee table next to an open Pepsi can and
old copies of Southern Living magazine on which Elizabeth
rested her bare feet. She was feeling lazy since Charlotte stopped
by earlier with news that Bobby Collins had asked her out (not
surprising actually) and she had said yes (unfuckingbelievable).

Elizabeth couldn't understand. Charlotte was too sensible
to not see what a pompous toad Bobby Collins was. Charlotte
had a life, friends, family, a good job, and a four-door vehicle to
get to work in. She lectured Charlotte on *all* of this.

"Lizzy," Charlotte said with an edge to her voice as she
swirled a spoon in her tea with a shaky motion. "You're always
comparing yourself to Jane and insisting you come up short, but
what you don't seem to realize is that everywhere you go there
are men paying attention to you. Maybe not the richest men in
town or the Bingleys of the world, which shouldn't bother you
because you insist that you don't aspire to go out with a guy with
money, but nevertheless you're popular with men. I'm not. It's
not like I have the options you and Jane do."

Elizabeth swallowed her words, wishing to repeat her
lecture.

"I don't really need a guy who's great company, just
tolerable company. That's all my mother has. I don't ask a lot, a
nice place to live and a real garden. Reverend Collins could be all

that I want given these criteria."

Elizabeth had felt a palpable tension as Charlotte got up to leave, a second cup of milky tea in her travel mug. They had parted on speaking terms but Charlotte was seriously unhappy.

There was a knock at the door that bumped Elizabeth out of her thoughts.

Reaching for a color-block afghan from the back of the couch, she wrapped it around her shoulders as a makeshift coverup.

Mrs. Bennet rushed across the living room, calling to Jane, "Hurry, my dear, he's here. Bingley is here early! Check yourself in the mirror before you come out!"

Remaining seated, Elizabeth prayed she smelled okay if Bingley leaned over to kiss her on the cheek as he did the last time he came by.

Mrs. Bennet swung open the hatch-like front door of the trailer and exclaimed, "Oh, Bingley, I knew it was you."

"How do you do, Mrs. Bennet?" said Bingley, walking in like he'd been there a hundred times before although it was only twice. "I hope you're well this evening."

"Yes, very well, I thank you, sir," said Mrs. Bennet, in a high pitched voice, "And I hope—" Her voice slipped to a lower range. "Oh! I see you brought a friend."

Will Darcy walked into the room several paces behind Bingley.

Elizabeth's feet slid off the coffee table and onto the carpet with a thud as magazines splashed onto the floor.

Mrs. Bennet spoke to Darcy. "Yes, it is indeed Mr. Darcy! I should say you are most welcome ... and so on and so forth. Let's forget about ancient history and all. Be that as it may, we're pleased to be entertaining a Darcy at our home." Mrs. Bennet turned a pointed, meaningful smile on Lydia and Elizabeth. "Isn't that right, girls?"

Lydia, seated in a recliner, giggled at their mother's contorted expressions.

Elizabeth felt lightheaded as she got to her feet. Good god, she knew Darcy could not but notice, with his critical eye, her tattered sweatpants, half-painted toenails and maybe even her cheesy garlic breath if he got close enough.

He greeted her with a slight nod of his head.

"Hello," she lobbed back in his direction as she stood frozen in place next to the blaring television set tuned to Lydia's favorite soap opera.

He walked past her toward the back window with a view of Longbourn Creek.

While conversing with Mrs. Bennet, Bingley dipped in to peck Lydia on the cheek. Then he stepped over to Elizabeth.

"Hey, how's it going?" said Elizabeth, letting the blanket fall back onto the couch.

Bingley gave her a quick hug and kiss that was over so

fast she was too distracted to notice anything except a split second feel of thin, warm limbs under plush fabric.

Through the front window, Elizabeth caught a glimpse of Darcy's black Aston Martin parked out front drawing the attention of a group of neighborhood kids.

Rubbing her arms to perk herself up, Elizabeth reached for the back of the TV, turning it off manually, eliciting a complaint from Lydia, "Come on, Lizzy! Nobody cares about your stupid etiquette."

With the elimination of background noise, the room was suddenly quiet enough for everyone to be a part of one conversation.

"I hope you were able to get the wallpaper you were looking for," said Mrs. Bennet to Bingley. "Jane said you have to have the finest quality in everything."

Bingley started to answer, but Mrs. Bennet, not bothering to listen for a reply, interrupted, "Oh, dear me, what was I thinking. I have to mention the flowers. Jane was so flattered. They must have cost a fortune. Of course, none of us can imagine what special occasion you're celebrating." She smiled broadly, winking at Bingley. "Jane told us nothing. Nothing at all. Although the Lucases think she's the luckiest girl in town."

Jane, who had just entered the room, blushed as Bingley turned to her with a smile.

Darcy was standing motionless near a ding in the wall

made by one of Mrs. Bennet's exes throwing a mug during a Super Bowl party.

"Buying flowers is nothing to Bingley," interjected Lydia, who looked bored. "He bought the biggest house on the beach."

Bingley smiled with an awkward chuckle.

Darcy frowned, glancing up at the ceiling in the corner of the room where there were water stains from the leaky roof.

"Now, Bingley," said Mrs. Bennet, not allowing Jane to get a word in. "Pray tell your sister I loved the purse she donated for the silent auction." She directed Lydia with a familiar shooing motion that meant she was to get their guests beer from the fridge. "Caroline's picture was on DerbyCentral.org. My Jane's was as well but it wasn't posted as it ought; you couldn't see her face. How Jane would love a Hermès purse like your sister's! Your sister has such fabulous clothes, Bingley. Jane would look so beautiful in a gown like the one Caroline wore to last week's benefit at the country club. All my neighbors are always stopping by to tell me how rich and great Jane is going to be someday."

Darcy shook his head no as he was offered a beer by Lydia, who pertly smiled at him with a confidence that impressed Elizabeth. No sign of lingering embarrassment from the way she acted with him when he drove her home after her late night out drinking with drag racers. Luckily, her recklessness of that evening hadn't been repeated after Elizabeth bribed her with a new smart phone that would stay on only as long as she didn't drink or ride with drinkers.

"Oh, well, if your friend doesn't like beer," said Mrs. Bennet, "I'm sure we can get him a glass of whiskey. Or does Mr. Darcy drink bourbon?"

Elizabeth cringed as her mom put on a Southern accent that sounded like something out of a high-end brothel.

"Thank you, ma'am. I'm fine," said Darcy.

Will's height alone made him seem out of place. The ceiling seemed too low, in danger of closing in on them as he stood erect, one hand in the pocket of his rust-colored flat-front slacks.

"You know, the Bennet family has as long a history in Derby as the Darcys," said Mrs. Bennet. "My mother was the belle of the Old Confederate Ball just like her mother before her. Old Mr. Jefferson Darcy gave her a wreath of jasmine on the occasion. And all the other great men about were keen on her. She had so many rich beaus."

Darcy had a look of disinterestedness on his face. At least he didn't look appalled as Elizabeth stood in dread of what her mom would say next.

"They say," continued Mrs. Bennet, "she looked like my sister Phyllis, but I never saw it. Not that I would ever talk about my sister Phyllis around the Darcys. We never talk about that, do we, Jane?"

Bingley, who had started to whisper to Jane, smiled at

Mrs. Bennet as if he were completely unperturbed by her, used to her saying bizarre, inappropriate things that made little sense to him.

Moments like these, Elizabeth tried her best to keep quiet and stay on her mother's good side because to take her up on anything, like how bad it looked to be bragging about how people said Jane will be rich someday, only made her louder and more adamant. She prayed her mother's sense of decorum would prevent her from getting any closer to Darcy's father sleeping with her sister.

Mrs. Bennet, of course, if she were to give her opinion, would say that Mr. Darcy Senior treated her sister and her unfortunate son abominably, but at the same time she privately expressed hopes that Will might someday right wrongs by redistributing the money he would inherit from his dad.

Elizabeth, desperate to change the subject, heard herself croak to Darcy, "I meant to thank you for hosting us on your boat."

Bingley laughed out loud. "Oh, don't refer to his sloop as a *boat*, Elizabeth. He'll be offended if you talk of it like it can be classed with an ordinary fishing vessel. It's a ship, not a boat!"

Elizabeth smiled, eager to adopt Bingley's joviality given the awkwardness she was feeling. "Well, to be sure, it was so big I was tempted to call it a barge."

Darcy, unflaggingly stoic, seemed to wake up in the eyes

as Elizabeth spoke.

Lydia turned to him. "What is the name of your boat? Jane promised I'll be invited next time. And, Bingley, you have to have another party at Netherfield because Jane and Lizzy didn't take me along last time."

Elizabeth felt jealous of her younger sister's nerve.

"It's the Admiral Nelson," answered Darcy, succinctly.

"That's the stupidest name I ever heard," said Lydia with hooting laughter.

Perhaps it was his haughty accent that set her off. Perhaps nothing. Elizabeth didn't want to know. She was wishing Lydia was an only child.

She looked at Darcy for a reaction but he was only frowning, his eyes suddenly caught by Mrs. Bennet's collection of cow figurines. He bent to examine them sitting on a shelf. They all had one thing in common, disproportionately large udders. Udders as openings for salt and pepper. Udders as hooks for jewelry. Udders as hand cream dispensers.

Elizabeth could hardly keep herself from running out of the room as his face registered awareness at what he was looking at. She was dying.

"It seems like the rain has finally let up," Elizabeth said, looking directly at Darcy and ignoring the shelf. "You can't sail in the rain, can you? Have you ever crossed the Atlantic by yourself?" Pulling up her sagging athletic pants, pretending they weren't slovenly, she taxed her brain for more questions.

He nodded in response, saying nothing at first, but his expression seemed to soften as he studied her, which she wanted to attribute to him sympathizing with her discomfort.

"You mean without a crew?" His hair fell over his left eyebrow. His was businessperson short but with enough of a wave to be swept back a little. "We always have at least a small crew. My cousins and I have tried to take her out ourselves, but not far, down to Florida and back was our longest trip."

Elizabeth swung her arm toward Bingley. "I hope you two get a chance to go out again soon ... without any wimpy girls on board to ruin things."

Bingley laughed, squeezing Jane to his side. "You wimpy girls are good company."

Darcy intently stared at Elizabeth for a few moments.

Held breath stagnated the air between them.

Elizabeth felt a bead of sweat on the side of her forehead.

He finally opened his mouth. "I didn't realize you had an interest in nautical sports."

"Oh," Elizabeth felt her mouth dry up. "I—"

"Of course she does," interrupted her mother before Elizabeth could come up with a clever answer. "We might not have oceanfront property here at Longbourn but we have a long history of producing sailors. Half my neighbors have sons who've served in the coast guard and many Bennets have worked on commercial liners. My cousin is in charge of all the dessert buffets on a cruise ship. Just because *your* hoity-toity part of Derby has a yacht club doesn't mean it has a monopoly on shipping."

Darcy said nothing, his eyes coolly assessing Mrs. Bennet. Perhaps looking for signs that she was genuinely inane, as opposed to purposefully absurd.

Elizabeth panted. Her mother was staring down Darcy, preparing to expose herself again, and Lydia was rolling out of her chair onto the floor like a ditz.

"Even though no one's itching to go just yet," Elizabeth said loudly, "You probably ought to, Jane." Elizabeth glanced at Bingley, then Darcy. "Your friends at the club are probably waiting for you at this point." She waited for agreement from Bingley but he hesitated.

Darcy took a step forward, seeming ready to be going, which made Bingley start to move as well.

"Have a good time," Elizabeth said softly to Darcy as everyone started talking at once.

Darcy paused in front of Elizabeth. "Would you like to join us? We can wait for you to get ready. We didn't mean to exclude you if you'd like to come along."

He was like a Greek statue come to life: hard features suddenly animated by slight movements of his mouth, chin, brow and nostrils, all aligned in classical forms.

"Oh, no, but thank you for the offer," Elizabeth answered, her cheeks burning. All she wanted to do was take a long cold shower and not feel his piercing eyes on her ever again. "I would only make you late. Jane is looking forward to dining al fresco with the whole gang." Elizabeth exhaled with a forced chuckle. "I'll hold down the fort here."

Mrs. Bennet looked confused and discontented. "What are you running on about, Lizzy? You're not making sense. The gentlemen are welcome to stay and have supper here with us if they like. We have brisket. Pooh pooh to that boring club. We can play a nice game of lottery."

But there was no way Elizabeth would let her mother do such a thing to Jane as to force their company and their food on Bingley for the evening. "Mom, they're going to be late for their reservation. We don't want that, do we? Jane is going to a special lobster dinner."

Mrs. Bennet relented, "Well, if Bingley has set plans ..."

Darcy bowed slightly as he said goodbye and headed out the door with Bingley and Jane.

That's it. Elizabeth decided to put her social life out of its misery and skip the town's Beach Ball. She'd give her two tickets to Charlotte so she could take Mr. Collins out for a night on the town.

Reverend Collins would probably enjoy himself

hobnobbing with wealthy Derbyites, more than Elizabeth was enjoying herself flailing around in that cacophony of discomfort that was being in the same room with Will Darcy. Just yesterday her DJ friend from work had told her that people were saying she was a hanger on, weaseling her way in among Bingley and his fancy friends because of her sister. She could nip that in the bud by staying home for the weekend. Practice her oboe. Walk around Longbourn picking wild flowers. Take a ride to the vintage record store an hour inland. She needed to actively avoid Will Darcy.

Chapter Seven

As Elizabeth drove down Beach Avenue in the direction of Netherfield, the whistling of the wind joined with the rumbling engine of her newly spruced up Vespa, all waxed and buffed with an aerodynamic basket not yet weighed down by instruments attached with bungee cords.

She pulled into the small parking lot attached to Derby Realtors, where she had an appointment to look at current listings for studio apartments. After hopping off her scooter, she used a chunky silicone-covered lock to secure her bike to the bike rack.

As she stowed her helmet in the back, she heard someone yell, "Nice ride," and looked up to see a spry young guy on foot waving at her.

"Thanks, bro," she hollered back, feeling exhilarated. After a rare traffic-free ride from Longbourn, she was up for a chat with a stranger.

Turning on his heels, the young man walked over to her. "Hi, I'm Wickham."

Up close, his clear skin reminded her of Jane's blooming complexion, and Elizabeth guessed he was about her own age. "Are you in Derby on vacation?" she asked, motioning toward the touristy boardwalk area which was just up the street.

"Oh, I'm a local, or at least I used to be." His twinkling blue eyes complimented his smooth, ready-for-prime-time voice. "I grew up around here and come home as often as I can."

Elizabeth was certain she'd never seen him before and that she would have remembered him if they had gone to Derby High together. But then again it wasn't like she'd ever had her finger on the pulse of the local social scene.

"So, will I see you at the Beach Ball tonight?" he asked.

She sighed. "Oh, unfortunately, no. Ticket scalpers are charging $300 for a ticket that's supposed to cost $50, so I'm out."

"If that's all, I'm your man," he exclaimed, pulling an embossed card from his pocket.

Elizabeth recognized it because she'd received two of the exact same in the mail and passed them on to Charlotte.

Elizabeth Famous

"I have an extra ticket," he said, reaching out to her, holding the ticket aloft in front of her without a quivering hand or any impatience in his posture.

She blushed, impressed by his exercise in confidence without pushiness.

There was nothing presumptuous about him as he smiled with an alluring softness. "Throw on a sweater. There'll be a breeze at the beach. And meet me there."

She wore a simple, high-waisted sun dress with a light blue floral pattern. It wasn't particularly dressy but she liked the way it looked on her and, more importantly, the only reason to say no to his offer was that she had nothing new or fancy to wear, and he seemed to approve of her simple yet classic dress.

"Sure," she said. "I'm game! But are you certain you want to give it to *me*?" She hesitated as she looked at the ticket he still held in front of her, his arm never lagging. "There are *many* women strolling around downtown who'd love to accompany you."

He laughed, a melodic, charming laugh that she heard from her scalp to her toes, tingly and electric. As she did an assessment of his handsome face, she thought he was just about the cutest thing ever.

"Please, take it. It'll be fun," he sang excitedly with good-natured liveliness. "It's been burning a hole in my pocket since my, uh, friend gave it to me a couple weeks back." He reached out and swiftly yet gently lay the ticket in the palm of her hand.

She hadn't realized how elegant and yet masculine a man might render the simplest gesture. He moved with such graceful panache she couldn't imagine spurning his advances. He must be living some sort of charmed life with no one ever turning him down.

Elizabeth texted Charlotte to apprise her friend of her new plans for that evening, adding, "I hope you find Collins as pleasant as he is steady and that I'm totally wrong about him."

But she knew she wasn't wrong about Bobby Collins. Being candid with Charlotte was no longer possible. They could never again share confidences if Charlotte claimed to find Bobby Collins companionable. There was something so depressing about overlooking Collins's deportment because, unlike most people at Longbourn, he had a savings account.

#

A little after ten, Elizabeth bounded down the boardwalk, pulled along by the lure of catchy hip hop songs, a whiff of burnt sugar, and glowing orbs hanging from tall posts.

To get to the trellised entrance tent, she had to step around spectators set up on blankets outside the roped-off party area to enjoy an overflow of entertainment.

A large rectangular swath of beach running all the way from the grassy dunes by the boardwalk to the densely packed sand near the high tide line was laid out with tables and chairs covered in flowing white linen.

The annual Beach Ball hosted by the Derby Recreation Council featured gourmet chocolate S'mores with homemade marshmallows, a big city DJ, and watermelon martinis, and this year they added a silent auction of designer accessories and gift certificates donated by local shops.

Elizabeth walked over to snoop at the seashell-bedecked gift baskets with sign-up sheets for bids. A month-long trial membership to the yacht club had a bid over a thousand dollars. A full season membership to Rosings Pool Club on the outskirts of Derby was almost ten thousand. Slippers donated by the designer shoe store weren't bid on yet.

Searching the dense crowd for familiar faces, she couldn't find Jane although she was supposed to be there with Bingley, whom she'd gone out to dinner with beforehand.

Presumably they'd snuck off somewhere to be alone.

Bingley seemed more and more taken with Jane. They spent every free evening together and talked on the phone every night before bed. Jane no longer demurred when someone intimated that Bingley was crazy about her; she just smiled. They had the easiest love affair in history and couldn't seem to find anything irksome about each other.

A man standing in a clump of guys holding bottles of imported beer said in a clear bass voice, "Hey, it's the band teacher!" as Elizabeth passed by.

She immediately recognized him as a single dad she'd seen at the concert on the last day of school. His tiny daughter, who took private lessons with a colleague from the high school, was the star of the school's brass section. According to school gossip, her dad had full custody as his ex-wife was in rehab for prescription opioid addiction.

"I knew I'd see you here," he said, his hands stretching his chino pockets. "All the younger teachers are here tonight."

"Just great," Elizabeth said sarcastically. "I thought this was going to be a cool party."

He laughed too hard. "Save a dance for me?"

Her face warmed at the idea. At parent/teacher conferences he had been affable and unassuming after mentioning he was an attorney at a law firm downtown. She knew he picked up his daughter on time every day after school. He was a good-looking guy, if a bit awkward. A catch really, although she was worried about somebody from school saying they saw her flirting with a parent.

"Sure thing!" she replied after a pause. "Fetch me later."

Spotting Charlotte standing by herself, Elizabeth trudge through the combed sand in her cork sandals all the way to the other side of the party space to a makeshift cash bar constructed out of a surfboard.

A drink garnished with a lime slice was waiting for her,

along with an empty bar stool. Charlotte, conscientious as always, had already laid out a tip for the bartender.

Bobby Collins must be off talking up another partygoer and giving Charlotte a breather. She looked happily alone.

"You're the best!" said Elizabeth, resting one hand on the bar stool as she raised the other in a toast.

"Salud," said Charlotte, looking spiffy in white capris.

Elizabeth took a long swig of margarita. "Either I wore the wrong shoes or I'm out of shape but walking over here was quite a workout."

"It's all in the plan. We need you to stay planted in one place so all these guys hovering around can get to you," said Charlotte.

Elizabeth laughed. "You have to promise to dance with me if I can't handle all the attention as an unchaperoned female!"

Charlotte shook her head as if she just remembered something. "Lizzy! Did you really meet someone just walking down Beach Avenue?"

Elizabeth laughed. "It was *so* strange. Nothing like that has ever happened to me before."

"Yeah, right," said Charlotte with an annoyed curl of her lip. She wore a thick coating of liquid foundation, had blown out her hair, and, as always, made a lot of effort with her appearance, although she often complained that her efforts did not pay off. "This guy just gave you a ticket right then and there ... after talking to you for half a minute?"

"I swear. I'm not making it up," said Elizabeth.

"Did you make some joke about being sexually frustrated?"

"No, not at all!" exclaimed Elizabeth with a laugh.

"And where is he?"

"Late maybe. You would have noticed him if he were here. He's not just run of the mill handsome; he's beautiful."

"I bow to you, Lizzy," said Charlotte, her face shiny as she shook her head.

"It was stupid luck. He liked my Vespa. Probably ogles girls on motorcycles. I'd sworn I was going to chill at home this weekend but after meeting him, resistance was futile."

"When you disappear with him at the end of the night," said Charlotte, "don't worry about offending me by not saying goodbye."

Elizabeth noticed people milling about near tented daybeds set up next to white mangrove trees, but she couldn't make anyone out as they were in full shadow. One might be her new friend, who'd texted her an hour ago to say that he was looking forward to seeing her that evening.

Elizabeth pointed at the six outdoor mattresses. "I wonder if any couples will have the nerve to sprawl out on those," she said to Charlotte.

"I wouldn't worry about anyone around here not having

the nerve," Charlotte replied with a sweep of her eyes at some young women standing nearby. "Did you know 'upscale beachwear' meant swimsuits?"

There was a girl wearing swim shorties with a sparkly bikini top and another in a swim dress with high slit skirt. The outfits were conservative bathing suits during daytime hours, when you only wore such a thing if you wanted to be allowed to lunch in a cafe without a cover-up, but their Lycra getups seemed yowza at a charity event.

Charlotte suddenly froze, her eyes wide as she grabbed Elizabeth by the upper arm, pinching her.

"What is it?" said Elizabeth, hurriedly looking in the direction Charlotte was facing.

Will Darcy was standing right behind her.

Elizabeth tried to sound casual as she whispered to Charlotte, "Silly, girl! You frightened me. I thought Bobby Collins had started breakdancing or something."

Turning on Darcy with a haughty expression, Elizabeth said loud enough for him to hear, "It's only Will Darcy. And we might have expected to see him here tonight. Nothing out of the ordinary."

"Good evening," he said with a bob of his head.

"Hi, *Darcy*," she replied, watching him flinch as he always did when she called him by his surname alone, over-pronouncing both of the two syllables. "You can't avoid me."

Will nonchalantly shook off the bartender who offered to make him a drink. "Am I trying to?"

"Yes, always," she laughed, not knowing what she said.

His dark eyes roved the dance floor environs then turned to gaze hard at her.

She returned his look quizzically. Did he walk up to her with something particular to say, maybe a message from Jane and Bingley?

He leaned against the bar, looking relaxed, but he said nothing.

A girl looking barely out of high school, dressed in an emerald mermaid skirt and holding a basket of long stem pink roses offered to sell him one for his lady. He gave her a slight once over, didn't respond to her solicitation, then returned his eyes to Elizabeth. "Would you introduce me to your friend?" he asked.

Elizabeth was confused for a moment then realized he meant Charlotte, not the mermaid girl he had been checking out. "Yes, of course, this is my neighbor Charlotte Lucas. She works in the loan department at Derby Savings Bank," said Elizabeth, not sure why she was spouting resume material instead of something fun like Charlotte's genius at arranging impromptu scavenger hunts for the kids at Longbourn.

"Quite of few bank officers are here tonight," Darcy said to Charlotte. "I assume you know Ted Nietzsche."

Charlotte opened her mouth and mumbled something unintelligible.

"She's, uh, a junior loan officer," said Elizabeth, covering for Charlotte's muteness.

"Res...sidential loans," explained Charlotte, barely raising her eyes to Darcy as she stammered.

Charlotte was so smart and funny but couldn't get over the idea she wasn't good looking enough to talk to very attractive people. She only spoke to Jane because they were childhood friends.

Elizabeth decided to try to make Charlotte laugh. "You didn't follow the dress code, Darcy. I hope Bingley did. You two need to learn to follow instructions."

Charlotte gawked.

Will did *not* flush with self-consciousness. "You'll forgive me," he said, his eyes narrowing.

The invite encouraged men to wear Hawaiian shirts, or at least oxfords with embroidered sea creatures, but most men at the party, including Darcy, stuck to the masculine palate of tan, brown, grey or navy blue stripes.

Elizabeth poked Charlotte with her elbow. "I see Jane and Bingley!" Looking at Darcy, she added gaily, "They look so cute together, huh?"

"I'm sure I can't say," he replied, sounding unenthusiastic.

"Oh, come on, if I asked you if you like my outfit — or

Charlotte's — you'd be polite enough to agree, wouldn't you?" said Elizabeth with a little hop.

"I didn't notice how they're dressed. I spoke to them for only a minute."

"Seriously? You *have to* admit they're a cute couple. Jane said today is their anniversary."

His eyebrows scrunched together. "I'm certain they're *not* married."

"You know what I mean," Elizabeth sneered at him exaggeratedly.

"Do I?" he asked, his chin flicking upward a bit. "I know ladies sometimes make a big to-do about an acquaintance of five weeks but men are rarely so inclined."

She laughed loudly at his chauvinism. It suited him perfectly and hopefully would ward off any unsuspecting woman who might cross his path. "In my experience, it's quite the opposite," she said. "Women are reluctant to raise their expectations having been disappointed by a man more than once."

He almost smiled, then reverted to his quintessential staid countenance. "I'd have to ask for particulars before I can gauge the legitimacy of your disappointed expectations."

Elizabeth laughed out loud, not worried about offending him although she thought it was ridiculous how stiff and formal his replies were.

Speaking of stiff and formal. Reverend Collins appeared, smiling at Elizabeth as if life could get no better. "Dear madams, I'm pleased to announce that my patroness, Catherine Darcy herself, is expected tonight. Of course, she has reserved a table with her niece Georgiana Darcy ..."

An up-tempo dance song sped into its hammering chorus, and Elizabeth's ears vibrated as she tried to make out Collins's words.

Darcy did not wait for Bobby to finish a single run-on sentence, even as Collins name dropped some of Will's nearest relations. "Excuse me. I see someone I know nearby."

As Darcy walked off, Charlotte gave Bobby her full attention, listening to all he said without breaking eye contact, despite Elizabeth's attempt to jostle her.

The crowd around the bar suddenly thickened, and Reverend Collins didn't seem to know what to do with himself without an ample allotment of personal space.

Huffing, he repeatedly excused himself and apologized for standing in the wrong place as he turned in circles. "Is this okay? I hope this is okay. Is there room for your friend Elizabeth? Should she stand on my other side?"

Charlotte offered to find Reverend Collins a seat at a lighted plexiglass table nearby.

But he, in his shiny dress shirt and tight slacks, took the initiative and grabbed a singleton empty chair for himself and left Charlotte standing.

Scooting his chair under the white box table as far as possible, he said, "Oh, am I out of the way now? I do hope I'm out of the way." Then he started chatting with his neighbors, apologizing for taking a seat without explicitly asking their permission.

He had effectively turned his back on Charlotte.

Elizabeth immediately motioned for her friend to follow her to the parquet dance floor. Feeling they'd escaped, she was ready to celebrate.

Charlotte smiled but kept saying something about finding a seat near Collins.

Elizabeth set the pace for dancing with a low key boogie befitting a public school teacher.

As one song ended and the opening chords of a new one sounded, Charlotte hollered, "Oh, Lizzy! Will Darcy must like you. He never talks to anybody."

"No, trust me. If you knew the topics of the very few conversations we've had, you'd never think that."

Charlotte frowned. "Are you sure?"

When the music slowed for a couple's dance, the elevated dance floor cleared, and Elizabeth stepped back down onto the now uneven sand and waved goodbye to Charlotte who insisted on returning to Reverend Collins.

Before she made it a half dozen steps, Elizabeth found herself claimed by the single dad from her school and returned to the dance floor with him.

He whirled her into a waltz-like slow dance with spins and box steps. It was a lot of fun but silly too. She made sure there was nothing sexy about her dancing.

After two songs, and a bit of small talk, he mentioned returning to his friend who was celebrating a promotion, before asking with blushing hesitancy, "I'll see you around?"

"Of course. Talk to you soon," said Elizabeth, trying to be encouraging.

A little tired, she wandered over to the lounge area where couples were indeed now lying with legs intertwined on the beds she'd noticed earlier.

Grinning at the intimacy of the cuddling, she thought of how she really wanted a boyfriend.

An empty platform bed with pale pink curtains flapping in the wind faced the ocean. Elizabeth slid her cotton-clad butt along the waterproof cushion and spread out, shielded from the party by the drapery.

She noticed a well-groomed older man wearing a giant gold watch and sitting alone on a cushioned wicker sofa about five feet away.

Charlotte, who always filled Elizabeth's ears with information and commentary on who's who, had pointed this guy out earlier as the big wig from the bank whom Darcy had mentioned. Ted Something.

He seemed a little out of it, several empty beer bottles on the cocktail table in front of him. Charlotte had said he was a distant relative of the Darcys, but Elizabeth saw absolutely no resemblance.

After removing her shoes and checking her phone for texts from Wickham or any other guy who might scoop her up, Elizabeth reclined, looking up at the stars.

Then, out of a slit in the curtain she saw something move. It was Bingley walking up to this Ted guy and taking a seat across from him in a coordinating white chair.

Bingley's back was to Elizabeth, and he didn't seem to notice her on her grandiose outdoor bed.

She lay flat a minute, hidden and motionless, wondering how to announce herself. She hadn't even had a chance to greet Bingley that night. When he'd come to pick up Jane earlier that evening, Elizabeth had been in the shower.

Before Elizabeth could come up with a witty comment with which to Jack-in-the-Box herself, the older man started speaking loudly to Bingley, practically shouting.

"...Any guy with a half million in net worth is in their sights, like sharks with blood in the water. Usually getting pregnant *accidentally* then getting a judge to order DNA testing."

"I find that hard to believe," said Bingley with a cool voice

151

so unlike his usual friendly tone. "I mean, people have tried to say things to me on occasion, but I don't pay attention to idle gossip."

"It's all of them living over'n Longbourn trailer park," said the man, slurring his speech. "That girl's mama's got three or four different men on the hook for child support, a different guy for each of her girls. Drives off the baby daddies once she gets her checks. Bennets have lived along the river in Longbourn for generations, never move out of there, even after they get a settlement. If one gives birth to a useless son who they can't pimp out like the girls, they send him off to work for a living on a cargo ship. If we built a fence around that whole damn dump at Longbourn, we'd be rid of half the homewreckers in this town."

Bingley sounded flustered. "Will, did you hear all this?"

Darcy had joined them! He hadn't been there when Bingley first sat down.

Elizabeth couldn't look, waiting with bated breath, terrified of what he might say, wishing she could think of an excuse to sit up and interrupt the conversation, but at this point how could she without being called out for eavesdropping?

Imagine the drunk guy recognizing her as a Bennet and screaming at her as she was forced to protect herself by brandishing a sandy shoe.

Had Darcy seen her? If he was standing where the direction of his voice suggested, he might be able to see her lying there looking dead to the world. What was worse ... spying or getting so smashed you pass out on a cabana bed? Maybe she should pretend to be drunk.

Bingley pressed Darcy, "I don't think I ever heard you put it so bluntly, about Jane's family, I mean. I know you said there's some sort of history, but you didn't want to get into details. But, uh, what do you think about, uh, what this gentleman is saying?"

Oddly, Darcy was silent, not answering Bingley straight away.

The older man started in again, blustering about "greedy bitches" but before he got very far Darcy said, almost inaudibly, "Others in town would tell you something along the same lines."

His tone of voice was resigned and weary, as if he were shrugging his shoulders. *What can you do? It's just the way it is with those Bennet girls.*

Elizabeth pushed off the pancake-like cushion beneath her and stretched her legs out before her, then jumped up, looking in the direction of Darcy's voice.

He was standing across from Bingley, who still had his back to her. Darcy was looking right back at her, not seeming surprised to see her pop up.

He knew she was there. And allowed them to talk that way about her family in front of her without stopping them!

Even if he'd only walked over at the latter half of the drunk man's tirade, he had the audacity to agree with him despite the fact he was blabbering on in a crude, exaggerated manner and very possibly harboring some sort of grudge against the Bennets given his irate tone.

Was the softness of Darcy's voice when he answered Bingley because she was there?

She turned away without a word and walked over to the rope that surrounded the party area and stepped over it onto the unlit beach, away from Bingley's notice she hoped and in spite of Darcy's.

She headed toward the waves.

They roared like a storm might be coming later that night. Maybe some dangerous riptides to pull late night swimmers out to sea.

She once had too much time on her hands and roamed around the darkened Derby Beach at night. She remembered meeting a boy who complained about getting his kayak marooned near Pemberley and being chased off the property.

From the darkness, she people watched, admiring the fabrics of the other women's expensive dresses. She spotted the male parent she'd danced with. He was standing with other men dressed in tan kakis. He might be interested in her but clearly wasn't going to go any further that night. Why hadn't he asked for her number?

She wiped her teary eyes. Somehow, hearing people around Bingley say out loud what she always tried to keep from hearing was not only painful but liberating in a way. Her family's reputation was laid out on the table. She and Jane could walk away from it, reject it.

From an early age she and Jane knew that their mom's choices never brought her much happiness. Only impoverished, grumpy guys like Jane's dad seemed to care for Mrs. Bennet. As grade schoolers, Elizabeth and Jane would take turns visiting their Aunt Gardiner's family up north in Maryland and knew they wanted something more like what she had: a happy marriage to a hard working guy who owned a hardware store.

Elizabeth thought about what Darcy said. She had believed it was possible he didn't trash talk Jane, that he was not interfering as he'd proclaimed to her the night he brought Lydia home from drag racing. Why would she have so much faith in him?

The fact that Bingley seemed surprised by some of the older drunk guy's words proved Will hadn't said all that much before tonight. But there was some indication he might have changed his tune and started sharing. He seemed displeased when earlier that night Elizabeth suggested Jane and Bingley might be a real couple with an anniversary to celebrate.

Why couldn't Darcy say something kind about Jane when confronted with the rantings of a drunk guy?

Elizabeth paused at the thought of Ted the Banker's point about the rarity of Bennet sons. She thought of the unwanted

"Bennet" male whom Darcy's father and her aunt created some twenty odd years ago? Richard was never at Longbourn now. When he got holidays from the navy he used his leftover settlement cash to party in Fort Lauderdale.

Her aunt may be partially culpable for how Richard's life turned out, including his criminal record and his anger at the world, but Jane certainly was not.

Elizabeth passed back over the rope. On a clump of grass almost swallowed by sand, she found an empty table set up as far away from the lounge section and Bingley and Darcy as possible. Listening for waves to crash, she felt calmer. She and Jane couldn't escape their family's past, so her sister would have to show Bingley she wasn't being pressured by their mother to go after his money but truly liked him. And Elizabeth would try to find a guy she could open up to about her numerous insecurities.

Someone approached out of the corner of her eye.

It was Wickham.

Turning, she greeted him with a full smile.

"Hey, gorgeous, why are you sitting here by yourself?" He was dressed like he never worried about his appearance but always looked hot with dirty blond hair and light blue eyes. "I'm sorry I'm late."

"Not at all. Things are just getting started." She hadn't

been thinking of him with enough anticipation. He was stunning.

"I hope you don't mind company," he said, taking a seat next to her.

"Of course not! It's welcome!"

They jumped into conversation. She asked lots of questions and he followed up on everything she said with apropos replies.

He'd been visiting friends up north on New York's Long Island for most of the year but was now living with a friend who worked at the nearby Derby Casino. He was quite familiar with Derby, all the hot spots and local hangouts, having spent much of his time in the area from birth. He said he was hoping to meet new people and really enjoy himself while in town.

He had a talent for offering compliments without phoniness, and his easy, playful sense of humor and vivacious laugh brought Elizabeth out of her funk. His smile was like that of a guy who ran for town council without taking any positions on the issues and won.

He asked her what she did for a living and about her weekday schedule. With any luck they'd arrange to go out on a date sometime soon.

When he offered to get her a daiquiri, she nodded enthusiastically and said, "That would be awesome," wishing she had thought of it first and offered to get *him* a drink.

On his way back, carrying two icy drinks, the contents

sloshing over the rims of the glasses, he stopped and did a double take. He visibly exhaled, before walking up to Will Darcy, who was now smack dab in the middle of the party space with Jane and Bingley.

Wickham rearranged the wide glasses he carried, propping them against his chest, and reached out his hand to Darcy.

Will appeared blindsided, kill written on his face. He turned away from Wickham without extending his hand.

Elizabeth couldn't believe it. She'd never seen Darcy so openly rude, so livid.

Did Wickham steal his girlfriend? That wouldn't be enough to justify such a look. It was a look you'd give someone who used your pet for target practice.

As Wickham returned to her, she asked, "Is everything okay?"

"You saw that, didn't you?" he said, laughing it off. "I have to confess I'm not all that surprised about being blown off by Will Darcy. We know each other, go way back. But things have soured between us, as you can see."

"I can't imagine—" But she stopped herself, not wanting to be presumptuous with a guy she had such high hopes for.

Wickham chuckled. "Will can be a difficult person to deal with."

He then changed the subject to her music, asking what

instruments she played.

After a few minutes chitchat, he abruptly switched back to the topic of Darcy. "I really should not say anything against Will Darcy considering how amazingly kind Mr. and Mrs. Darcy have always been to me."

"Really?" Elizabeth exclaimed. "I don't know the older Darcys."

Wickham told her of how, as a boy, he lost both his parents, who had devoted their lives to the upkeep of Pemberley, and that he was almost adopted by the Darcys after his parents' deaths. "Will started acting out with violent jealousy of me, so they put the adoption process on hold and I returned to my grandmother's house."

Wickham continued with a doleful smile. "I had been living at Pemberley because my grandmother was ill. She got better, thank god. But while I was at Pemberley, Mr. Darcy bought me a pony, and Will was so angry that I had to give it to him to care for in order to avoid a huge fight. But his parents are truly the best people. They paid for all my schooling from grade school on up."

"I can't say I'm totally shocked by what you say about him," said Elizabeth, "although you make him sound more *petty* than I imagined."

"The truth is that none of those childhood battles between Darcy and me matter now. What really gets to me is what happened a year ago. His father had helped me get my dream job at the thoroughbred racetrack near the Derby Casino. I was in the accounts department. Will found out and traveled all the way home from France to meet with my employer and have me fired. With no reference I haven't been able to find a similar position."

"That's outrageous." Elizabeth nearly jumped to her feet, then settled for leaning forward while remaining seated. "How can he get away with that, with going out of his way to maliciously harm your prospects?"

"He's a Darcy." Wickham shrugged, good-naturedly, as if his motto was *Don't worry; be happy.* "He doesn't let me near his sister, Georgie, and yet she was always so fond of me as a kid. He's tried to turn his parents against me; they don't invite me to the house as much anymore."

"I believe Georgiana is here tonight but I don't know her at all. I barely know what she looks like."

"Oh, she is here. I ran into her on my way in." Wickham pointed to a girl in flowing purple chiffon standing near Will.

Elizabeth stared.

A little less attractive than her tall and cut brother, Georgiana had a bland look about her, like she wasn't distinctive looking and could blend into a crowd.

Wickham laughed. "I hope Darcy doesn't have me thrown out. The last time I said hello to her at the yacht club he got the bouncer to escort me out."

"What is she like?" Elizabeth asked, not taking her eyes off young Miss Darcy.

Elizabeth had heard stories about her doing things like buying a single star fruit at the gourmet grocer and paying with a hundred-dollar bill. Her reputation was that she kept to the same well-heeled school friends she'd known her entire life.

Wickham exhaled audibly. "I wish I could say she's a lovely young woman, but in some ways she's worse than her brother."

"Really?" Elizabeth exclaimed, looking at her. Georgiana's expression was not at all high-handed like Will's.

"Hopefully she has a chance to outgrow the Darcy pride and become more open to people in general," he said.

Wickham spoke with such affability, it would have been easy to believe everything he said about Darcy, even if Elizabeth hadn't already known first hand of his arrogance.

"Someone should confront him," said Elizabeth. "Make him defend himself. Someone should tell Bingley about the things he's done to you. Why do people always let him get his way? Just because of his money? All his scowling wouldn't protect him from me if he hurt one of my sisters."

"Who are your sisters?" asked Wickham enthusiastically. "Are they here?"

"Oh, I have two sisters. Jane is standing near Will; she's

dating his friend Bingley, although I wouldn't say she's a friend of Will's. And my younger sister Lydia is over by the surfboard bar," said Elizabeth. Earlier Lydia had texted to say she met a guy with a yacht club membership and was on the chase.

"Darcy likes to have his own way," said Wickham, voluntarily returning to the subject of Darcy. "That's for sure. All men do, I suppose. He just has the means of getting what he wants no matter who it hurts."

She smiled, not wanting to be too glum or seem too affected by what he said.

"Do you want to dance?" he asked as the music started up again.

She agreed and they walked out onto the dance floor.

He was easy to touch, like a happy puppy, and Elizabeth moved to the music while brushing her hands against the hairless skin on the underside of his arms.

She joked with Wickham about how being disliked by Darcy was an attractive quality to her. Noticing Darcy looking in her direction, she laughed to herself at the idea of putting on a little show for him, rubbing up against Wickham with her hips.

After another drink and laughing with Wickham about the epidemic of beach chic décor overtaking every home in Derby, Elizabeth said, "One thing I don't understand. It seems like Will Darcy would try to keep a positive profile if he wants people to do real estate deals with him, which seems to be his ambition from all I've heard."

"With his equals, he behaves well and is generous," said Wickham. "It's only dispensable folks like me he feels he can cheat."

Elizabeth couldn't wait to get some time alone with Jane to share what she'd learned. Although her enthusiasm for divulging was dulled by the idea that sweet Bingley might be friends with an unscrupulous narcissist.

#

Bingley stood with Darcy at the center of the Beach Ball's sandy event space and motioned in Elizabeth's direction. "You said that Wickham fellow's a charmer."

"A charming rat," said Will, unable to resist vilifying Wickham, but not wanting to get into specifics with his friend.

Despite Bingley's current interest in Jane Bennet, Will harbored a secret wish that his sister and Bingley would end up together as a couple when she was older, so he didn't want Bingley to know about Georgiana's history with Wickham. It was for the best if everyone involved forgot about it.

"What is it you have to accuse this Wickham fellow of?" asked Bingley.

"I'm not at liberty to share," said Will, "but he's had some pretty dishonorable dealings with my family."

Wickham and Elizabeth returned to the crowded dance floor, drawing quite a few eyes as they started to dance cheek to cheek, whispering to each other as they casually touched. Elizabeth smiled, looking carefree, and Will wondered why she wasn't flippant with Wickham as she always was with him.

Elizabeth's girlfriend from earlier joined in and they all danced in a makeshift circle that included Wickham. Elizabeth's petite mouth open wide as she said something to her not very comely but sensible-looking friend. Charlotte, that was her name. Wickham was buzzing around the ladies, using his gallant act to full effect.

What were the odds that Wickham of all people would notice Elizabeth that night ... with so many people around to distract her and interest him? It was a repellant coincidence. There was no saying what sort of self-serving gossip he'd been entertaining her with as they mingled.

Bingley stepped up. "I'm going to go fetch her away from him if he's really a cad. Jane would want me to."

Will swung his head. "I don't advise it. And, please, if you're thinking of playing matchmaker, your performance would reflect no credit on either of us."

Ignoring Darcy's advice, Bingley walked over to grab Elizabeth by the hand, talking energetically until she took his arm and walked with him to where Will stood.

Jesus, could Bingley be any more obvious? Wickham will see Elizabeth standing with me; he'll try to get her drunk and talking.

"... You're the life of the party!" Bingley hollered to

Elizabeth over the music. "I had no idea. But we wore out Jane. She went to freshen up, but I think I'll have to take her home soon. Do you need a ride?"

Elizabeth smirked but not unpleasantly. "I know better than to play second fiddle with you two." As usual Elizabeth's natural sweetness disarmed her archness, but there was something off. A pained look fleetingly crossed her face as she made small talk with Bingley.

It could not be that Elizabeth was so fortunate as to be disappointed by Wickham already.

She was certainly not thrilled with what she'd overheard earlier out of Ted Nietzsche from the bank. Will had seen her scowl when she popped up from the curtained lounge she'd been lying on. Not that she could be surprised by what that gentleman had intimated. She was not stupid; she knew what locals said about her family.

Jane returned, looking drained.

Bingley found Jane a seat away from the smoking bonfire where guests were still roasting marshmallows.

When Jane pulled at Bingley's shirt, encouraging him to share her seat, he shook his head no and just leaned on the table beside her, looking off in the distance.

Will thought of the pointed questions Bingley had asked earlier that night about the Bennets' dealings with his family. Bingley had seemed troubled, yet he must have heard people allude to Bennet scheming many times during his time in Derby. Anything Will had confirmed for him was not totally new to him.

Will took a step toward Elizabeth. "Can I get you something from the bar? Some juice or seltzer perhaps?"

She looked at him for a second, saying "No thanks," then bopped to the music, seemingly ignoring him. She wasn't exactly dancing but swaying her hips to the beat while standing in place.

She thinks she's being aloof, but even when she says the most provocative things to him — "Who's babysitting you for the remainder of the evening?" or "I won't touch your money" — the meaning of her words was defused by her charm.

At just the right angle to scrutinize her figure, Will noticed her shoulders and waist were narrow in comparison to her full hips and rounded butt. His thoughts were not subtle; the urge to take her into his arms staggered him. He imagined looking down at her face, being on top of her, inside her.

He leaned in, hovering near her rolling shoulder, "Do you want to dance?"

"With you?" She turned, the back of her hand against her forehead as if she might faint.

"I never dance if I can help it," he said, "but if you'd like to—"

"Assuming you might be able to stumble into some dance moves," she said, "I don't think it's a good idea. We wouldn't want to cause a scene. The ladies can only handle so much liveliness from you before they get overheated."

He smiled in reply. He wanted to challenge her, say that her performance just now, her pretend dancing and fainting, was for him alone and no one else and he knew it. She wasn't causing any sort of scene. No one looked at them.

He took a sip of the drink he'd been absentmindedly nursing for half an hour, wishing his mouth was on her. "Do you go to concerts at the band shell in the park on Sunday evenings?"

"I've never gone but maybe I ought to ... are they totally free of charge?" she chirped.

"Uh..." He wanted to try to appeal to something other than her snarkiness.

"Maybe I'd go if there was someone grounded and nice to join me. I'm not impressed by a guy's finances, contrary to what your banking pal said." Her bright eyes upbraided him. "It's much more important to me to find someone who's not a total asshole."

The funny thing was he'd probably be willing to discuss his own finances with her if only to remain in her company for the night. "I reckoned your interest in classical music would be enough of an inducement for you to attend the concerts."

"Classical music is best for training beginning instrumentalists, but it's not my genre of choice."

"And your choice is?"

"I don't trust your interest. You might take some sort of

pleasure in despising my taste."

"No, I assure you that's not the case." He gestured toward the hip hop DJ playing chart topping tunes for the dance floor crowd. "Do you like this music?"

She looked up at him. "Actually, polka is my very favorite." Her left eye twitched with mirth. Then she added in a more serious tone, "And I like a little jazz."

"Really?" He knitted his brow. "So do I."

Jane stood up. She was ready to leave. Bingley said goodbye with exhausted-looking Jane standing at his side.

After they were gone, Elizabeth opened a bottle of water, took a sip and spun around.

Will didn't want to relinquish her company, but after dodging several girls air kissing, he called to Elizabeth, "Do you want me to help you locate ... uh...your friend Charlotte?"

Before she could answer, Lydia Bennet rushed past him, getting in Elizabeth's face, waving a tiny card in the air. "Look, I stole Denny's credit card and now he has to try on one of my dresses before I'll give it back. Oh my god, I'm going to die of laughter."

Will had never noticed Elizabeth's diminutive sister before this summer, but in the past few weeks he'd encountered her several times, each time astounded by the volume of her laughter.

Lydia didn't acknowledge him, but this was not out of

rudeness. She didn't see him. The screen of a cell phone was a bright light at this beach party where the only illumination was dim paper orbs and firelight.

Elizabeth underhandedly passed Lydia some cash. "Call a cab if you need to. Promise me."

"It was so funny," said Lydia, stuffing the money into the back pocket of her white short shorts. "Pratt pointed at a cocktail left behind by some other girl and said, 'I dare you to drink that!' And you won't believe what I did ..."

Shaking his head, Will turned away and eyed the thinning crowd on the dance floor. Discarded raffle tickets smashed under foot. Tables sunk off kilter in the sand. A beaded purse slung over the back of an uncomfortable-looking s-shaped chair. Georgiana had been here at the party before Wickham showed up. Will pitied what must be Elizabeth's worries about Lydia. Younger sisters could be heartwrenching.

When he turned back around, Elizabeth was alone. She took a wobbly step closer to him in the uneven sand. "I forgot to mention. Tonight I met an old friend of yours."

His stomach muscles clenched. "Did you?"

"You know Wickham, don't you?" She raised her voice. "Wickham George is his full name, I believe."

"I know of him, but he's not a friend."

"Yes, he said you and he have had a falling out."

He felt his eyelids wrinkle, hating that he probably looked

like his father did when someone spoke to him without first being introduced. "Wickham has a gift for making friends but he's rarely able to keep them."

"It's a shame he lost your friendship and in a way that will hurt him for years to come. He's the kind of person who could use a little help, considering how he was orphaned."

"Elizabeth, I should warn you not to believe all that man says, no matter how sympathetic you may be to his stories of woe. His capacity for wile is boundless."

She looked stunned for a moment, her chest rising and falling under her high-waisted cotton dress. "Well, I don't know ... I don't see why I wouldn't give the benefit of the doubt to such a cool guy."

Will thought of how she had never given him much benefit of the doubt — she'd been questioning him, challenging him from the day they met at Netherfield. "Being overly trusting with Wickham may leave you unhappily deceived."

Her mouth widened. "I think I'm generally a good judge of people, and I like your ex-friend."

He shook his head. "Elizabeth, perhaps your thoughts, after a good night's sleep, will be clearer. The consequences of being duped can be devastating, especially for someone such as yourself."

Her eyes flashed anger.

He was willing to have it out with her. They were dancing

around conflict, not quite exposing themselves to each other, rarely putting anything on the line.

"What can I do?" She raised her shoulders like a cat backing up. "My humble background gives me a soft spot for the downtrodden who have endured unkindness at the hands of the powerful."

"Unkindness?" He looked away, furious at the idea that Wickham might have complained to her about his family. "Elizabeth, you should not unquestioningly believe whatever Wickham is currently spouting." He felt impotent. "Not to mention, why do you take such an eager interest in a stranger's affairs?"

She mugged. "I'm sure that I, as a vulnerable female, must benefit from your manly advice. But I'll try to limp along and make decisions for myself."

Despite her satirical bent, she never seemed cloying or fake. She was quirky and real. And somehow mystifying.

She scared him and not just because she wasn't taking his counsel. He was intrigued by her. He had no influence over her, and yet he wanted her to be eager to please him like other women.

"I don't believe repeating myself will do any good." He heard a tinge of emotion in his voice and knew he must end this conversation immediately. "But I hope you carefully consider what I've said. I don't want you to get hurt by him as others I know have."

She looked away. The sky had turned black in the past quarter hour and there were murmurings about a forecast of early morning rain.

He groaned internally, sickened by her interest in Wickham and by his own reactions to her. He cared far too much about what she felt and what she did. "I must say goodnight, Elizabeth." His voice was forced calmness.

She nodded, her sharp eyes meeting his for an instant. "Goodnight."

#

Restless and not feeling ready for sleep, Elizabeth found Wickham and invited him to follow her back to her house in his blue compact. There would be no harm if hanging out turned into a little make out session.

Her mom was away visiting Aunt Gardiner for the weekend. Lydia, according to her texts, was eating pancakes at a diner with Pratt and Denny. Jane was with Bingley in the back bedroom, the only place in the trailer where you could have one-on-one privacy.

Elizabeth and Wickham got the couch.

He was so charming, saying all the right things, but Elizabeth had drank a lot and was unnerved by her argument with Darcy and had some concerns about Bingley.

Sure, Bingley seemed cool as ever when she'd spoken to

him after she got home. He made a couple comments to her about how it might not be a great idea to invite Wickham over if she'd only just met him, but she took this as a protective big brother thing. However, Jane seemed genuinely worried about something.

At that moment, her sister's plaintive voice could be heard coming from the back room along with Bingley's slightly raised voice. It was not loud enough to make out his words but he sounded somewhat upset.

Wickham was a diametrical contrast. Kind of a dream actually. Robust and so turned on by her. The feeling of being attractive was so exciting. But she wasn't actually ready to go all the way.

He would be the seventh guy she slept with, but she wanted to wait till the second or third date. She wasn't ready for intimacy involving her very sensitive private parts.

As she and Wickham kissed, he reached for her hand and directed it to his lap. Not wanting to leave him frustrated, she fumblingly gave him a hand job on the couch.

The ardency of his groping hands on her body made her feel warm all over. And she got enjoyment from his pleasure.

After getting off, he went to take a shower.

Things were quiet in the back room now.

As Elizabeth and Wickham said goodnight at the door, he repeated how he wanted to see her again as soon as possible.

This was the best she'd felt in weeks. Soon she'd get laid for the first time that summer.

After heating up a frozen burrito, she checked DerbyCentral.org and was happy to see that there were already photos of Bingley and Jane from the Beach Ball that night.

#

A few days later, Bingley still hadn't called Jane after their loud conversation in the back bedroom. Jane gave in and made the call herself, contrary to her normal policy, and they made a date, but he cancelled last minute.

Elizabeth tried to talk to Jane about this as their mom had a panic attack. "Oh my gosh, he met someone else. He's dumping Jane for someone else. Who could it be? He hasn't called in days."

Jane voiced no complaints about Bingley, and Elizabeth couldn't get her to say anything that might explain his upset voice wafting down the hallway the night of the Beach Ball.

Caroline texted Jane with a photo of her brother and Georgiana Darcy, mentioning that her "dear friend Georgie" had recently taken an interest in Bingley as she'd always hoped. "They're perfect for each other, and her family adores my brother."

Elizabeth had to leave the room as Jane sent a polite message in reply to her dear friend Caroline. If Elizabeth had stayed in the room, she might have grabbed the phone and texted the brother that he was inexcusably hurting Jane with his sudden radio silence.

On Wednesday, Elizabeth and Wickham went out to the movies and had the best time laughing and leaning into each other during the kissing scenes but the date ended with no sex.

The next day after work, Elizabeth spied Wickham with Bridget from the shoe store, canoodling outside a popular southwestern restaurant downtown.

She drove straight home, shocked but not feeling as upset as she might have if they'd gone all the way.

Yes, she'd been imagining having sex with him as soon as they saw each other again, but, to be fair, it wasn't like they knew each other very well or very long.

They'd only texted a few times and talked on the phone once, in addition to the Beach Ball date and the movie date.

If his interest in her was so fly-by-night, it was best she found out now before they did it. He must be the kind of guy who couldn't keep his hands off you when you were near but forgot about you when another woman crossed his line of sight.

He was not for her.

Bingley and Jane had finally gotten back on track and were out together that night playing tennis on the clay courts at the country club.

Mrs. Bennet stopped complaining of phantom pains in her side and began talking about plans for a family trip to the Gardiner's house at Christmas which would include an invite for

Bingley.

Wickham called Elizabeth the next day to say he was sorry, explaining in a longwinded, regretful speech that he'd been anxious to go out with her again, only waiting for her to have a free night, but then he ran into an ex, Bridget King, and they decided to give things another go.

As she ended the call, she was happy to find she didn't care all that much. When talking about his career plans, he said something about feeling directionless and less motivated than before Darcy got him fired. He told her he had no current plans for work, which was normally a red flag she ignored at her peril.

His explanation for this ostensible laziness was that he wanted to have a good time after all he'd suffered, or at least that's what he told Jane and Mrs. Bennet when he stopped by for a platonic visit, sharing his sob story with them and half their neighborhood friends.

Everyone, except Jane who seemed confused and anxious, agreed that Will Darcy was wicked for treating his childhood friend and his parents' favorite so heartlessly.

After ordering meat lovers pizza, Wickham and her family sat outside on the patio playing rummy and laughing over encounters they'd had with Derby tourists. The well-dressed gentleman who asked Elizabeth what state he was in. The college girls who wanted to know the visiting hours at Pemberley.

Wickham was a socially and verbally gifted man,

entertaining them all at once as if each were his main object. They all agreed on how much they liked his company, even Jane who was concerned that Wickham and Darcy had suffered a terrible misunderstanding that must be rectified. But Jane did go so far as to admit to Elizabeth that if what Wickham said about Will Darcy was true, Bingley might be injured by association.

Elizabeth said goodbye to Wickham that evening with a genuine smile, despite his having just jilted her.

In their bunk beds, Elizabeth and Jane rehashed all Wickham told them about the Darcys. The mystery of why they'd never crossed paths with Wickham when he was younger had been solved. He actually wasn't so much of a Derby resident as they originally were led to believe. He lived with his grandmother in a town a half hour south, only visiting Pemberley frequently, and at age ten was sent away to a fancy boarding school by the Darcys.

When Jane told Elizabeth she was sincerely sorry that things hadn't gone anywhere with her and Wickham, Elizabeth joked, "Oh, don't worry, a much less agreeable man would do for me."

Chapter Eight

Rosings Park's original claim to fame was its scenic woodlands and plantation house that predated the war between the states, but it was now known for the exclusive pool club cut from the sizable ancestral property belonging to Will's great aunt Catherine's branch of the family.

Will was in the neighborhood of Rosings because although his aunt Catherine couldn't rope her own grandson Cornel into spending Saturday afternoon with her, Will had sat down with her in her overly air conditioned dining parlor for a luncheon of pureed sweet potatoes and shredded chicken served by a waitstaff of three. Afterwards, still shivering, he helped his aunt by lugging crates up a spiral staircase to her library's crawlspace.

Now, at five o'clock, having finally escaped his aunt's press gang, he swung by Rosings Pool Club to meet Anne de Bourgh for dinner at the poolside bistro.

Technically he was single, although he and Anne spent at least one evening a week together. At the start of the summer he'd been sure he wanted a relationship, but he just couldn't commit. Telling Anne he needed time before taking things to the next level, he resisted calling her his girlfriend when his parents asked.

Thankfully, Anne wasn't emotional about much, including fidelity. She was eternally pragmatic. If time was what he needed, she was willing to wait a year. She found it amusing that he occasionally took out Bingley's sister Caroline. The fact that Anne was so understanding made him more inclined to think he could be happy with her, going so far as to chastise himself for stalling.

Walking to the sheltered dining area, Will scanned the pool surround for Anne, who was normally at least 15 minutes late. The hostess sat him at a table by the pool's edge, and he noticed a small stage set up near a row of willow trees by the perimeter fence. On it, a dozen kids sitting in rows of chairs and holding shiny instruments started playing a Beach Boys tune. Judging from their slicked-back wet hair, they had been swimming in the Olympic-sized pool before their performance —pink flamingo floaties were strewn about the pool and water had been splashed on the stone pavers set among blue grass. Above the kids hung a banner reading "Wintergreen School of Music."

The young performers, some still dressed in swim trunks, wore green T-shirts with music notes. A percussionist in the back gently tapped a drum kit, but woodwinds and brass made up most of the troupe. A conductor faced the musicians, a stand set up in front of her with sheet music flapping in the light breeze. She was dressed in what seemed like a 1930s-style bathing suit covered by a colorful Polynesian sarong. As the kids banged out the chorus of "Surfing USA," their leader bounced on her toes and waved her arms to keep tempo. It was an energetic performance; she was clearly young as conductors go. When she turned her head slightly, Will recognized Elizabeth's smiling profile.

For over a week now he'd had a reoccurring nightmare about what might have happened between her and Wickham after she was so pleased with him at the Beach Ball. His imaginings of her sweet face and his sleaze-ball ways were nauseating and in clinical detail. Now he felt his heart pounding in relief as he studied her soft, curvy shape bopping to the catchy tune. Funny enough, her lips moved, mouthing the lyrics of the song although it was a wholly instrumental performance.

The Beach Boys medley finished, Elizabeth spun around, nodding "thank you" to a spattering of applause. She spoke into a microphone, "Our final piece features an oboe solo. 'Hope you enjoy it."

A small girl carrying a black oboe walked forward, and the band began a slowish song Will couldn't make out. There wasn't much sound coming from the soloist's instrument, just as thin, barely audible quacking. Elizabeth grabbed another oboe set up on a stand and stepped over to accompany the girl.

A loud, full-bodied sound rose above the rest of the band and the jazzy melody *"The girl from Ipanema goes walking"* became recognizable. Elizabeth's fingers moved quickly over the silver keys of her oboe, and the percussionist sped up. Her clear, insistent sound reverberated throughout the cluster of dining tables.

When the music stopped, the small girl next to Elizabeth mirrored her wide smile and proudly took a diminutive bow.

Not a minute later, Anne appeared, dressed in a pink scalloped skirt, and Will pulled himself away from staring at Elizabeth as he kissed Anne on the cheek.

He and Anne ate, talking mostly about his parents social calendar and church events.

After, Anne requested they move to the bar for a drink. The pool was empty, but the pool club was crowded with the after dinner crowd. Apparently, many club members wanted to score a hook up now that high season was in full swing. Not the Will could blame them.

The bar area had long, rectangular bar-height tables. Anne led the way to one with caste iron scrollwork that looked like it'd been personally chosen by Aunt Catherine. The communal table had only two available seats, which is why Anne scootched onto an empty bar stool right next to Elizabeth Bennet.

Jesus.

Elizabeth sat facing away from them, talking to a man with a scruffy beard. She had changed into a tight saffron shirt and loose shorts. Her students were no where in sight. Sent home before she met up with a date? She sure knew how to pick 'em. The guy had a huge cartoonish tribal tattoo on his bicep.

Breathing in deeply, Will shook his head.

Anne was oblivious. She knew nothing of Elizabeth. He was certain he'd never mentioned her to Anne.

He adjusted the tuck of his cotton-silk mélange shirt, hoping Elizabeth wouldn't think he was stalking her, then rested his hand on the back of her ornate seat and said "Hi."

Elizabeth's mouth dropped open like she was about to start playing her oboe again.

Anne was talking to a bleached-blond waitress about drinks.

Elizabeth's startled expression transformed into a force

smile, her hand gripping the table edge. "Oh, hi," she replied.

Holding her eyes, Will reached for a bowl of bar snacks, fingering the ridges of a shelled walnut. "Your students were great."

"Thanks," she nodded. "They were so excited to be invited here to play." She looked like she was about to say something more but hesitated. How had he failed to notice the way her dark eyes sparkled when he'd first seen her? She was so damn attractive in the most unique way. Such brilliance written on her face. And yet he missed this the night they met.

As he took his seat next to Anne, he thought of the way Elizabeth had dismissed his advice when they last spoke at the Beach Ball and wished she'd say something conciliatory.

Anne finished with the perky waitress, and glancing to her left, said "Hi" to Elizabeth as if they were somehow acquainted.

Were they? How could that be?

"I think we met before," Anne said. "I don't recall exactly ..."

Will imagined Lydia drunk and throwing up on the shaded property at the corner of Beach Avenue and Ocean Drive that belonged to Anne's family. Containing a sprawling white cottage set back far from the street, the large lot had recently become a loitering spot for young people hanging out downtown.

"...Were you at afternoon tea at Catherine Darcy's last season?" Anne asked Elizabeth.

For years Anne and her mother had attended events at Rosings Park. Aunt Catherine liked to gather small groups of people to dine on under-seasoned food while she administered advice about how to get sand out of carpet and the right number of shelves in a curio cabinet. However, Will was certain no Bennet had ever received an invitation to one of her soirees.

"Me? Uh, no," said Elizabeth limply, looking nonplussed as she bounced her crossed leg.

"Are you a friend of Caroline's?" Anne smiled, turning to look at Will for an instant.

"Bingley Townsend's sister?" said Elizabeth. "No, not really. I believe we might have crossed paths when I was walking downtown with Bobby Collins and he was, uh—"

"Oh! That's it. Outside the salon on Main Street. You were with Reverend Collins dragging an enormous violin down the sidewalk," Anne simpered, her eyes crinkling.

"He, uh—"

"Bless your heart!" Anne interrupted. She slid her chair a couple inches closer to Will's. "It's nice to see you again. How is that quaint man? He's a special one, isn't he?"

Elizabeth blanched. "He insisted on helping me move a donated bass to the middle school."

"Yes. So true," said Anne with a flip of her hair. "But you'll excuse me." Motioning toward Will, she added, "My friend's here."

Elizabeth's flinch was barely perceptible.

Will tried to think of something to say to her.

It was astounding that Anne spent even a minute considering whether to pursue the acquaintance with Elizabeth. They had nothing in common in their sartorial choices. Elizabeth was casual like a folk musician and Anne had a shawl collar and tasteful pearl jewelry.

What's more, Elizabeth didn't have an upper class Southern accent like pampered princess Anne. Elizabeth's voice was decidedly that of someone who'd grown up working class. She sounded educated but no one would mistake her for old money. At the same time, she didn't sound like she'd spent all her life in a trailer park.

Elizabeth studied Anne's profile a moment longer, then with a shrug, swiveled toward the slouching man she was with. He belched.

Why did she lower herself to guys like him? She was underestimating her appeal.

As Anne corrected the waitress for putting the wrong garnish in her drink, Will accidentally made eye contact with Elizabeth's bearded date.

He swung a beer bottle in the air and bellowed, "Hey, dude, what's up? How's it hanging?"

Will swallowed an annoyed exhale. His lips sealed, he barely nodded in reply.

Elizabeth looked awkward. "So, uh ..." She spun a little in her chair, moving left then right.

Why was she with this dead-eyed slacker?

Anne's phone rang and she got up to take the call, carrying her gin fizz with her as she walked several paces from the table.

Will rubbed the bridge of his nose.

A platter of mini desserts Anne had ordered was placed in front of him by the waitress, and he welcomed his table-mates to share in the feast of miniature foods.

Will felt boxed in with Elizabeth, her confused-looking date, and five other nondescript people he didn't know from Adam. He hated engaging with strangers, trying to catch their flow of conversation and pretend to be interested in the concerns of people unconnected with him.

Elizabeth took a tiny piece of sponge cake topped with purple icing and said with a tilt of her head, "This is Larry. He's an electrician for the public schools. We just met recently."

What would make her think he wanted to be introduced to Larry? "Excuse me," said Will. "I didn't mean to interject myself in your private conversation. Please don't mind me."

Elizabeth's date didn't seem conscious of the cut, but Will noticed Elizabeth's cheeks flush.

He truly did not wish to blow *her* off, but he wasn't going to vie for her attention while she was getting to know another man.

Elizabeth turned to Larry the custodian. "As you can see, Darcy and I are not the best of friends. You might say we hate each other."

A croaky laugh was her new friend's reply.

Will looked at Elizabeth. "I'm sorry?"

"Nothing," she mumbled under her breath, her eyes growing stormy.

He searched for the words to explain himself to her. He was not interested in meeting Elizabeth's dates, even if in general he wanted to be on better terms with her.

The man with Elizabeth spoke way too loudly in Will's direction. "Hey, Mister, did you hear the joke about the town pharmacist? He makes a payment on his speed boat every time the Bennet sisters come to get their birth control prescriptions refilled." Spit flew out of his mouth as he laughed.

So Elizabeth was hanging out with a scumbag.

She didn't laugh, just rolled her eyes.

As Will studied the pair more closely, it seemed they might not be a potential couple. Just sitting around at the pool club perhaps.

Anne returned to the table after finishing her call. Reaching around Will, she took a blue macaron.

He watched her eat.

She remained standing. "I'm going to powder my nose. Back in a minute." Anne caressed his arm before walking off.

The guy with Elizabeth tried a line. "Come on. You must have a boyfriend. Tell the truth," he crooned. "DJ said you stopped going out with him."

"It's been a while," she replied, not looking concerned by his persistence. "I'm very selective." Her voice rose satirically. "My dates must appear in more than one of Derby Central's lifestyle pages before I allow them to be photographed with me. It's a huge responsibility to date me."

Her new pal seemed to have no idea what she was talking about, and Darcy realized she might be taking a jab at him as the reputed town golden boy.

She certainly didn't understand his life as well as she thought. Most days involve endless paperwork and arranging with lawyers to file briefs. If he was lucky, the day ended with muffled sex followed by boring conversation about restoring a mantle clock.

"You're full of shit," cried Elizabeth's dazed slacker after a delayed reaction — the man must be getting smashed. "Stop talking like you're all posh. Your underage sister goes around begging people to buy her shots."

"Ask Darcy," said Elizabeth, turning in Will's direction. "He too has oppressively high social status. His choice of a consort affects everyone in town."

The guy with Elizabeth looked baffled again.

Will thought of mentioning his family's conscientious philanthropy, numerous mayoralties, and generous land grants to the town. But he smirked at Elizabeth instead. "I've known you long enough to realize you sometimes enjoy espousing views that are not your own. You don't actually believe any such thing about me."

She laughed, her eyes haughty. "Yes, but you won't be so unkind as to expose me as a phony in front of the whole table or else I might retaliate."

He leaned forward, his voice low. "I'm not afraid of you."

Elizabeth gave him a saucy smile. "You ought to be afraid." Her eyes were wild.

Will's voice caught in his throat as he looked down at her breasts which were prominent in her tight top.

Dampness permeated the air as grey clouds formed overhead, and the dude with Elizabeth tried to regain her attention with whooping noises.

She ignored him. "I was just going to start talking about horse breeding, nautical miles, and military academies." Her nose flicked up in the air on her last word.

Chills. She was mimicking the flat intonation of Will's voice. *Parodying him!*

His lip curled as he slid his arm across the table toward

her. "It might be good for you to occupy your time with such worthy pursuits."

"Worthy pursuits?" she motioned toward Anne who was walking toward them. "You mean, like curating a collection of beautiful women?"

"Damn right!" said the tattooed electrician, trying to dive back into the conversation at the words "beautiful women."

Anne sat down, blocking Will's view of Elizabeth on fire.

His chest felt heavy. He adjusted his chair to peer over Anne's shoulder and give Elizabeth a pointed gaze he hoped might stick with her for a while.

He couldn't listen to what Anne was saying about her parents' new etagere. He was dying to continue sparring with Elizabeth Bennet.

"I'm tired," Anne complained, picking up the last sliver of almond shortbread. "I've been shopping with Mama all afternoon and it's so crowded here. Can you walk me out? I wish your dad's driver was available, so you could drive me home in my car."

"Sorry," said Will. "I drove myself. But of course I'll walk you to your car."

He took out money to cover the drinks and food on the table and wished he could think of an excuse to touch Elizabeth as he passed her by but merely said, "Good evening."

"Bye," she replied, curled in her seat, looking tiny and

alone in the bearded loser's company.

If not for Anne and his dignity, he could have continued following Elizabeth around all evening, interrupting all her conversations. *Damn. This was not good.* Anne wouldn't be spending the night with him. And worse his thoughts and feelings were elsewhere.

#

Under a canopy of fir trees, pavers in herringbone design led through the green copper gates of Rosings Pool Club. Rain had been threatening all day and a light drizzle started coming down as Elizabeth pulled out her clunky old phone and, walking slowly, checked for texts from Jane.

Jane had stayed home that day despite having wanted to come see Elizabeth's students play.

Two days earlier, on the first of August, Bingley had paused work on Netherfield to return to Texas because a flood had damaged his parents' ranch near Austin. Before he left, he and Jane had several tense conversations — the first one the night of the Beach Ball. He told her he was having trouble getting over the fact she hadn't been forthright with him about certain aspects of her family history.

"I can understand not mentioning it when we first met," Bingley had said, "and that in general you're a bit *uncomfortable* about your family having a sort of distressing reputation around Derby — I've noticed this, of course — but when we started talking about our future you should have found a way to bring it up."

Elizabeth had tried to reassure her sister, who whimpered over Bingley's departure, telling Jane there was no way Bingley would be away more than a week, that he'd soon be back in her arms. She and Bingley were too good together to not work out any bruised feelings he had about Jane not being frank with him.

Jane had seemed resigned, saying forlornly, "Mom had been so adamant about not telling him anything and once I avoided mentioning it the first time, it just never seemed like the right time. It's my fault. When people at the club dropped hints, I pretended I didn't hear."

Now, as Elizabeth left the pool club, muggy air mixing with the cooling effect of the rain, Jane forwarded Elizabeth a new text from Bingley:

I've decided to stay home for longer than originally planned, maybe not come back to Netherfield for a few weeks. I've been invited to visit friends in Rome, and I'm considering a bit of traveling. Sorry. That's all I can say for now.

Oh, Bingley. In the summer a few weeks was an eternity.

It made no sense. How could Bingley, whom Elizabeth had always liked so much, act in such a way? The Bingley she knew would never send snippy text messages, casually mentioning he wasn't planning to return to Derby for a while because he was going on a spur of the moment vacation to Italy.

Elizabeth immediately called Jane.

Jane wouldn't hear of sending any sort of complaint in reply. And she would not plead with him to "forgive her and return to Derby," as Mrs. Bennet demanded in the background.

Jane's voice was shaky over the phone. "I'll have to accept whatever decision he makes."

Thunder turned from rumbling to cymbal crashing and the rain started really coming down.

"I'm coming home now," said Elizabeth as she ended the call.

She jogged down the tree-lined road from Rosings Pool Club to the bus stop.

Bent over, catching her breath, she hid in the back corner of the bus shelter, next to a perfume ad, and heard her phone ping.

A text from Jane read, I didn't want to show you this while you were enjoying yourself at the pool club but since you're on your way home ...

Jane forwarded another text from Bingley:

As I said before, yes, I have spoken to Will. He didn't want to tell me the whole story but I kept insisting he tell me more. And now I feel like I can't trust you, Jane. Imagine my reaction when I learned that your aunt, of whom you speak so warmly, followed a married man around town until she found him alone after an argument with his wife and then got him in bed with the intention of getting pregnant. What about the child your aunt brought into the world for the purpose of extracting a settlement and then tossed aside? It's so outrageous I can't even write it down.

Elizabeth dug in her purse, rummaging to find an extra quarter for the bus fare and burning with anger.

How could he? Will Darcy was throwing Bingley for a loop with stories of how Aunt Phyllis forced his poor defenseless father to cheat on his wife. And Jane was guilty by association.

She would not have thought Bingley was so naive. Didn't he see that Will and Caroline wanted to turn him against Jane because they were snobs and thought Jane wasn't good enough for him? The only part of all this Elizabeth hadn't figured out yet was why it took Will Darcy so many weeks to tell Bingley these stories about Aunt Phyllis tampering with prophylactics. Why hadn't he done this to Jane on day one?

What have I been doing, hanging with Will by the pool? Anyone who noticed me back there might think we were friends.

It was growing dark.

A black car with streaks of water running down its tinted windows pulled up next to her and stopped.

Her pulse sped up. Some man from the club was going to use the rain to try to pick her up?

The window lowered halfway. Will Darcy's dry face

appeared in shadow. "Do you need a ride?"

She hadn't seen him since a half hour ago when he'd walked off with the thin woman in pink with beautiful fair hair. Elizabeth had thought he was long gone.

"You're all alone ...," he observed helpfully. "Normally, you're with one of your sisters."

"Yep. No sisters." She propped her hand against the bus stop enclosure, standing back from the edge to avoid the rain. She wished she could make him say something about his interference with Jane and Bingley.

He stared expectantly, wisps of rain blowing on him.

"Where's your friend in that cute pink outfit?" she asked loudly, competing with the blustery wind of the storm.

"Anne drove home in her own car a while ago. I was leaving too when I ran into my cousin Cornel. He lives around here." His voice was steady and as always clear and articulate. "I'm heading downtown, but I could swing by your place and drop you off if you like."

"I'm fine taking the bus," she said, feeling she must be polite despite the unsaid things floating in her head. "Oh, I almost forgot." She pulled bills out of the tapestry wallet she used as a clutch purse. "I'm glad you stopped. I can pay you back." She handed him two twenties.

"I'd really rather not. It's not necessary; I assure you," he said calmly.

"I insist," she said. Back at the club, she had watched him put a few hundreds on the table to cover the exorbitant bill.

Lowering his window fully, he took the damp money from her outstretched hand, holding it away from himself as if he didn't want to take it, then dropped it onto the center console of his sleek car. "You're sure about the ride?" he asked

A car rode by, splashing muddy puddle water onto the curb.

Elizabeth sidestepped. "I'm fine. Truly. Goodnight, Darcy."

He cocked his head to the left, then righted himself, clenching his jaw. "Don't *Darcy* me, Elizabeth." His teeth were white and straight like he'd kept every orthodontist appointment. "Call me William if you want to be formal. I rarely hear my name unabbreviated, yet for some reason, after you started it, a lot of people have been addressing me as 'Darcy' of late and they rarely did before." His elbow pointed at her from its resting spot on the car windowsill, the slightest grin softening his cut features.

She felt a pang. Three sentences in a row on the same topic was a dissertation coming from him.

Frowning for an instant, she thought of when she and Jane first met him and Bingley at Netherfield: Jane and Bingley had hit it off like soulmates who'd never send frosty texts to each other. "According to Ms. Manners, whatever you ask me to call you, I must," she said. "So if you request that I call you

Dingleberry, you're Dingleberry. If Prince Regent, you're Prince Regent."

"I can think of quite a few things I've wanted to call *you*," he said, with a sort of swagger. "But I've resisted."

"I don't want to know," she shook her head, suddenly feeling the full effect of the muggy wet heat and wanting to be dry.

"Get in," he commanded, leaning across the interior of his car to open the passenger side door. "You're getting soaked."

"Yes, but—"

"Elizabeth!" He exclaimed. "Get in. The doors open for you. Water is coming in."

She exhaled, then skirted around the front of his car.

As soon as she pulled the heavy door closed, he started driving, pulling onto the road leading to downtown Derby as she fastened her seatbelt.

To get to Longbourn, you took an exit several miles ahead. She was sure he knew this as a native of Derby, so she didn't mention directions.

What were they going to do now, discuss Bingley's travel plans? No, they'd probably just make out in her driveway before he dropped her off. She snickered to herself about her absurd series of run ins with Will Darcy.

The sound of the rain was muffled inside his car with its winged Aston Martin emblem and an array of knobs and dials arranged like modern art. She couldn't recall ever riding in a new car before and only knew of the new car smell by report. It wasn't anything to write home about. His car smelled like leather and hand sanitizer.

She listened to her own breathing and, after a minute, her ears adjusted to the acoustics of the small space and she could hear the sound of his breathing as well.

He broke the silence abruptly, his voice raspy. "You like to play around. Why don't you and I stop beating around the bush and have some actual fun?"

"What?" she exclaimed. "Fun? With you? I doubt it."

"You're all talk?" he asked with a drawl, his face taut. "No action?"

Her stomach dropped. "What do you mean by that?"

"I'm asking if you'd like me to take you somewhere ... the new hotel on the beach perhaps?"

Whipping her head to face him, she stabbed the heels of her wet sandals into the car's mat. "Don't make jokes like that. You might frighten some helpless girl." She exhaled loudly, wanting to seem confident.

Had he been drinking? She'd only seen him down one glass of something.

She waited for some acknowledgment of his nonsense, but he looked shockingly subdued. So much so she started to hyperventilate.

"*You*'re not helpless, are you?" he asked with the slightest grin.

She closed her eyes, lightheaded. Reaching for the back of her neck, she dabbed sticky sweat mixed with rain.

What in the hell? Was this actually happening? She was sitting next to Will Darcy, moving at forty miles per hour in an enclosed space and being propositioned with clichés?

When she opened her eyes, they were slowing down for a red light, and he was looking at her, his expression haughty, as if he'd expected an answer to his romantic inquiry by now. "So?"

She imagined herself opening the door and stumbling into the woods, falling face first in a stream like Ophelia. But the babbling brook running toward Longbourn was too shallow for even a dead man's float.

She struggled for her voice, realizing she had a premonition of this. "Eh um, you think I'd agree to go off to a hotel with you for ... *sex*?" She gulped. "After all I know about you, after all the things you've said about my family, all that has happened with ..."

"Yes, well, considering our families, it *is* awkward to ask, probably foolish given your family's reputed modus operandi. That being said, I thought it might be an experience if you were up for it." He shrugged his shoulder like sleeping with her was no big deal. Take it or leave it.

His eyes were on the road as he started the car moving

again, accelerating, seemingly callous and unconcerned. *This was on-the-prowl Will Darcy?*

"So you're asking me to go hook up with you while insulting me, and my, uh, my family?" She barely got the words off her tongue.

"What do you want me to say? I'm not going to lie about your family's known predilections. If you don't like my idea of the hotel, I'm sorry for troubling you with it."

Was he really expecting to get laid with this method? He didn't sound even a bit conflicted about his offensive approach. This couldn't possibly be the way he made a move on pretty-in-pink Anne.

How could he think so poorly of her to believe she'd consider such an offer? Could he be so ridiculously sure of himself to think she'd jump in bed with him if he showed the slightest interest in her? *Oh my god.*

She thought of Bingley's messages to Jane. Bennets give it up to rich men, hoping for a payout.

This was not to be endured. "Do you actually think I'd be willing to go off with you ... when, to your arrogant ass, being a friend to Bingley is telling him some story about how my family was part of an extortion plot against your dad?" she huffed. "That's a lie if you think Jane has anything to do with that, that she endorses that. Just because she looks like my aunt doesn't mean she has any part in my aunt's activities. It amazes me that you think I would overlook the fact that you hurt my sister and hook up with you ... *for fun*."

He glanced at her, wide-eyed.

"Oh, and I almost forgot," she continued, "do you think I'd be interested in you after what I learned about the cruel way you acted toward a guy who's had none of the many advantages in life you've had?"

The car bucked a little as he slowed down to exit the highway. "You mean Wickham?" His voice was scorching. "For your sake, I hope the rumors about you and him are not true."

Gone was his restraint. His temper was out. But she didn't fear him, or she couldn't accuse him of ever seeming capable of violence, so she didn't shut up. She was the type of person, with the type of experiences, who would shut up if she felt physically threatened.

"What rumors?" she asked. "Oh, I can guess. Rumors that I let him in my pants, just like you seem to think I would with you ... at the drop of a hat? Snap your fingers and I come crawling. Those are the rumors you mean. The rumors that I'm easy."

Stretching his neck from left to right, chin in the air, he appeared much less like a viper ready to strike, a little penitent even, but, as always, condescending.

"Please, Elizabeth, let's hit reverse," he said, his voice softened and a touch rattled. "I believe there's been some misunderstanding."

After turning onto the road leading to Longbourn, he pulled the car over, out of the way of traffic.

The rain tap tap tapped on the roof, and he turned on the hazard lights as they sat in the warm and dry car, silent for a minute.

He turned in his seat so that his whole body faced her.

It was too tempting not to look him up and down. He was so well made, intimidatingly built, with broad shoulders and a lean torso. His legs and thighs square, fitting the driver's seat like he was in a cockpit, even as he now slumped, looking defeated, his eyelids lowered. "Several things you've said to me I construed as interest of a certain sort."

She flushed in disbelief. "Things I've said to you?"

He nodded his head, looking calm but as though he were suppressing fiercer emotions. "Yes, things you've said over the past couple months."

"I've said nothing to you that could possibly make you think I want to get fucked in a hotel." Seeing stars, she shook her head, riled up again. "I don't believe that. The truth is that you look at me and think, *there's a girl who's much less than me* — I know for a fact you publicly declared me to be plain and unworthy of your attention in front of a crowd at Netherfield. You think *because she comes from a family that sleeps around and she herself has some sort of reputation she'd blow me if I asked.*"

"Not at all," he said, strikingly loud although he didn't

seem to be wincing at her vulgarity. "I was basing my suggestion on specific instances in which I believed you were trying to ... I guess it was your playful way of speaking." He breathed deeply, sitting up a bit, leaning ever so slightly in her direction. "I wish I have phrased my request more delicately, if only in hopes you might have considered it."

She could have punched the roof. "Oh, Darcy, you are mistaken if you believe you could have expressed yourself in any possible way that would have convinced me to go off with you."

"Really?" He had the nerve to look not only offended but skeptical.

"Oh, yes, I'm one thing you'll never be able to get your hands on, Will Darcy. Not under any circumstances. Not if you could land a Stradivarius. Not if you moved my entire family out of Longbourn onto beachfront property. I would not let you touch me for anything in the world."

He went white, opening his mouth but not speaking, like a drowning swimmer gasping for air.

"If I've been a bit chatty with you once or twice, it was innocently meant and out of concern for my sister." Her hands and legs shook convulsively. "Ever since I first knew you, since I saw you at Netherfield, I've seen what you are, so cold and arrogant and insensitive, someone I have zero interest in romantically."

She jerked her face toward the steamed up passenger-side window.

Done.

There was nothing else she could say.

No way to be clearer.

No way to express her feelings more forcefully.

He put the car in gear and, sounding mortified, said, "I'll take you home."

The silence was excruciating as they pulled back onto the road and slowly moved down the dark street toward Longbourn.

As they reached the neon sign for Longbourn Creek Estates he said, "I promise you you're mistaken, if you believe I intended to insult you, Elizabeth,"

His words were like music to her ears, but only for a split second.

It was hopeless. She was sick. For the rest of her life she'd be tortured by their conversation that night, by his shock that she wouldn't drop to her knees if the great Will Darcy said he wanted her.

Her face fully averted from him, she tried to stop feeling like she was going to retch.

The humiliation of who she was, a humiliation she'd tried to mitigate her entire life, had blown up in her face. His look of surprise when she turned him down would be engraved forever on her self-esteem. His gasp of incredulity upon learning she was not his for the taking would scar her for life.

Will Darcy offered to have sex with her, claiming she was asking for it, had been giving off take-me signals. He thought she'd be fine being taken to some hotel room to suck his dick. He had no actual interest in her besides wanting to ejaculate in her once or twice, but, that would not be a problem, she'd be up for it.

If she never saw him again it would be too soon to atone for this. The wound to her ego would never heal ... because he was a Darcy, he was Will Darcy, handsome, rich, intelligent and too good for her except if he chose to use her as a functioning cum depository.

She sniffled as she choked on tears. With cloudy vision, she looked out the window at Longbourn: the white lattice work hiding trailer wheels, the bent vertical blinds, the personalized golf carts, and the TV screens with people screaming in agony as guns fired. She knew the potholes of Longbourn by heart.

He stopped the car in front of her house, leaving the engine running as he turned to her, saying, "Truly. I wish you well, Elizabeth."

She shook her head, wanting to tell him that she didn't believe him, that she didn't believe he had a single good intention. But this wasn't true. She heard the sincerity in his voice.

His little show of kindness made it worse. She'd rather he curse her, so she could dismiss him as a sociopath. She didn't want him to be anyone worth having, to have any manners, to have anything witty to say, to have anything worthwhile about him. She wanted him to be nothing. Not some popular guy who thought she was a quick fuck, but never girlfriend material like pink Anne.

She pushed open the car door, ducked her head into the rain and jogged to the yellow trailer.

The bolt connecting her twin bed to Jane's upper bunk stuck out halfway. Ten years ago when their mother found matching twin beds at a yard sale, Elizabeth had gone through every last wrench and screwdriver in the house trying to make the brackets hold the bunk beds together flush. But no luck.

The protruding bolt scraped her finger as she grabbed it and twisted ineffectually, humming a scale she'd played with her students earlier that day.

She imagined what might have been with Will Darcy. After some awkward undressing and friction when he first entered her, she'd be on her back with him in her face, his gorgeousness so much more than any guy she'd gone all the way with. She'd get to feel his penis inside her. Such an honor. He'd offered her the chance to experience him naked, making her the envy of all her acquaintances. And a worthless twat.

She couldn't still be that disgraceful girl of seventeen who couldn't get out from under the scourge of being a Bennet girl.

Fatherless because her dad didn't find her worth sticking around for. Dating a guy she met at a bar who slapped her before she submitted to sex in stunned silence. And maybe worst of all, laughing with her mom about less popular girls while trying to get guys to buy her clothes.

How could it be that Will Darcy saw her as that exact same loser? Why wasn't she seen as an educated professional, a great success story? What would it take for her to be respected by a man like him?

Chapter Nine

Standing in front of a quartet of rising seventh graders, Elizabeth gave the group of summer students an exasperated smirk and put her hand on her hip. "Did *anyone* practice this week? I know hanging out with friends at the beach is fun but learning to play an instrument offers a potential lifetime of enjoyment."

A rap at the door made her give off reading the riot act.

Walking out from behind the conductor's stand, she headed over to the door, thinking the music director, her boss, had come to observe her class.

She pushed open the heavy wood door and Will Darcy grabbed it by the inside edge, moving out of the way as it swung wide.

She was slack-jawed in disbelief. The taste of M&Ms sour in her mouth.

He stepped into the room, wordlessly, uninvited, barely glancing at her class. His eyes were cold ice. The etched aesthetics of his face in full effect with a glowering, haunted look. It occurred to her that he might be exhausted.

"Would you do me the honor of reading this letter?" he said with the formality of a royal courier.

She didn't move a muscle.

"Don't be alarmed. It's an apology," he said as he held out a folded piece of thick paper.

She took the letter into her hand.

He looked around the room for a moment, his eyes pausing on her giant bag lying on the floor with "Miss Elizabeth" embroidered on the side and a folded music stand sticking out, then he turned on his heals and walked out, closing the door behind him.

Her students were paying full attention now.

"Oh my god! Is he your boyfriend?" asked the clarinet player with dangling curls.

"He's cute, Miss Elizabeth," said the flutist, resting her instrument upside down on the carpeted floor. "What's his name?"

The clarinet at the end of the row laughed, "Do you feed

him M&Ms?"

"I know his name. He's Will Darcy of Pemberley," said her best student, a fellow oboist.

Elizabeth didn't answer any of their questions. "Okay, back to work! Turn to page 27 of your lesson book."

Dear E,

My conduct of the other night was such that I must apologize and ask you to forgive my coarse offer. It was impulsive and unfortunately gave you an entirely false idea of my impression of you.

If I've ever, in the past, behaved in a way less than cordial toward you or said something I oughtn't, it was not due to any lack of respect for you but my own awkwardness about how to relate to you given our divergent backgrounds and my confused thoughts regarding you. In point of fact, I admire you and your opinions, even those I disagree with.

Feeling compelled to defend myself, I must address the two allegations you made against me. I hope you will excuse my presumption here, but I believe justice demands your consideration.

First, you said I hurt your sister by sharing

information about your family with Bingley. Quite the contrary, I have for many weeks consciously refrained from sharing more intimate details of what I know about your family, or your aunt in particular. Only recently, Bingley came to me and requested not only my knowledge of facts but my opinion regarding his relationship with your sister. I answered him honestly, and with honorable intentions. I did not give him information because I jumped at the chance to expose your family or separate him from your sister — although your mother has said things in my presence which could be called alarmingly suspect. I spoke openly to Bingley because I had concerns for his welfare. I admit to you, in confidence, that I advised him against the connection with Jane because of a certain incompatibility between his personality and hers.

Bingley is the most trusting person, while your sister is placid and malleable, having a tendency to adapt herself to suit those she finds herself in company with. Around your mother, Jane cares for makeup and clothes; around Bingley, she's excited about antique furniture. I studied her and I didn't perceive any particular or strong emotions toward my friend. In general, she does not seem to be one who is deeply touched by anyone outside her family. Bingley has gotten into scrapes before by being overly gullible — he once lent his girlfriend a laptop computer the night before an important document needed to be filed in court and you can imagine how that took a turn for the disastrous. With regard to your sister, I warned him to be cautious and step away for a period of time.

I believe I had a right to share my thoughts with him. He's an adult. He could take it or leave it when it comes to my advice and is not beholden to me. But you declared that I hurt Jane, and being as close as you are to your sister, you may be better able to judge the degree to which she cares for Bingley. If I made a mistake in my advice to him, it's not an indelible one. I know he intends to maintain contact with Jane, and presumably they can settle things between them on their own if their feelings are truly the lasting sort. In the future I will not offer suggestions to Bingley either way for fear I may be unclear as to your sister's true sentiments.

Second, you alluded to Wickham George. I realized the night of the party at the beach that he'd made some sort of claims about my mistreatment of him, but I'm not sure exactly what sort of falsehoods he's peddling, so I'll relate a history of my relationship with him.

Wickham and I grew up together. His mother was a loyal employee, working and even living at Pemberley until her premature passing. His father held odd jobs at Pemberley and was reliable before suddenly disappearing from town soon after his wife's sad departure — I believe he too passed away but that was only a couple years ago.

My parents took an interest in Wickham from an early age. Over the years, they have done much to better his situation in life. They paid for his education, including sending him away to a private military school. They offered him assistance in his chosen career path and invited him to Pemberley often. They enjoy his company and have never observed Wickham in less guarded moments as I have. They know he's had problems with gambling and profligacy but feel sorry for his personal loses and assume his smiling personal qualities are an approximate representation of his inner feelings.

My parents and I agree on many things, but we do not see eye to eye on the subject of Wickham. He and I have never been close, despite my parents' wishes. There are

213

numerous reasons I've lost respect for him. I'll give just two examples of vicious behavior I've witnessed. At eighteen he brought to me his pregnant girlfriend who was in distress after an attempted abortion and insisted I drive her to the hospital because he "didn't feel like it." Second, I'll never forget my conversation with his grandmother, Mrs. Emily George, about how he'd convinced her she was suffering from dementia because she found things missing from her house when he was staying with her.

Despite my personal estimation of him, I have tried to honor my parents by assisting Wickham. I've handed him checks to cover his debts. I have bailed him out of jail for disorderly conduct. Most recently, I found him a lucrative job at a thoroughbred racetrack, which he lost because he bet on horses while working, which could have gotten him in legal trouble if I hadn't intervened on his behalf with his employer.

He rarely if ever has appreciated my efforts. He is want to denigrate me in proportion to the difficulty of his financial situation, which I know is usually bad. He has told my parents he doesn't think he'll be able to get by if they do not gift him some portion of the Pemberley property, which you must acknowledge is a rather audacious request.

He is someone I would not wish to have any personal connections with, but I accept that my parents feel an obligation to him, and I will continue to carry out their wishes as they plan to do more for him. I accept this as their choice without believing he deserves their favor or patronage. But he has it, and he has come to rely on it.

Now we come to the worst part. Unbeknownst to my parents, Wickham has recently made attempts to hurt my sister. I cannot say for certain if the bad blood between us had something to do with his actions toward Georgiana, but I fear it may have. I can't go into the particulars in writing, but she was away at college by herself for the first time when Wickham came to visit her in March. I can say in vague terms that he took advantage of his connection to my family, tried to pressure her to elope with him, and sent her life into a tailspin, albeit a temporary one. But I must relate the remainder of the story to you in person if you wish to hear it. Otherwise, I never talk of it.

Wickham has a talent for charming people and passing himself off as a harmless hedonist. He is in fact scheming, manipulative and often cruel. I would advise you not to trust him in any capacity. I tried to communicate this to you at the Beach Ball, but I believe I was too flustered at the time to express myself as clearly as I ought.

Finally, I now agree with you that the idea of anything between us was ill-conceived on my part. I hope we can be friends, but I realize that first I must convince you it is not the case that a low opinion of you caused me to take the opportunity to ask you out. I swear to you that it was quite the opposite. Since I first met you at Netherfield, I've always found you to be a lively, well-meaning and sensible person, and it was wrong of me to make you feel otherwise. I should have been more sensitive to your situation, and I should have behaved like a gentleman. Again, I sincerely apologize.

W. D.

Alone after her last group of students left, she reread the note for the fifth time.

At first she couldn't believe he intended to defend his behavior toward Jane as anything other than a superiority complex. To suggest Jane did not have real feelings for Bingley! He even implied that Jane might be feigning feelings for Bingley because of his money.

Outrageous.

She picked up her oboe and tried to play a note but it squawked. A cramp in her neck made her stand and stretch.

Perhaps their mom did start out with the idea of Jane going after Bingley because he was well off. When he first came to town and everyone found out that this young man purchased a huge house on the beach and planned to renovate, Mrs. Bennet had encouraged Jane to throw herself at him. They heard Bingley looked nice but they didn't really know anything about his character or personality. Their mother was prodding Jane to go for him because of his wealth.

Elizabeth's hand shook as she practiced keying a difficult sequence, staring at the sheet music propped on the collapsible stand in front of her.

Mrs. Bennet's urgings had no bearing on what Jane actually did or how she felt. Jane sincerely liked Bingley from the get go, from the first night at Netherfield, and she now cared for him deeply. She was a miserable, altered person since her parting from him. And Will Darcy did this to her.

The reed in Elizabeth's mouth was dry, and she rewet it with her tongue.

Charlotte had once said, "I know Jane wants to counter the impression she's a Bennet girl, but her triumph in fooling the world about the strength of her feelings for Bingley is lost if she deceives him too." Elizabeth had laughed. Now she wondered if Jane could be a bit willowy, too easy going. Overly persuadable.

Oh god, she had to admit that Darcy's conduct might be less an outrage if what he wrote in his letter was true from his perspective. He was trying to help his friend by separating him from a pliable, disingenuous woman being pressured by her mother to ingratiate him. It was a serious misinterpretation on his part but maybe an understandable one in a certain light.

Elizabeth walked to the window overlooking the school's parking lot, forgetting the piece of music she'd been trying to make her way through.

What about Wickham? Was it possible she'd been gullible in believing Wickham's stories about the Pemberley family because he, unlike Will, seemed to appreciate her looks and spoke so pleasantly to her? She was hit by the humiliating thought that she had wanted to believe Wickham's stories about Will because of her early decision to dislike everything about Will Darcy.

Yes, Darcy was off-puttingly prideful at times; he had an exaggerated sense of his self-worth and smarts; and he had called her plain. But this was not evidence of the kind of gross immorality Wickham accused him of. She'd never seen Darcy act vengefully or ruthlessly, and she'd seen him in difficult situations, like his bringing lascivious Lydia home from drag racing. Jane had heard that his car was damage that night but he hadn't complained of this to her family. Imagine the bill for a new paint job. On his yacht, when they had to disembark because of Jane's seasickness, there was not a complaint or unsympathetic look directed toward her or Jane. When she confronted him over his dad's treatment of poor Richard, he said it was a sad situation and seemed sincere. During the trailer visit when her mom went off about Bennet women having rich beaus, he remained subdued under a barrage of provocative statements from her mother. Most tellingly, when she herself had ripped him a new one in his car in the rain, he'd actually wished her well at their parting.

Did she actually believe he was the kind of person who went around wantonly hurting people's chances of making a living out of spite? Why would Darcy want Wickham fired from a job? He must want him to not be so dependent on his family's resources.

Now that she thought about it, Wickham's account made little sense. His adoption story must be bogus. A quick google search of Wickham's mother, who was buried at a local cemetery, showed that her husband had only passed away in the past few years; maybe Wickham's father was a deadbeat, but Wickham had lied about being an orphan at an early age and having the Darcys try to adopt him. Elizabeth should have known this. Wickham's grandmother was still living and what southern grandma would think of relinquishing custody of her grandson to anyone, even the Darcys?

Wickham had shown her, and anyone who was interested, an angry text message from Darcy as proof of his animosity and injurious conduct: "You will not get away with what you've done." Wickham had said Darcy was on the war path over his parents wanting to give Wickham assistance.

But the date of the message back in April seemed to coincide with the situation Darcy described involving Wickham pursuing his sister while she was away at college. It seemed plausible that Wickham the ladies' man had been fooling around with Georgiana Darcy. Maybe he tried to get hitched to her for her money?

As far as Elizabeth could remember, Georgiana left the Beach Ball around the time Wickham tried to greet her brother. But how could Will Darcy keep his sister Georgiana, an independently wealthy young woman who inherited land and money from her grandfather at birth, away from Wickham unless this was her choice? Darcy could not get Wickham kicked out of places like the yacht club without cause. He couldn't pull out his photo ID, show his family name, and get people fired. These stories from Wickham beggared belief. If she hadn't been prejudiced against Will Darcy, she would have realized this.

Elizabeth separated the pieces of her oboe, packed them in the hard plastic case, and snapped it closed. Then she gave in and unfolded the letter from Darcy again.

Will Darcy would not make up a story like this about his sister. What he wrote of Wickham and Georgiana must be true. Will Darcy had a reputation in Derby for being arrogant but no one other than Wickham accused him of being a liar. And he was definitely a good son and a good brother.

The honesty of Will's letter was astounding. He trusted her with such personal matters involving his parents and sister. As well as unflattering confidences about himself. And something that had somehow been lost on her while she'd been sitting in his car being hit on was that *he must really like something about* me *as an individual to overcome his previous lackluster impression and want to sleep with me.*

He'd never addressed her accusation that he called her plain at Netherfield, but he didn't deny it. Would he choose someone he was only mildly physically attracted to for a mindless hook up? Other very good looking women would fuck him if he wanted quick sexual gratification. There must be something about her personality that interested him because her looks weren't enough of a draw. He'd wrote that he was *confused about her.* What a thing to say.

His offer of sex wasn't as insulting as she originally thought. Maybe she should be flattered that despite initially rating her as just okay, despite the snide things she said to him including her attempts to taunt him, he had actually liked her enough to get up the nerve to make such a proposal ... to a

Bennet.

Amazing.

And she was not innocent in all this. For almost the entire summer she'd been getting her jollies out of making fun of Will Darcy. Call it trashy or even *ignoble*. She'd always thought of herself as the clever one who didn't suffer fools gladly. But she wasn't more insightful than Jane; she was jealous and small-minded. Will Darcy wasn't actually a bad guy; he hadn't in fact acted like a complete ass at Netherfield or after. From a charitable point of view, he hadn't been cruel to Jane. He was reserved and stoic and guarded. His judgements were moralistic and stringent perhaps, but he wasn't an awful person.

Until that moment she'd never really known herself. Despite all her attempts to slice and dice Will Darcy, she'd gotten both herself and him wrong.

#

On Thursday after work Elizabeth received a text from a number she didn't recognize. It read, Hello, Elizabeth. This is Will Darcy. How are you?

She hopped onto her bed, lay back on her lumpy pillow, and typed, Um, I'm doing sort of okay. Better than I thought after a rough weekend.

Darcy: I hope my letter made a difference, a positive one

Elizabeth: Are we texting buddies now? I didn't

222

know you had my number

Darcy: I had to ask around for it

Elizabeth: Who betrayed me?

Darcy: I think I'm supposed to insert the smiley face emoji here. Is that how this works?

Elizabeth: A smiley face gave you my phone number?

Darcy: It was Bingley, actually. I apologize on his behalf if he wasn't supposed to share it. He believes I am responsible and wouldn't have recognized me from the way I behaved the other night

Elizabeth: You kicked back too many mint juleps at the pool club?

Darcy: Frankly ... I don't really know what happened. I was not drunk. I was intrigued by the conversation we had while you were sitting with Larry the Electrician and found myself wanting to continue it

Elizabeth: ... in a swanky hotel room.

Darcy: I know my explanation doesn't make a whole lot of sense

Elizabeth: I'll help ...

Elizabeth: Pink skirt was not going home with you so you looked around for a backup plan and there I was

Darcy: No, that's not it. That's an excellent example of your self-deprecating humor, but that's not correct

Elizabeth: Let's go for door #2

Elizabeth: AKA the conceited explanation for why you asked me to go to a hotel with you

Darcy: Oh god no

Elizabeth: No?

Darcy: I dread it

Elizabeth: Ok. I won't do that to you

Darcy: The conceited explanation is so awful I can't type it

Elizabeth: Now you have to. I must know. And in clear terms. No beating around the bush and hemming and hawing and stuff like "I don't know what came over me ...

Darcy: May I change the subject by requesting the pleasure of your company at a jazz concert my parents are hosting?

Elizabeth: Jazz? I didn't know anyone in Derby threw jazz parties

Darcy: Yes, it's a benefit and I was hoping you would be my guest

Elizabeth: I'm going to copy and paste our previous texts ...

> **Darcy:** The conceited explanation is so awful I can't type it
>
> **Elizabeth:** Now you have to. I must know

224

Darcy: To answer and have to write something like "I thought you'd be game" is too much. I don't want to know what you think of me

Elizabeth: Would delusional be unkind?

Darcy: Ouch

Elizabeth: Take your medicine

Darcy: Okay, I took it. Now tell me if you'd like to attend a jazz concert on the 17th of August at Pemberley

Elizabeth: I have a question. Theoretically speaking, when exactly do I go with you to the hotel, before or after I have sex with Larry, who seemed to want to drive me home after Rosings, and this other musician guy, a DJ, who was at Rosings too and who definitely wants to hook up with me ... because I might get worn out by the end of it all

Darcy: I know you're not interested in Larry

Elizabeth: Who am I interested in according to you? I mean, besides you, obviously. Since you have opinions about this. Please tell me who I want to hook up with according to your astute observations

Darcy: In the screenshot you sent, I noticed you input my name as "Darcy." That's not what comes up on caller ID. There are many Darcys in this area code. What would you do if I got married and had a wife? Oh, look it's "Darcy" calling ... or is it his wife "Darcy" calling? ... or maybe it's his sister "Darcy" calling?

Elizabeth: I'm glad you asked that question and ignored my other question because it gives me the opportunity to tell you that your wife is not going to take your last name so it won't be a problem

Darcy: How are you privy to that sort of information?

Elizabeth: I speculate based on my knowledge of you. You'll piss her off too much to be willing to follow stale traditions

Darcy: The question remains, why would you save my name on your phone as just "Darcy" with no honorific or given name?

Elizabeth: I don't know. But I'm thinking of changing it to @SSH()LE. Do you like it?

Darcy: fuck that

Elizabeth: Hey! I'm surprised at you

Darcy: You shouldn't be. You know firsthand I have a way with women

Elizabeth: Okay, I admit it. That made me laugh

Darcy: Whatever it takes to get you to respond to my invitation

Elizabeth: You must be totally fed up with me by now. Even I feel annoyed with myself. If you want me to consider an invitation, send it to my email address

ElizabethBennet@DerbyCentral.org along with links to
the performers who will be there.

Darcy: Ok. I will

Elizabeth: I'm all aflutter with anticipation

Elizabeth: still fluttering

Darcy: Is it just me ... or have you and I stumbled
into some uncharted territory?

Elizabeth: We're no longer talking about the jazz
concert at Pemberley Estates, correct?

Darcy: It's just Pemberley. The name, I mean.
Names are important

Elizabeth: Yes sir

Darcy: I should let you go to bed. You have
students awaiting your instruction tomorrow morning

Elizabeth: Yes, and they enjoyed your visit the
other day. But I have a question. Does "uncharted
territory" refer to that empty beach you keep all to
yourself?

Darcy: Has anyone ever told you your intelligence
makes you less intelligible?

Elizabeth: Well, you too are a puzzle ...

Darcy: I'm glancing over the things you've written
tonight and can't stop rereading your message about all
the men you met at Rosings wearing you out

Elizabeth: If you only knew the half of it ... I

haven't even brought up Bobby Collins

Darcy: Ha!

Elizabeth: He's a quaint one ... I think that's what your friend Anne said

Darcy: You are having an easier time here because I showed all my cards in the letter I wrote you

Elizabeth: Is it an awkward position for you to be in?

Darcy: Yes of course

Elizabeth: Normally you get a straight answer

Darcy: often

Elizabeth: You don't venture into uncharted territory unless it's part of a girl?

Darcy: Yes, that's exactly what I was driving at, Elizabeth

Elizabeth: So the uncharted territory you referred to is my vagina?

Darcy: No, but that would make for an interesting conversation

Elizabeth: Now we're getting somewhere

Darcy: someplace Larry will never go

Elizabeth: I am such a nerd. I'm glad I memorized the part of your letter about wanting to be friends and didn't type anything stupid above.

Darcy: Did you give any thought to what I wrote?

Elizabeth: I believed you. Unfortunately for me because it makes me look foolish. Except about Jane. I can't discuss Jane with you.

Darcy: I'm sorry but I understand

Elizabeth: As your friend, I accept your apology

Darcy: Great. But some of the things I wrote are already less apropos. May I amend them?

Elizabeth: I'm scared to go to a party at Pemberley

Darcy: Just come hang out with me and listen to some jazz. It's going to be a large gathering, lots of overdressed people milling about with cocktails

Elizabeth: I have a confession

Darcy: go ahead

Elizabeth: I've assumed the worst of you many times

Darcy: Perhaps I've deserved it ... many times

Darcy: I have a confession too

Elizabeth: Yes???

Darcy: I wish I had simply asked you out instead of fighting with myself so much about what to do and then saying something asinine about a hotel

Elizabeth: *stunned silence*

Darcy: Imagine if I wasn't such a simpleton at Netherfield when you said "But who's going to tuck you in tonight, Darcy?" I don't remember your exact words but it was something like that

Elizabeth: You thought I was flirting?

Darcy: No, I thought you were being yourself and then I made you dislike me by acting like a humorless dolt

Elizabeth: It wasn't the work of one evening. You making me think you're a jerk, that is

Darcy: You thought I was uptight, I believe

Elizabeth: Uh, actually, most of the time I was openly antagonistic toward you

Darcy: I rarely if ever took what you said that way. You don't come off as antagonistic

Elizabeth: Are you for real? I guess I am kinda surprised I didn't get more acrimonious blowback from you, given the things I've teased you about

Darcy: I did realize you were sometimes dissatisfied with my behavior, thought I was being reserved or haughty. But in all honesty, I didn't think any of that would make you think less of me to any great extent. Can you believe that? I didn't think I had to make an effort. Things are always so easy for me that I didn't think I needed to try to ingratiate myself

Elizabeth: That's a lot to say. Are you suggesting you should have tried to please me?

Darcy: I'm trying to imagine a way in which you would have responded positively to my offer of the other evening

Elizabeth: Oh, I can explain that to you. You see I have these little things inside me called vaginal muscles, and they do this thing called clenching up when they're trying to tell me BEWARE that will lead you to nothing but trouble so do not screw him because you know the ending to this story already, Liz

Darcy: I'm fascinated by these wise muscles

Elizabeth: They can be a burden sometimes

Darcy: I'm dying to ask you questions I ought not

Elizabeth: Right back at ya

Darcy: Please, ask away

Elizabeth: If you're so horny, why aren't you texting your girlfriend in pink?

Darcy: I'm not. I'm simply saying what I want to say

Elizabeth: I don't know. I'm pretty sure you were on a date with someone dressed in pink the other night at Rosings. I don't know Anne at all really but Bobby Collins, who likes to bother me sometimes for his own freakish amusement and does things like grab my shopping bag filled with Q-tips and insist on carrying it for me, says she's your fiancée. But I know he's an idiot so ...

Darcy: I'm not dating anyone exclusively. That's far from the mark

Elizabeth: What are your intentions toward me?

Darcy: Right. I wish I could be more clear on that but I think we need to talk again. In person. If you can bear my company

Elizabeth: Are you proposing sex again?

Darcy: You're so funny. I was thinking more along the lines of some jazz

Elizabeth: okie dokie

Darcy: I'm really up in the air. I don't always understand you. Sometimes you're vulnerable and other times not ... Not that you're hiding who you are but you're so tenacious about one thing but lax about another. And why do people in your family still go around saying things about going after men with money while you and Jane are mute?

Elizabeth: I'm not "going after you"

Darcy: I realize that. Please don't be defensive. I didn't make any sort of accusation. I'm just concerned about the unsettled family drama that regularly intrudes, and you are rightly steamed at me over some things I've said. Not to mention, the things that seem unfair and defamatory to you and Jane may seem like legitimate precautions to me and my friends

Elizabeth: Are we talking about holes in condoms now?

Darcy: God no

Elizabeth: You call out my family for being mercenary and then tell me not to be defensive

Darcy: I did and I have no excuse to offer other than I've seen things. This is not my first rodeo

Elizabeth: hmm

Darcy: There's only one option

Elizabeth: Go fuck yourself?

Darcy: Please don't be angry, Elizabeth

Elizabeth: sure, whatever you say

Darcy: please

Elizabeth: What's the "one option" you mentioned?

Darcy: Up until now I tried the approach of ignoring this as much as I possibly could but that didn't work

Elizabeth: Ignoring what ... our family feud?

Darcy: No, ignoring my interest in you

Elizabeth: oh

Darcy: I wasn't successful. In fact, I ended up hurting you with the things I said to you the other night because I was so hell bent on acting like it meant nothing

Elizabeth: oh, I see

Darcy: So, therefore ...

Elizabeth: yes?

Darcy: I think we should get together and see what

happens. Come to the jazz concert

Elizabeth: okay

Darcy: Right now I don't think we can say what is possible and what's not. What do you think?

Elizabeth: I've thought of you as a toxic know-it-all whose opinions don't have any effect on me so this is all new for me

Darcy: And what do you think now?

Elizabeth: About getting to know you better?

Darcy: Yes. Exactly. Is that a possibility for you?

Elizabeth: I think so

Darcy: It's a tribute to you that you haven't spent time overthinking things like I have

Elizabeth: Oh don't worry. I'm going to be doing that as soon as I get off the phone

Darcy: I've kept you up very late

Elizabeth: Yes, you kept me up into the small hours of the night bothering me with talk of how you're interested in me

Darcy: I'll let you go to bed. See you on the 17th at Pemberley?

Elizabeth: Uh most likely. Do I need a printed invitation?

Darcy: No, just your name

Elizabeth: My name is on your guest list?

Darcy: Yes, of course, I put it there

#

All week was delicious anxiousness. Wanting to see him, anticipating it in her belly and, disconcertingly, the place she mentioned during their text chat. She was so crazy excited there was sure to be disappointment ... *The opening chords of a Miles Davis rift swell as Will gawks at a mysterious red-haired debutante in a ruffled ball gown and Elizabeth slumps off to join the wallflowers.*

Elizabeth couldn't convince sluggish Jane to come with her. She was still down in the dumps about Bingley and didn't want to go back to Pemberley, where she'd gone diving off the rocks before Bingley left.

Everybody in Derby was talking about Georgiana Darcy's trip to Italy to sightsee with Bingley and Caroline, speculating about what it meant. Miss Darcy was the type of girl Bingley was expected to be with. Jane had never been invited to visit him at his home in Texas, nor did she have the money to travel.

Elizabeth told Jane the obvious, that Georgiana was too young to be the object of such gossip. But at an outdoor birthday party at a neighbor's Gulf Stream trailer, all the church ladies were discussing a future wedding at Pemberley between Will's best friend and his sister like they were anticipating a royal wedding. "Mrs. Bennet may think her daughter will get him but ... she's more likely to get a grandchild to care for."

The day before the jazz concert, Elizabeth was still scrounging around in search of a dress. She hit the jackpot with a $35 tags-on dress at the clearance section of a wedding store at the mall. The one-off bridesmaid dress in a deep shade of indigo had an extra layer of fabric in front and nothing in the back so it had to be worn without a bra, but its square neckline wasn't overly revealing. The only downside was the cheap, thin fabric but at night this wouldn't be as much of a problem as it had been for the summertime bridesmaid who'd refused to wear it.

Charlotte offered Elizabeth the use of her car so she wouldn't have to arrive on her bike. The Vespa would seem like a joke, drawing unwanted attention from the older Darcys' friends, and her dress wouldn't straddle a bike — side saddle was not an option.

Elizabeth was sure she could get Charlotte a spot on the guest list at Pemberley but, when asked, Charlotte wasn't enthusiastic, just got quiet.

Sitting sideways on the Bennet's lumpy couch and not meeting Elizabeth's eyes, Charlotte covered her mouth with a paper take-out coffee cup and mumbled, "I'm still seeing Reverend Collins."

Elizabeth kept her mouth shut and listened. This was shocking news because she had ratted on Collins when he had asked her out behind Charlotte's back a few days after the Beach Ball.

"I can let you borrow my old car because I got a car loan with Bobby's help on the financing. We're going to pick it up today. My parents' van is on its last legs so they're going to take over my old car."

This was a blow, but Elizabeth tried to handled it better than she did the first time Charlotte broached the topic of Bobby Collins.

It was not her decision to make. Collins was not any sort of real imposition on her.

Eyes lowered, Charlotte said, "I'm not a romantic like you, Lizzy. I know he asks other girls out but he's not very successful so ..."

"I only want what's best for you. If Bobby Collins makes you happy ..."

"I've never been to so many nice restaurants. I even got to visit Rosings Park on Sunday."

"How was it?" asked Elizabeth, a little shocked at how fast things were moving for her friend. "Did you meet the great Catherine Darcy?"

"Yes. And it was very grand, just as you've heard. The grounds are so far 'round, you never see a neighbor. Could you imagine? Our neighbors know how many times a day we brush our teeth."

"I've always wondered; do they have a colossal swimming pool on the grounds of Rosings Park? Because if not, there's something missing."

Charlotte laughed. "I didn't see one. If there is, it's not as large as the one at the pool club."

"Don't be scared to tell me things, Charlotte," Elizabeth said in a softer, serious voice. "I may freak out but I come around if I'm in the wrong. Just ask Will Darcy."

"Oh, speaking of you sexting Will Darcy ..."

"No! Stop!" Elizabeth laughed. "I shouldn't say another word about it. I'm creating gobs of unwarranted expectation."

"Uh, well, I have to beg your pardon about something having to do with his majesty. I'm not sure what came over me but halfway through luncheon at Rosings I hadn't said one word so I was dying to speak and mentioned that my friend was going to be Will Darcy's guest at a jazz party at Pemberley, and his aunt — she's his great aunt actually — seemed indignant about it. I kept thinking to myself, *it's only a first date*."

"Not even that," Elizabeth interjected. "Just a meet up actually."

"Well, his aunt reacted like you were an impertinent hussy out looking at engagement rings."

Elizabeth mugged. "Charlotte, you troublemaker!"

"I know. It's just that Collins is always talking about you and I had some news, so ... it came out."

Chapter Ten

The front of Pemberley house was more imposing than welcoming, but Elizabeth was drawn in, skipping up the white marble stairs to the giant-sized entryway doors.

She wanted a glimpse of what she'd seen in magazines: crashing ocean waves at the end of a cavernous hallway lined with spindly tables just sitting around not really serving any purpose.

She grabbed the bronze door knocker as a valet came rushing up behind her.

"Miss, if you wouldn't mine, this way please," he said, courteously directing her to follow the crowd filing around the side of the house.

Delaying for a moment, she looked up at the Corinthian columns that seemed to strain under the weight of the two story building. A bit of ivy crept up their pedestals and the stone under her feet was worn and ancient looking. Will's parents were purveyors of culture, pillars of the community. *My dad died of an overdose and my mom collects dairy cow figurines.*

Elizabeth made her way along a vaulted portico, following a Greek-key-patterned mosaic walkway, passing slowly under arch after arch. She was hobbled by her gown which was several inches too long. And the elderly couples walking in front of her dressed in sequins and black tie were walking at a snail's pace.

The covered walkway opened onto a rectangle of lawn trimmed so short it looked like carpet. She stepped onto the grass and stopped, looking up at the night sky sprinkled with stars for a moment. Off to the east, mere steps from the house, unobstructed by anything, was a mind-blowing swath of natural beach and boundless black ocean beyond.

The one-of-a-kind view was ignored by most of her fellow guests. Were they really so jaded? Perhaps they'd been to Pemberley many times before. Elizabeth stared, wondering what it would be like to wake up in a bedroom on the water, just hop out of bed and go jump in the ocean. Trying to catch her breath, she strained to hear the waves crashing. But all she heard was the band, which had started playing an instrumental medley.

Candles in lanterns illuminated banquet tables set with silver trays. Champagne bottles were lined up on a polished-wood bar. White upholstered lounges sat directly on the grass. Nothing was overly showy or ostentatious like Charlotte's descriptions of Rosings. Not a gold scroll or baroque statue in sight. You might call it simple and elegant.

The party space was enclosed on the inland side by a stone wall with iron gates. It looked like it might be a leftover from the Civil War, but Pemberley was a more modern building, built by Will's great grandfather in the late 19th century. Fitzwilliam Darcy had been a carpetbagger from the north who made his fortune buying and selling land in and around Derby.

Elizabeth walked over to where the musicians were set up on a blue stone patio. She noted the concert grand piano, wooden stands decorated with carved harps, and giant planters camouflaging an amplifier system. An opened bottle of wine sat by the alto sax's shoe. Only at Pemberley do musicians who drink while performing choose Merlot.

Pemberley house provided a stunning backdrop for the performers with its tall verandas and classical architecture -- symmetrical, regal and bright white. The band rolled out some classics but were treated like background music, perhaps guests were waiting for featured soloists to take center stage.

Elizabeth could delay no longer.

It was time to look around and find Will.

All her hopes for the evening were on the line. Memories of his arrogance and coldness intruded but her expectations were for something more as she replayed the things he'd communicated since Rosings Pool. There was this spark between them that had somehow flared up after that horrendous episode in his car in the rain. Maybe there had been something of a flicker before that in the way she was always paying so much attention to him, but it had been counteracted by her prejudice against him.

She spied the hosts, Will's parents, mingling near their palatial home with thick crystal Champagne flutes in hand, so she headed in the opposite direction toward the rows of chairs set up facing the jazz performers. The general audience section was the place for her.

As she placed a hand on the back of a white banquet chair, she heard her name in Darcy's clear, low voice, "Elizabeth."

"Nice place!" she said before even seeing him, as she turned in the direction of his voice.

He wasn't alone. Two young women with hair pulled back in chignons and wearing complicated bias cut designer dresses stood nearby.

"Hello," he said softly, his sharp, intelligent eyes capturing her full attention. "I'm so glad you made it."

"Thanks for inviting me" she said, feeling drawn in by his tall presence.

242

"Is Jane with you?" he asked, not exactly beaming but there was a warmth in his expression she didn't often see.

"No, I'm alone," she said, her breath coming faster as they continued to stare at each other.

He nodded wordlessly.

It wasn't a hot night and there was a breeze coming from the ocean, so there wouldn't be an excuse if she started sweating, but she couldn't think of anything to say. Finally, she glanced at the youngish women standing with Darcy and sputtered limply, "I didn't even bring Lydia."

"Can you make it a whole evening without a sister?" he smiled.

She laughed, joyful in not feeling like he was making fun of her family so much as that they had started an inside joke.

The raunchier parts of their recent conversation sprung to mind as her eyes swept over the soft wave of his hair and the close cut of his suit. He fit in with the place, was at home here, if anyone could be easy in a place like Pemberley.

"Would you mind if...?" His expression changed to hesitant, not so intense. "May I introduce you to my sister?"

"Of course," Elizabeth replied, her cheeks burning.

His sister! The girl standing near him, whom she'd been defensively ignoring, was his sister. Now Elizabeth recognized her from the Beach Ball. Georgiana up close was less imposing than her many photos online. Her face with her hair up seemed more sharply angled.

Will's smiling grey eyes reflected a gleam of light from a nearby lantern. "Elizabeth, may I present my sister Georgiana." He turned. "Georgiana, this is Elizabeth Bennet, whom I've mentioned to you."

"It's nice to meet you," said Elizabeth buoyantly, a little concerned that his sister would have no desire to meet her and might feel this introduction was sprung on her.

Georgiana was pretty, but her face never varied from the same neutral expression. "Hello, it ... it's so nice to mm ...meet you."

"How's your summer?" Elizabeth asked. "Enjoying all Derby has to offer?" She glanced at Will. "Have you risked your life sailing on your brother's little boat?"

"Oh, yes, of course. I ... I love to. He ... he's the best skipper. It's never a risk. I ... I promise you."

Elizabeth smiled at her ardency, thinking maybe she shouldn't make fun of Will to his little sister. Georgiana was like one of Elizabeth's delicate female students who must be handled with kid gloves.

And why had no one ever mentioned her stutter? Not Jane or anyone. It was only slight so perhaps it didn't always register, but the elementary school's speech teacher would label it a treatable condition.

"It's so nice of you all to host a jazz party," Elizabeth

bounced on her toes. "Believe me, these musicians you've tapped are thrilled to have this sort of audience."

"It's our pleasure," said Georgiana, all sincerity. "We love to see ss...so many people here at Pemberley, don't we?" She turned toward Will. "Normally the house feels so empty, but when our parents throw a party it comes alive." She smiled brightly, spreading her arms. "Th....this is who we really are. Events like this for the children's hospital are so important."

Although it was a bit of a struggle for Georgiana to get so many words out, she spoke so sweetly it was impossible to feel sorry for her, and Elizabeth felt the compliment to herself of shy Georgiana making such an effort to chat with her.

"I was thinking as I walked in about how much I've always loved concerts," said Elizabeth, feeling obliged to offer up something heartfelt in response. "I don't have many memories of my dad, who passed away quite a few years ago, but I remember every one of the times I got to hear his band."

"What sort of band was he in?" asked Will, his blunt, inquisitive tone such a contrast to his sister's.

Elizabeth blushed, not sure how much she wanted to say to Will about her father. "They did some improvisational jazz stuff but mostly cover songs. He played guitar." God, she recalled that nonsense Will had overheard on the subject of her father, when Collins questioned whether she even knew his identity while accosting her at the shoe store.

245

Will looked at his sister. "I mentioned Elizabeth's a music teacher at West Derby Elementary, didn't I?"

Elizabeth's eyes widened. It was almost beyond belief to have Will Darcy encouraging his sister to get to know her, but that's exactly what he was doing.

"Oh, of course. I forgot," said Georgiana, looking more relaxed the more she spoke, her stutter almost completely gone. "What a wonderful thing, to be a teacher. I'd love working with children. Y...You are so fortunate. It's a gift."

"It's a blast, usually, although I have to keep a sense of humor when things go crazy and half my students forget their instruments the day we're supposed to play at the Derby Arts Festival. Or that time a dog ran onto the parade route during the Veteran's Day Parade and tripped one of my trumpets and then the Board of Ed wanted me to apologize for being a reckless drum major."

Will laughed out loud while his sister looked baffled.

"Reckless drum mm...major?" Georgiana asked, stuttering on the last word of the phrase.

The young woman dressed as if she'd coordinated outfits with Georgiana suddenly grabbed her arm, yanking her with a giggle, and Elizabeth and Will watched as his sister turned to wave goodbye apologetically as she stumbled away with her friend.

Elizabeth looked up at Will. "What I'd give to know all

you've told your sister about me." She felt dampness on her forehead.

Will moved a step toward her with a tenuous elegance like he might spring at her if they were cats. "Yes, but she's completely loyal to me, so you could never get anything from her I didn't want you to know." His voice was smooth, no tremor to it like his sister's.

A waiter carrying a tray with glasses of champagne headed toward them.

"Oh, but you never know; something could slip out by accident," Elizabeth said, hoping he didn't think she was alluding to Georgiana's speech impediment.

A grin slowly spread over his face. "What is it you suspect I'm not telling you?"

She blushed and blushed again, thinking of their text conversation when she outrageously mentioned her vaj. "Dark, shadowy things," she finally murmured.

His grin caused his cheek to dimple.

The people around them were minding their own business, talking amongst themselves, but if she touched him she would draw attention. *Ooooh, who's that girl with Will Darcy?*

But for the first time she could imagine touching him. It was almost painful not to as she stood so close. She could almost rub her hips against him if she arched her back.

Darcy's countenance wasn't exactly encouraging. He was

as imposing as ever, but a steadfast hint of a smile was a pleasant addition to his haughty mien, and she couldn't help but eat it up, smiling at him like they had a secret.

"Do you want to try some oysters? I can get you something to eat," he offered.

"I'll settled for a glass of Champagne," she said as the waiter made his way to where they stood. She reached for a glass, serving herself from the half full tray.

"Not sticking to seltzer today?" Darcy asked.

She swayed her dress from side to side, knowing it was nothing special yet wanting him to glance down at her body as he'd already done two or three times. "Ha, you always mention that like it was so brazen to ask you to fetch me a glass of water at Netherfield, but I thought you were *offering*!"

"I think you just wanted to send me off on an errand."

"What? So I could be alone with Cornel?" she exclaimed.

"No, no, not that. To get rid of me. Dismiss me."

"Oh, yeah, you're probably right about that. I knew you hated Bennets."

He shook his head. "No. I certainly never hated *you*." He said he never hated her like he was saying he liked her.

She had to reach out to him somehow. Emotionally or physically. Say or do something to let him know she was trying to believe he didn't actually lack minimal respect for her as she once firmly believed. To say that perhaps she'd misunderstood him. At that moment, she didn't want to just make a joke or say something pert.

Reaching for his hand, which she knew was being forward, she skimmed his fingers with the lightest touch.

Not having seen her arm move toward him, he flinched. Then, looking down, he seamlessly enveloped her hand in his as he realized it was her.

A wave of achy pleasure shot through her.

His eyes raised to hers, his expression tense. "You know, Elizabeth, I was thinking—"

"Hello, Pemberley!" A man holding a trombone leaned into a microphone. "The main event is about to start."

Elizabeth stepped to Darcy's side, lightly leaning against his arm as he kept his grip on her hand.

Concertgoers looking for empty chairs started to brush past the two of them as they stood at the end of a row of white chairs.

Darcy brought her hand to his chest, rubbing it against his smooth lapel, then leaned forward, breathing on her skin.

Her neck strained as she turned to look up at him, and he returned her look with hard eyes that said he wanted to do something to her.

A man in a turban slapped Will on the back. "Mr. William, where do we sit? There are ten of us."

Will immediately switched gears, motioning to a half

empty row of chairs. He pointed out a block of ten seats and the Indian family filed in.

An older woman dressed in red silk with gold embroidery jumped into conversation with Will about his plans for constructing cottages in West Derby.

He told the woman about breaking ground in the fall as he put his hand on Elizabeth's lower back and nudged her toward a chair next to him.

The scratchy sound of a microphone being turned on drew their attention to the low impromptu stage where the musicians were moving chairs and stands.

Will's father shook hands with a tall man holding a bass violin, and, after adjusting the microphone to his height, welcomed everyone to Pemberley for a night of jazz.

Fredrick Darcy was on a smaller scale than Will, shorter and a less imposing physical presence than his gorgeous son. He appeared to be a tidy, well-dressed dapper man, not a philanderer who abandoned his unwanted son. But maybe there was an alternate way of looking at things and what he was actually guilty of was plying his illegitimate child with lots of hush money to keep his wife from leaving him.

Mr. Darcy's speech had practiced flair, and he made the crowd chuckle when he mentioned filling donation envelopes. He seemed like one of those reflexively polite people who without exception acted nice, but Elizabeth knew this didn't necessarily mean he was genuinely kind.

The Vice Principal at Elizabeth's school was warm and friendly when you first met him, the exact opposite of Will on first impression, but once he caught a whiff of your cheap perfume or heard a faint echo of your Jersey accent he despised you on the inside.

Elizabeth was thankful Will's dad was far off and seemingly not part of her plans for the evening. She'd be terrified to have to talk to him.

"... My son William and my daughter Georgiana have done so much in preparation for this evening. Can we get them up here?" said Mr. Darcy into the microphone which blared his words to all corners of the outdoor space.

Will had to leave her to go up and stand by his dad and sister.

Forty minutes later, Elizabeth made her way to an arched exit in the fieldstone wall bordering the party area. She limped along slowly, frowning as she held up her gown.

After onstage introductions, Darcy had been obliged to take a seat with his parents on the veranda, sitting next to his mother who wore a subdue peach gown, but Elizabeth wasn't unhappy with him. It was hardly a mere request when his dad called him up.

Elizabeth had saved a chair for him in the row with the

Indian family, waiting for him to return, but he hadn't, and she conversed between numbers with her community-minded Sikh neighbors about skyrocketing rents in Derby. The man in a turban nodded along as she told of her own struggle to save up enough for first and last month's rent plus security deposit. "It's almost $7000!" she told them, not disguising her frustration over not being able to save so much in the course of a year.

The woman in red sitting next to her smiled. "How is it you know the Darcys? Are you friends with Will?"

"We're just acquaintances," Elizabeth had said.

Turning around for a last glance of Pemberley before leaving, Elizabeth looked past the musicians to the stately house, wishing she'd seen the inside.

"Elizabeth!" Darcy came out from behind a clump of guests mingling by white-cushioned settees and jogged up to her. "Are you leaving? There's a solo coming up I think you'll enjoy."

"I'm going." She shook her head exasperatedly. "I'm a total klutz and stepped on my own dress when I was walking around looking for the ladies' room."

Turning, she showed him the tear along a seam toward the back of her skirt. A panel of fabric had halfway ripped off, exposing her right leg all the way up to her butt cheek when she wasn't holding the gown together with a clenched fist.

She laughed at herself, overdoing the mirth a bit for his

benefit, but really feeling let down. "I made this big deal about protecting my dress from other people then stepped on the train myself."

"Let me fetch the housekeeper. I'm sure she has a needle and thread you could use," said Darcy, his brow furrowed.

"I think I better just tuck my tail between my legs and go home. It's too embarrassing to risk flashing everyone." She was adamant about going and hoped he wasn't going to be overbearing trying to convince her to stay.

He moved behind her, his hands lingering at the seam of her skirt, examining it closely, much more closely than she might have wished given its embarrassingly cheap construction.

She felt air on her thigh, but he didn't tug at the material or do anything to further expose her, just touched her leg as gently as she'd touched his hand earlier.

She blushed, shaking her head at the hopeless condition of the dress. "A lot of sewing would be required to fix a thirty-inch slit."

"Here," he said, wrapping his arm around her and holding the material of the dress together so she didn't have to continue holding her hand behind her back. "We can sit right here." He motioned toward a bench built into the stone wall. "It's dark, and we can listen to the next set, then go inside and get something for a temporary fix. Maybe black duct tape."

She laughed but saw he was serious.

"I'll hold it together for you," he said, courteously leading her a few steps to the long low seat.

As he helped her sit, treating her like a helpless princess and the pea, he kept hold of her dress and glided behind her in a single motion, wrapping his arms around her, never removing his grip on her torn dress.

It was too much, she leaned her head back, resting it on his shoulder and closing her eyes for a moment, trying to completely relax and enjoy the feeling of being in his arms.

He felt solid and warm but not overly hot behind her. His arms were weightless, his muscles flexed so he didn't rest himself on her.

They weren't exactly out of view but they were far behind the audience, elevated a bit with a good view of the dark Pemberley beach. The branches of a huge tree on the other side of the stonewall were high over their heads.

She went limp against his chest, knowing he'd get the message she was into his embrace.

His fingertips were on the skin of her thigh by the slit but he wasn't overtly touching her there, just gripping her dress.

A breeze came from the direction of the beach. Looking down, she saw the damp skin of her upper chest exposed to the night air, but she didn't coverup. She was shivering with euphoria as he squeezed her and the music began again.

His left hand relaxed, resting on her belly.

She elbowed his abs playfully. "I think my stomach is more cushiony than yours."

His hands awoke, broadly sweeping across her leg and thigh, then moving up her body, to her hips and waist, before stroking both her arms simultaneously.

Her muscles twitched. "Should I hit the gym?" she whispered, wanting him of such discriminating tastes to comment on her body, knowing he'd have to say something nice.

"No, you're the perfect medium."

She savored the solicited compliment, glancing at her torn dress lying in a little crush of fabric that thankfully didn't expose her.

"Does that mean you need to soften up a bit in order to achieve a happy medium like me?" she asked coyly.

"No, men are different," he said as he gently explored her, his hand matching the curves of her body.

"What do you mean?" she whispered, turning to look at him, hearing her breath coming out in little puffs.

He was motionless for a moment. Seemingly calm. "Women's curves have a purpose. There's no point to a man's beer belly."

"Wait, you mean like nursing babies ... and menstruation ... Darcy, are you serious?" She tensed as she chuckled. "I always thought you were a whiz at being pedantic, but I didn't realize you'd take it so far." She rolled her eyes to the sky. "Although ...

perhaps it's true I need little reminders from a guy like you lest it ever slips my mind what I have to deal with every month."

He laughed, shaking. It was a joy to inspired such a laugh, his firm stomach muscles moving against her back. She was pressed against him, practically sitting between his legs now.

She turned to look at his laughing eyes. "Silly, the right answer is something about how you find me attractive just the way I am."

"Of course I do," he answered immediately.

She was emotional, how could she not be, but she didn't feel physically vulnerable even though she was literally surrounded by his muscular body which was much bigger and could crush her into anything from this position.

"But wouldn't it be trite for me to sit here and tell you how good you look?" he asked, sounding sincere.

"I have doubts after what you said when you first saw me."

"Oh, right. You mentioned that before, and I was too distracted to remember to reply. Is that the nasty comment your mom once referenced?"

"Actually, my friend Charlotte's sister overheard you slighting my looks when Jane and I first arrived at Netherfield."

"Really?" He seemed surprised. "I'm sorry if I said something boorish. I actually don't remember what I said. I think I was annoyed with Bingley going on and on about Derby having the best looking women he'd ever seen. Should I ask exactly what was attributed to me?"

"Don't worry. I laughed it off," she said, concealing a bit of her real feelings. She turned to face him, mirroring his pensive look.

"I didn't know you then," he said gently. "My first memory of you is seeing you upstairs when you tripped off the stepladder. I know that's when I heard your voice for the first time. After that night, every time I've been around you, I've thought you were more and more striking. I've never met anyone quite like you ... not just the way you look, everything."

"Oh." She breathed slowly, taking him all in. "I guess that's good to hear. Sorry to bring it up again. It's just not my favorite memory of you."

"I'm fortunate in that I enjoy all of my memories of you," he said in a serious tone, both of them ignoring the music now. "Well, except ... you know... when you were crying in my car."

"Give me a good memory," she said with a little sniff.

His shoulders slid forward as he cupped her chin with his right hand. "Your eyes are so ... I always have to stop myself from staring at you too long."

She melted, closing her eyes.

He kissed her hard, digging his fingers into her hair. Then he seemed to think better of it and pulled back a bit, kissing her more gently, his hands moving slower, fingertips grazing her scalp.

She turned sideways in his lap, keeping her hands down, not reaching for him yet, just letting him act.

He changed the angle of the kiss, adding more pressure then softening it again.

She breathed into his face, like she was falling into a trance until he nipped her lip, and she stifled a happy giggle.

With a deliberate movement, confident and leisurely, he moved his hands over her body covered in purple-blue fabric. Straying to her backside, he paused where her skin was indented by the elastic of her underwear.

She felt emotion behind his touch, like his slow hand was his way of whispering sweet nothings, which she knew wasn't his style.

When he pulled back to study her face, she balked. She didn't want him to read her. She wanted privacy from his scrutiny. Privacy so she could enjoy him. She leaned in to kiss him, their tongues colliding, warm and intimate.

Gasping, she tried to give back as good as he gave her, although he had fuller lips and seemingly more practice French kissing.

She shuddered as his fingers drew on the bare skin at the edge of her dress, skimming her breasts.

She turned to see if anyone was watching them. No one was. They were in shadow. Away from the crowd. Hidden on a bench built into the dark stone wall.

He reached for the torn opening of her dress and she scooted over so he had extra fabric to move his hand under her skirt without showing anything to someone who might glance in their direction with a camera light on.

He squeezed the firmness of her upper leg and molested her inner thigh, which she allowed, shamelessly opening her legs for him.

She was clear about his intentions, but she didn't want him to try to climb on top of her as she was certain he would do if he let himself go, reverting fully to drive, instead of proper public behavior.

She felt turned on, but if they ended up going somewhere to have sex, she was scared how the first thrust of intercourse with an aroused, not totally in-control man would probably hurt quite a bit. No matter how ready she was, at the moment of penetration all her fears would wash over her and she'd tense up. She hinted at her problem before, but she could imagine trying to explain to him how she often clammed up during vaginal penetration and felt pain. She didn't want to think about it.

Thus far, she hadn't touched him much, so as he kissed her neck, she forced herself to reach for his hair, so short and conservative but with that bit of natural wave that wouldn't be tamed. Its soft silkiness gave her a more pleasant object for her musings.

As repeated final notes of "Blues In The Night" blasted out the subwoofers, he stopped kissing her and looked in her eyes, his face an inch from hers.

She smiled at his blurry image.

He breathed in, his lips brushing against her forehead.

The band leader announced an intermission to set up for some swing dancing on the veranda.

"I should probably go," she whispered, knowing she'd be disappointing him, but it was a good way to check if he had undisclosed anger issues — she was still probing this new warmer side of him. "I can't go inside the house with you because I'd have to walk up those marble stairs with a torn dress trailing behind me for all to see."

"There's another entrance on the side," he said, sounding concerned but totally calm and unperturbed.

"The one that goes into the kitchen for the waiters?" she asked dubiously. "I'm sure I don't want to get in their way; they're working hard."

"It goes to a hallway with stairs to the upper floors. I'll take you up to fix your dress and then we can take a walk on the beach."

She nodded, internally preparing her overexcited body to be ready to say no to sex. But she had every hope he'd back off gracefully when she told him.

#

Will couldn't believe what was happening.

He led Elizabeth, who seemed to be having a Lydia-style laughing fit, through stairwells decorated with tromp l'oeil and papered paneled hallways to the upper floor of Pemberley house.

So much for Bennet girls sizing up his family's ancestral home. Jane couldn't have cared less about the architecture or furnishings when she was here; she only had eyes for Bingley during her visit when Will's parents were away. And Elizabeth wasn't paying any attention to her surroundings or processing much of anything except the location of his hands on her body.

He ushered her into the corner guest chamber with its overly floral decor. Normally, he loathed the room but its formality made it seem like the proper place to take her so as not to seem like he was just trying to get her in bed.

Sitting her on the cushioned window seat with a view of the ocean, he closed the wide open window to be safe, and said, "I'm going to go find the housekeeper. I'll be right back."

In five minutes, he returned to find her in the exact same position he left her and handed her the fabric tape he'd gotten from Mrs. Jennings. "I can help you apply it."

As she twisted around, working to repair the dress while still wearing it, she did far from a first-rate job.

He tried to prop her up, but she laughed and stumbled in

his arms, trashing most of the tape.

He couldn't stop smiling, moving his hands over her body as she giggled at every touch.

Pulling her into a sitting position opposite him on the window seat, he reached for her, running his hand along the side of her dress, pretending to examine the structure. "So this gown is designed to be worn braless? Women's clothing can be so confusing. Visible undergarments. Invisible undergarments. Adhesive bras. Strange underwire contraptions."

She laughed. "Are we talking about your experience ripping bodices?"

He smiled. He would not allow her to back him into confessing to having undressed a lot of women. "I remember being around sixteen and seeing a woman walk across the lobby of this hotel in Saint-Tropez, and I couldn't figure out how she achieved this physically impossible position of her breasts, with no fabric underneath or above, just on the side."

She fell down laughing as she clutched the fabric tape on her dress with one hand and her stomach with the other. "Okay, Darcy, this will be fun. Let's talk about you masturbating after seeing a woman in a skimpy dress while on vacation as a teenager?"

His abs hurt from laughing. They were both Lydia now. He needed to get serious if he was going to fuck her.

She glanced behind her at the four-post bed positioned

between windows that looked onto the courtyard. The live music had started up again.

Studying the shape of her under her dress, he touched one of the thin straps holding up her top and then her soft, not boney collar bone.

She held perfectly still, like she was waiting for him to continue, so he pushed the strap off her shoulder.

Her face turned downward, almost shyly and she closed her eyes.

The front of her dress was open at the top corner. Not exposing her but open for his hand to slide under.

He did, feeling the shape of her, touching her breast like she was a soft fragile creature that might spring away.

But this was not enough.

With a little tug, the cloth of her gown folded over onto itself, exposing her left breast to his view.

There was a dip in the upper half caused by heaviness pulling it down, areola tilted upward. Flushes of reddish pink mixed with her tan skin.

He was instantly hard.

He should caress her roundness and say how beautiful she looked, but instead he grabbed her, squeezing her breast with his whole hand.

She let him. Holding still. Chest heaving. Ripe for the taking.

He pushed off the other spaghetti strap of the halter top dress, pulling down the entire front panel so she was topless to the waist, the curve of her torso so erotically feminine.

Her shoulders stiffened, and he thought of wrapping his arms around her.

She was breathing hard like she'd been running.

But he didn't relent. He gripped both her breasts, nudging them together, circling the tips with his thumbs, hoping she would go over the edge and have to open her eyes and look at him.

She moaned under her breath.

Suddenly releasing her, he moved closer, and she slid her legs out of his way so they were chest to chest.

He looked down as the fabric of his white shirt brushed against her nipples.

His mouth by her nose, he waited for her to open her eyes.

With his middle finger, he skimmed along the soft underside of her breast with a feather touch.

When she shivered like he was tickling her, he grabbed her, his hand causing finger-shaped indentations in her skin.

She leaned forward and arched her neck, pressing her breasts into his hands until he felt he might explode.

He reached for the hem of her mangled skirt and pulled it up to her thighs, slipping his hand under.

She scooted forward, pressing her whole body against him.

He unzipped the back of her dress, chucking it off with her help.

She wore some sort of stretchy yet cottony-looking white underwear that wasn't exactly sexy.

He pulled them halfway off and she jerked, seizing him with noodle-like arms around his waist.

He pulled back, looking at her face, trying to read her.

Erogenous torture mixed with concern. She definitely wanted more but wasn't thinking it was a clear choice.

He'd been good, hadn't let her feel his dick when she was on his lap outside. Hadn't really expected to go this far with her. But they were enjoying it. There was a comfortable bed at their disposal.

"I don't think I'm ready," she said, frowning and looking torn.

He nodded, immediately realizing she was right. It was rushed.

But it was physically painful to ease off and realize he wouldn't climb on top of her that night. "I didn't mean to pressure you."

"No, it's not that. Not at all." She pulled her dress up, pushing the thin, flimsy straps back onto her shoulders. "It's just that it's probably not a good idea unless I'm totally relaxed because, like I told you in our text chat, my muscles clench up."

"Yes, I remember exactly what you said about your wise muscles." He smiled, trying not to focus on his painful erection. "You even put it in writing for me."

She blushed. "Yeah. Can you delete that?"

"Not a chance," he said, his breathing slowing and his urge to grab her subsiding.

She hugged herself, seeming pleased by his accepting her reaction. "I had a bad experience with this guy I dated when I was much younger. He had a temper. A violent streak too, I guess."

He tried to read the details in her face. "That's awful." How bad was it? Was she talking date rape?

"I don't really feel like going into it right now, but he basically tried to push me around and I got out of there as fast as I could and never saw him again."

"What's his name?" He felt anger coming on. "Is he still living in the area?"

She shook her head. "No, no, don't worry about it. It was a long time ago. He has no effect on me now except this permanent need to take things slow."

"You're right." His hands, which had tensed into fists, relaxed. "It wasn't a good idea anyway. We haven't gone on a real date yet."

He led her down the back hall gallery, passing the realist portraits of his ancestors without comment.

Stopping before a pair of plate-glass doors, he took her hand and led her outside onto the balcony.

She looked around with huge eyes at the sweep of the coastline, and he waited for her to take it in.

Most people took a few minutes to adjust to the setting before resuming conversation. If he was having trouble closing a deal, he brought his prospective business associate out here for a drink and without saying much, the negotiations concluded.

Elizabeth sucked in her lips as she turned her head from side to side. Hopefully she was not unhappy with him for his aggressive behavior back inside.

"Let's go down to the beach," he said, escorting her to the narrow stone steps.

As she stepped onto the first floor veranda, just a few feet from the sand, she turned to him. "You should say something about growing up here because I can't imagine it."

"It was great but not everything," he said. "When I was a kid, I wanted to host a Batman birthday party out here, but my mom took over and there were taffeta tablecloths with daffodil centerpieces. I'm never totally myself at my parents' home. When I made the mistake of bringing a date home from college my freshman year, my dad gave an impromptu lecture on appropriate dinner attire."

She laughed. "No. Really?"

It was a joy to watch her smile. Almost as pleasurable as kissing her.

"Not that I'm complaining. Their home; their rules. No parties here like Bingley's blowouts at Netherfield."

She nodded as she crossed the veranda's wide-planked decking and took a cautious step down onto the beach. She seemed okay, not upset with him.

"Were you able to have a Wonder Woman birthday party at Longbourn?" he asked.

"Of course. If it's a cheesy birthday party theme, we had it." Her expressive eyes mirrored her animated voice.

He glanced down at her, imagining her dressed in the sexy Wonder Woman costumes he'd seen last Halloween — although they were nothing like what you'd see at a kid's party.

"You have your own place around here?" she asked, looking inland at the low lying, wild pasture leading to Pemberley's hills in the distance.

"Yes, I live in a small ranch-style home near the horse paddock."

She nodded, seeming to put on a touch of nonchalance. "Did your company build it?"

"We don't do single home builds," he answered. "My place was something I worked on by myself. Actually, that's not true either; I worked with an architect."

268

Guests from the party were strolling on the section of the beach closest to the courtyard, but there was no one on the beach to the south of the house, so he led her that way.

As they walked, he studied *her*, not the continuous changes in prospect that captured her gaze.

Yes, she fascinated him, but she was so different from him. They clashed spectacularly.

He needed to decide if and how to officially ask her out. If he should try to embark on something real with her, a sort of opposites-attract mashup. But the thought of anything serious was disorienting and fraught. And a casual fling was a pointless waste of time that might be hurtful to her and him both, not to mention the unnecessary drama for their respective families.

"How young were you when you got mixed up with that abusive older guy?" he asked, feeling a mystery ache in his bicep.

"Young. Seventeen. It was awful but I was lucky to be able to quickly get away from him."

"Same age as Georgiana when Wickham went after her."

She nodded. "Oh?"

"When I found out they were dating and convinced her to break things off with him, he told her he wanted to marry her, and when she said no, he announced to her that he had some sort of venereal disease and that she needed to get tested right away. It turned out he made it all up and never had a positive test, just wanted to get back at her for summarily dumping him."

269

"That's ... brutal." She stopped walking, just stared at him in disbelief. "It's hard to believe all these stories you've told me about him. And considering your sister is clearly a very sensitive person, that makes it worse. I mean, she's not Lydia who'd tell a guy to fuck off if he pulled something like that."

He nodded. *Oh, god.* He was thinking about *not* asking her out. Not yet anyway. He wasn't ready. Or he couldn't make up his mind. He foresaw disaster whenever one of his pessimistic thoughts intruded.

He turned to look at the ocean, thinking of the real magnitude of his decision. He did not want to have to tell her what he was thinking. Not after the way he'd been touching her.

Glancing down, he kicked at a broken seashell, its sharp edge pointing upward. "You wouldn't believe how hard I've tried to get Wickham out of my life. I understand my parents are obligated to help him, but I don't want him involved in my personal life in any way, and yet he's like a weed that keeps coming back even after you think you've dug it out by the roots."

He looked at her, gesturing all around. "Wickham used to leave empty bottles of Jack along with used condoms on this part of the beach. I would go around cleaning up after him rather than have my parents see. If you had any idea what a sick, pathetic task that was." He walked toward the white bubbly trail left by a wave, thinking of how he'd swim out in the water to cool off if this were any other night and not a night of dress up for his parents' party. "God, I hate that you were involved with him," he said, glancing at her apprehensively.

Her eyes looked pained, and he had to look away.

With a suctioning sound, her shoe sunk into the wet sand and she tipped backward, stepping on the hem of her dress.

He shot out his arm for her to grab onto, then led her back to firmer ground. "Sorry, I know better than to walk so close to the surf. I'm distracted. I hope you didn't ruin your shoes."

She gave him a half smile, shaking her mangled, sandy-hemmed dress. "I don't really care about my clothes getting messed up, but I don't like you saying I'm tainted if I hooked up with Wickham."

"No, of course not, it's just that things are so thorny already, with our families and the dissimilarity between us. I just wish you'd never met him. I can't stand the thought of you with him, although it's probably impolitic of me to give voice to that." He knew he sounded like a relic. A 28-year-old with antiquated ideas about women's virtue and chastity.

"But, wait a minute, Darcy," she stood tall, or to her full height of maybe five and a half feet. "You don't have a right to ask about Wickham George and me. I don't think anyone has a right to insist on knowing those sorts of private details unless they're married or have evidence their partner had an affair or something. Otherwise..."

"Yes, I agree with you. And I also know that it's not

surprising if something happened with you and him. Everyone gets lonely. I've had more one-night stands than I want to admit." He hung his head. "I'm speaking of my aversion to him in particular and how I want nothing to do with him, and yet I can't seem to totally disconnect him from you."

She almost laughed, but it was scornful. "So I'd be great if you could just change a few things about me, like who I've dated, who I am ... what family I come from?"

"I certainly do *not* want to change you. But I wish I'd warned you about him more effectively."

"I get that you're trying to put a blunt edge on it, but it feels like what you're saying is that it's beneath you to be with a woman who's been *used* by some guy you hate. Like the two of you are dogs marking your territory."

"No! No! Please don't think that, Elizabeth."

She exhaled slowly, letting out a long sigh that sounded a bit like singing. "I feel kind of tired."

He turned to her, his forehead throbbing with a sudden headache, sickened by the thought of Wickham marking Elizabeth. "I'll take you home," he said limply.

"It's okay. I have a car," she answered.

"I'll drive you home in your car and then have someone pick me up at Longbourn," he said, determined to do something for her as appreciation for what a great night it had been before he blew it by mentioning Wickham.

She said nothing, just started walking with him toward the valet parking area.

The youngest of the valets was sitting and smoking, and Will called out to him.

He dropped his cigarette in a barrel meant for butts and jogged over.

"Can you bring Elizabeth's car around?" Will asked. "Actually, on second thought, bring my car too and have someone deliver her car to an address I give you."

He asked Elizabeth to write down Charlotte's address.

She did silently, and, when his car was brought to them, she allowed the valet to open the car door for her and then close it behind her.

She was quiet, fidgeting with her dress as if she worried about getting sand in the seat cushions.

"Please, don't worry about it." He thought of her tears the last time she was in his car and helped her brush away the sand.

Blinking her long lashes, she said, "Thanks for inviting me. I loved the concert. Including the setting. Pemberley is nice enough to make me want to put up with you."

He huffed a laugh, shaking his head. "May I call you sometime?"

Chapter Eleven

Every window of the yellow trailer was lit up and the screen door was flapping in the wind.

Elizabeth's throat dried up. "What's going on?"

Smoothly decelerating, Darcy pulled to a stop directly in front of her house. "I don't know."

Elizabeth hurried out of the car.

Mrs. Bennet came rushing out of the house, running across the tiny patch of lawn. "Oh Lizzy. We're in such a state. My baby! She's gone. All her things are gone ... What will we do? Oh, my Lydia ..." She burst into tears.

Elizabeth's heart sank as she grabbed for her mom, trying to hold her still. "Lydia's gone? What happened?"

Jane came up from behind Mrs. Bennet dressed in a nightgown and light sweater and greeted Darcy, who had followed Elizabeth out of the car.

Turning to Elizabeth, Jane said, "Lydia called to say she's left town and isn't coming back."

"She's run off," Mrs. Bennet squealed loud enough to wake the neighbors. "But lord knows where she is. My poor baby. She couldn't tell us. It's to be such a secret. She can't tell us anything."

Jane was calmer than their mother, but her face was strained, contorted from its usual loveliness. "Lydia said she could only be at the phone a minute but promised to call again tomorrow."

Elizabeth glanced at Darcy who'd positioned himself a few feet behind her. Turning to her mom, Elizabeth said, "I don't understand. Why didn't Lydia just tell you she was going away? You would have been fine with her taking a trip, right?"

Mrs. Bennet clutched her hands over her chest. "Oh, what a likable young man! Who would have believed he'd do such a thing to our dear Lydia? Everyone likes him. Even Lizzy admires him." She curled her lip at Darcy, who was standing mutely, his face impenetrably grave. "If only he had not been treated so dreadfully by his friends in Derby, he might not have left in such a hurry."

"*He?*" asked Elizabeth. "Whom are we talking about?"

275

"Wickham!" her mom screeched, seeming annoyed that Elizabeth didn't already know this.

Jane stepped forward, nodding, "She said she's run away with Wickham. We were all astonished."

Elizabeth felt struck in the chest by some unseen force. "Wickham?" she wheezed.

"They're hiding out because of his *gambling debts*," said Jane. "Some men came to his lodging to say he had to pay up immediately. Can you believe that? It's like out of a mob movie."

"Wickham?" repeated Elizabeth. "Lydia barely knows him. How in the world...?"

Jane nodded, her eyes pinkish red where they were normally white. "True. I've never heard her even mention going out with him."

"Have you been in touch with the authorities?" asked Will, speaking for the first time.

"Yes, we must report her missing," seconded Elizabeth.

"Will the police do anything?" asked Jane. "She's eighteen now."

"Oh, there's no need for that, my dears," said Mrs. Bennet. "Let's wait a while and hopefully he'll do right by our dear Lydia. He must take good care of her. She's so young and such a good girl. Maybe he'll marry her."

"Mother, she could end up alone and pregnant, or worse if some gangsters are after Wickham. We have to get her back right away. This is not okay," said Elizabeth.

Frowning, Darcy stiffly motioned for Elizabeth to step aside and speak with him.

She followed and could see his old aloofness had returned as he stood back on his heels, not getting close to her. He looked resigned in a way she hated. This was what he expected from her family.

"I know I should be going, but—" He hesitated.

A gloom fell over her spirits as she realized that although the Wickham and Lydia drama didn't astonish him, it would appall him. He'd always thought Lydia was out of control and had tried to tell her she ought to do more about her sister's conduct. "Yes, I understand," Elizabeth mumbled, unable to smile.

He must be thinking her family was a shameful cacophony of questionable behavior and sordid interactions with Wickham. He was definitely thinking that she herself fucked Wickham first and now Lydia was fucking him too.

"I have no idea what we're going to do," said Elizabeth, the air suddenly oppressively hot. "You know him too well to think his intentions toward Lydia are noble. What does he want with her?"

His face crumbled out of its stoic, resigned facade. His eyes brimming with emotion. "Good god, Elizabeth. I wish I had done more to warn you about him. I was too proud to go around town opening up about my family's private business, my private run ins with him. I said a couple things to you, alluded to the thing with Georgie in the letter I wrote you, but I could have done more."

"None of us should blame ourselves for Wickham's bad behavior."

"But you don't know it all. I didn't mention parts to you. I didn't think it was important. Or I loathe to speak of him so much that I avoided mentioning it. The night I brought Lydia home after drag racing, I had seen Wickham with Lydia in one of the cars. After what happened with my sister, I didn't think it was safe to leave Lydia in his company, but I didn't bring up his name to you because I assumed you didn't know him and, honestly, I hate so much to speak of him."

"It's true, I hadn't heard his name at the time," she blushed, embarrassed at how much more she did than learn Wickham's name. "I could swear I'd never seen him before the day of the Beach Ball, and I'm certain I never saw him with Lydia. Not once." She cringed horribly at the memory of her night with Wickham on the couch. She hadn't thought of it while with Darcy at Pemberley, even when the subject of Wickham was brought up; she'd been focused on looking at Will and she'd been indignant about the idea he might judge her for her past sexual experiences.

"You didn't see him before because my parents sent him

far away to a private boys' school and he didn't attend Derby High like you and I did." His voice had deadened. "He comes and goes a lot, staying with friends here and there, exchanging one group of friends for another. I should have said something to you and your mother about not trusting him when I first spotted him back in late June."

"You did say something at the Beach Ball but, of course, I was angry and didn't want to believe you. And even after your letter, when I started to believe he was trouble, I had no idea Lydia was in any way involved with him, other than a passing admiration she shared with just about everyone around Longbourn. She's been hiding her relationship with him from us — if she has one and this is not merely a bolt from the blue sort of thing."

He nodded slowly but it seemed his thoughts were elsewhere.

She waited for him to speak. She had a passing, far off wish that he might change the subject back to something about how he wanted to call her sometime or better yet see her again.

But he didn't.

She was losing him. At the beach he had said he might not be comfortable dating her because she seemed to have hooked up with Wickham. Now she was in a crisis because her little sister was foolish enough to throw herself into Wickham's power and run off with him. Darcy must think there was some kind of

Wickham fan club going on at the Bennet trailer. And it was true that whenever Wickham had stopped by they'd all laughed at his jokes uproariously like he was a fucking dreamboat.

Elizabeth hadn't seen Wickham lately, heard of him with Bridget but not much else. She had been dreading running into him around Derby after learning about the stuff from Darcy's letter. Charlotte told her Wickham was still talking to lots of people about Will Darcy while at the same time claiming he loved the elder Darcys and would never do anything to harm them in any way.

"I apologize again for staying longer than I ought," Will said, sounding formal. "If there's anything I can do, please don't hesitate to ask for my help."

"Yes, okay, thank you." She straightened, reaching for the torn seam of her dress and wishing he'd look at her the way he'd done earlier, but his eyes were hazy and unfocused.

He turned to go.

As she watched him drive away, she thought of how she may not hear from him after this. He might not text or call. Her family was going off the deep end with Wickham, and Darcy might head for the hills.

#

"Are you insane?" Elizabeth exclaimed, pressing the phone so hard against her ear that her tinted moisturizer stuck to it. "You want us to pay a blackmailer for an X-rated video of you and Wickham?"

"Someone stole my phone and it wasn't locked," said Lydia, who called home and asked to speak to Lizzy, saying there was "important business" to discuss. "They sent Wickham proof that they have the sex tape, and they're asking $5,000."

"Lydia, that's a lot of money! We should call the police and see if they can trace the message or something."

"Oh, lord, the bad guys will certainly post the video online if we call the police. Maybe Mom can mortgage the trailer to get the money."

"Lydia!" Elizabeth yelped. "You can't be serious!"

Static came through the phone as Lydia started crying. "Wickham says he'd be too ashamed to marry me if there's an X-rated video of me for everyone to see. He says we must find the money. If he's going to introduce me to the Darcys as his future wife and get them to write us into their will, there can't be a porno video of me."

"Marry you? Why would you want to marry him?" Elizabeth didn't even allow herself to fully digest what Lydia was implying about her intentions to repeat what their aunt had done and try to pressure Will's parents into giving her money.

"Because I love him," said Lydia over the phone. "He's my everything."

"Even if he tells you he won't marry you because a sexy video of you and him has been spread around online? He tells you something like that and he's your everything?"

"Wickham is here with me right now, Lizzy, and he heard you say that! He says he's surprised at you and said, '*How would you feel if there was a video like that of you?* Wouldn't you pay up if it was a video of you that was being passed around ... so that Will Darcy could see it?'"

Elizabeth seethed. "Lydia, why in the world are we talking about Will Darcy?"

"Everyone knows you were shadowing him at that jazz party at Pemberley. Mom said he brought you home and offered to help you find me. How silly! I was only running off with my dear Wickham."

"Darcy is irrelevant to this. What are we going to do, Lydia? If we could find $5000, how do we know it would actually get us the one and only copy of this video you're worried about? How do we know that it might not still be released online somewhere?"

"Oh, Lizzy, you don't want to spend your money to prevent a porno of me going viral? How could you be so self-centered?"

#

There were a dozen more phone calls back and forth, and Mrs. Bennet went to the bank to try to get a mortgage, but she was denied due to a lack of sufficient income. Elizabeth checked her bank balances. A total of $4,073.

During a phone call the next day, Lydia let it slip that she was in Las Vegas, but this was to go no further than their family or the runaways' safety would be in jeopardy.

"I think you all should fly to Vegas to see me ... and bring the money," Lydia said to Jane over the phone, pretending she didn't hear what she'd just been told about their mom's failure to get a mortgage. "Also, can you ask Elizabeth if she could possibly help pay for my plane ticket to the South Pole?"

"Your what?" Jane exclaimed. Elizabeth was listening in on Jane's call, her ear pressed against the outside of the phone Jane held.

"Wickham has got a job offer in Antarctica. He does have some friends, you know, although not as many as he deserves! He's going to run the snack commissary at a research facility there. It's like a little convenience store. So cute. We'll be selling chocolate bars and potato chips and stuff."

"Lydia, how can you afford this ... buying intercontinental plane tickets and all that? Aren't you both strapped for money right now?" asked Jane.

"I told you. Wickham still has some friends, even if Will Darcy has treated him horribly, as you all know!"

Elizabeth had to interrupt. "Lydia, please listen to me, I don't believe Wickham was telling us the truth about his interactions with Will Darcy."

There was a pause, after which Lydia said, "Really, well,

Wickham just heard you say that, Lizzy, and is very disappointed."

Not long after this phone call, Elizabeth got an email from BlueRussian@cheapemail.com saying he was the person in possession of the phone belonging to her sister and he just discovered that it contained a compromising photo of Elizabeth "making out with the same dude from the porno video, and if you want me to hand over the photo, wire me an additional 5k."

Attached to the email was a picture of Elizabeth in her blue and white dress from the Beach Ball. In it, Wickham held the phone taking a selfie of her and him in which you could see her underwear as her skirt was lifted up and his left hand was on her thigh. Her own arm was outstretched with her hand resting on the crotch of his jeans. It was suggestive but there was no nudity.

Elizabeth called Lydia who was holed up in her hotel room in Vegas. "Lydia, do you know the *name* of the person who's been calling demanding money for the X-rated video of you and Wickham?"

"He didn't give his name, silly."

"Did he email you?"

"Uh, yes, I think so. And he called Wickham's phone."

"What's his email address?

"Something about Russia."

"Oh god. He sent an email to me about a photograph from your phone. It's a photo Wickham took of himself and me the night of the Beach Ball."

"Oh my gosh," Lydia squealed and peals of laughter came through the phone. "I feel so terrible, but I know exactly what you're talking about! There was a photo on my phone of you two. Wickham sent it to me as a laugh ages ago, and now the horrible blackmailer must have it."

"He asked me for another $5,000 for the photo," said Elizabeth. "I think that's on top of the $5,000 for the video of you."

"What will you do?" asked Lydia.

"It's just a dopey picture. I didn't realize Wickham was taking a photo like that but whatever."

"It would be terrible if everyone in Derby saw it. Imagine when Will Darcy sees it. Oh, Lizzy, how could you bear it?"

"It's not X-rated. It's kinda lame to take an up-skirt shot without my permission but it's not a crime. You said the video of you is much more explicit, right? That in it you are naked and having sex, not innocuous stuff. Is that correct?"

"Yes, you can see everything," said Lydia, sounding horrified but maybe overdoing it a bit. "I remember Wickham moved the phone around for close ups of me everywhere and I wasn't wearing a stitch. Oh, Lizzy, I'll be so humiliated. I'll never be able to show my face again in Derby or anywhere else either. Wickham agrees I'll be an outcast. He said to tell you that if it happened to you, you'd agree it was unendurable."

"Unendurable, huh? Is that his word? Did he learn it during the one and a half years of college paid for by the Darcys?" She was not a fool; she knew that part of everything Lydia said to her was either stretching the truth or an exaggeration. "Lydia, why in the world did you have all this on your phone and yet there was no password protection? You told me nothing about the photo of me. I didn't know it existed."

"To be honest, I forgot about the photo, and I sort of liked to watch the video of me and my darling Wickham. It's pretty good actually. I just don't want anyone else to see it or Wickham will die of embarrassment."

#

Later, Elizabeth spoke with Jane as they lay in their bunkbeds in the dark. "I think I'll offer her a plane ticket back and see if she'll leave him, but I don't think she will."

"Yes," said Jane, sounding distraught, "but even if we can get her away from Wickham, we can't just allow that video of her to be posted online."

"I'm not losing sleep over the idea of Wickham breaking up with her if the video is circulated, but of course I want to stop the extortionist from carrying out his threat. Yet, how do we trust a criminal and how do we know it's not Wickham himself working with a co-conspirator to ask for money on his behalf?"

"Oh, Lizzy," Jane sounded traumatized. "You believe he's capable of such a thing?"

"I do after everything Darcy has told me."

Jane asked for specifics and, mentioning Georgiana in only the vaguest terms, Elizabeth went over some of the information in Darcy's letter as well as things he'd told her the night at Pemberley.

"And Lizzy, what about that photo Wickham took of you? You didn't know he was taking it?

"No, I noticed he had his phone out but I thought he was shooting our faces."

"Were you maybe a little ... tipsy?" asked Jane.

"Yes, I was out of it."

"Oh Lizzy."

Elizabeth chuckled. "If a photo like that gets around, I don't think I'll ever get another invitation to a party at Pemberley."

"Lizzy, stop joking. What about Will? Have you talk to him?"

"No," she said, dejectedly. She couldn't hide her disappointment. He hadn't called or texted or anything. "He has a hang up about Wickham and dating women who've been with Wickham. When he sees that photo, there will certainly never be a chance of us ever dating."

"Lizzy, we should get the money to pay for both."

"$10,000?" Elizabeth exclaimed.

"We'll sell the trailer."

"Oh Jane," Elizabeth sighed.

"Lizzy, you can't give up having any chance with Will now that you started to like him."

"I did like him. I do like him. But that's water under the bridge now."

"Why?"

"Because I'm not going to jump through hoops to prove I'm not a Bennet slut who's slept around. I did hook up with Wickham, sort of. I'd rather not get into details of what I did with him exactly because that's irrelevant and he's repulsive, but it was a sex act, and I can't try to hide who I am to make Will or anyone want me."

"You are not a *Bennet slut*, Lizzy. Don't ever agree with those horrible people who say that about us! And you could try to explain to Will that you made a mistake and would never do it again."

"Oh, Jane, he already said he was struggling with the idea of dating me because he was trying to break all personal connections with Wickham. Now my sister is sleeping with Wickham and talking about marrying him, and I will soon have a photo forever associating me with Wickham, which Darcy would have to look at for the rest of his life. The photo will end up on DerbyCentral.org. A photo of my hand on Wickham's dick."

"You do not have your hand on his ...! It's only on the front of his pants."

"And what's your point?"

"I don't know. But we have to believe there's a way the photo won't be released!"

"*I* will release it then. I don't want something like that hanging over my head waiting to come out." Elizabeth breathed hard. "I need to find some guy who can accept who I am: a foolish woman who makes out with guys because they agree with her about how Will Darcy is a snob."

"Oh Lizzy. We must try to stop it somehow. Stop being so principled about this."

"Oh, believe me, I've thought of it. Last night, I had this idea of disowning Lydia and running away from it all, pretending this nightmare wasn't real — but then I thought of how I'd miss you and you'll never leave Derby and Mom. Then I thought of throwing myself at Will's feet, asking for the money to buy my photo and destroy it. I even thought of how I might lie and say it wasn't me in the picture: 'You can't say for certain it's me; only the chin is showing' and 'Someone must have borrowed my dress.'"

"Lizzy, think of Will's parents and everyone in town seeing the photo. It's one thing to have exes but quite another to have intimate photos with them seen by everyone you and Will know. You can't expect him to be okay with that, not a guy like Will Darcy. Or take it further, if you wanted to marry someone like him someday, a conservative man, how will he feel about a photo floating around of his wife with another man? He'd want you to buy it and burn it."

"Oh stop! Why are you tormenting me, Jane?" Elizabeth flipped on the bed so she was facing the wall and pulled the covers over her head.

"We have to get rid of the photo somehow!" Jane repeated.

#

The next morning, they got a phone call from an unknown number. A man with a low voice that was nothing like Wickham's said he was Blue Russian and asked for their decision. Mrs. Bennet started shrieking so loud that Elizabeth and Jane had to run into the bathroom to continue the phone call.

Jane held onto the receiver because Elizabeth was threatening to grab it and curse him out.

"We only have $3,000 to give you for Lydia's video," Jane said plaintively and convincingly. Jane the actress?

"What are you offering for the photo? I'll make you a package deal," the man over the phone said. "$6,000 for both."

Elizabeth, who was leaning in to listen, said, "We don't want that photo and, anyway, it's been shared online already." Not true as far as she knew, but Lydia said Wickham had sent it from his phone to hers, so maybe he'd done this with other friends. "I'm planning to put it up on the town website to give my friends a laugh," said Elizabeth. This wasn't a total lie; the picture of her and Wickham had made Charlotte laugh.

Jane interrupted her, shushing, and tried to negotiate for both, offering the man $3,500 if he'd wait a couple days for them to come up with the extra money.

He wasn't having it. "That's nowhere near enough. You'll have to come up with more money or you're fucked."

"Lizzy," Jane whispered, covering the phone's microphone. "I could call Bingley and ask for the money. We haven't spoken on the phone a lot recently but we're still texting in a friendly sort of way."

Elizabeth shook her head furiously and grabbed the phone from Jane. "This is Elizabeth, the one with the cash, and it's $3,000 for the video and only the video. And we want delivery on our terms."

He grumbled a bit then seemed to come around, accepting their offer.

Jane hedged, raising her voice loud enough to be heard over the phone. "Maybe we shouldn't trust him."

"How do we know you're not a friend of Wickham's and he gave you Lydia's phone?" Elizabeth asked, speaking calmly. "Do you make a living by stealing phones and extorting money? I've never heard of such a thing. Why would we trust you're for real?"

"I'm in the business of amateur porn and some guy found a phone with some material on it. If you don't buy this video, someone else will."

"So you're not threatening to spread it online out of spite if we don't pay you but threatening to sell it to some porn site that will post it with other explicit videos?"

"I need to get money for it one way or the other. I don't care which. We all have to earn our keep. It's the American way. We're not socialists, are we?"

This guy definitely wasn't Wickham disguising his voice.

Mrs. Bennet was hysterical in the hallway outside the bathroom door. "My poor Lydia. This horrible man might try to kidnap her and force her into pornography and sell videos of her all over the world. What will we do?"

Elizabeth asked the caller to hold and, heart pounding, started thinking out loud in a huddle with Jane. "I don't trust him either, but, Mom has a point ... kind of. Allowing this to happen to Lydia might send her down a slope she can't crawl back up. If she's abandoned right now by Wickham, when she thinks he's a god, I worry about her getting strung along by some guys she meets at the casinos and making more of these sex videos so they can try to sell them. She's like easy prey after she's getting all this attention for having sex on camera. Going to Antarctica with Wickham isn't much better, but at least she won't be as desperate as she would be with the video out there for all to see.

If they go, they're stuck down there for a while because there's only one flight per season, in or out. Maybe she'll get bored at a scientific research facility with only a few men around and be willing to come back to us, assuming not every guy in Derby has watched her having sex. She might be happy to be back home with us if we can squash this video; this thing with Wickham might fade away. That's what we're really trying for. We definitely do not want her to marry him. Not that anyone believes he intends to. I believe he's clamoring to get this video destroyed to protect his future prospects. His hopes of getting money from the Darcys or marrying someone with money — he wanted to marry Georgiana. That's much less likely with this video, so he's saying stuff about 'protecting Lydia's reputation' in order to 'make her an honest woman someday' but that's just part of his ruse."

"Oh, please, Lizzy, I want my baby back," called their mother from the other side of the door. "And please send her and dear Wickham airfare so they can visit us before they go to the South Pole."

Elizabeth got back on the phone. "We agree to buy the video. We'll have our lawyer call you and arrange for a legal purchase. There must be some neutral location were the handover can take place."

"You better have all of the $3,000 you promised," said BlueRussian, betraying a bit of an Eastern European accent.

293

Mrs. Bennet was ecstatic. Wickham and Lydia could marry and start a wildly successful business together selling candy bars and gum in the Land of Penguins. But Jane and Elizabeth knew there wasn't enough money left for all they needed. Maybe Elizabeth could send money to help offset costs, but what about Wickham's gambling debts? Weren't those debts the reason he fled in the first place? How were they to be dealt with?

There was very little to be hopeful about even though they intended to spend most of Elizabeth's savings.

#

It was Thursday, August 22nd, five days after the jazz party at Pemberley, and Elizabeth was at her favorite cubicle in the Derby Public Library where she'd spent so much time during college. After cancelling Lydia's cursed cell phone, she looked over her finances and calculated her upcoming bills.

She was there to research copyright law and extortion law and read about contract disputes involving pornographers and their actors. She had a call with code-name BlueRussian scheduled for later that evening when they'd make final arrangements for the return of the phone with the video on it.

From her peripheral vision she saw an elderly woman approach her.

"Miss Bennet!"

Elizabeth looked up.

"Do you know who I am?" asked the very tall woman, probably six-feet tall.

"Uh," she wracked her brain. "No, sorry, I don't."

"I'm quite certain you've heard of me. I'm Mrs. Catherine Darcy. My late husband's brother was Will Darcy's grandfather, which makes me one of Will's nearest relations."

"Oh," Elizabeth blanched. "Hello." She was uncomfortable with Catherine Darcy's curt almost rude tone of voice, but she could expect no less given what she'd heard of her.

"You cannot be unaware of why I have come to speak to you."

Elizabeth grinned to herself — was Darcy's aunt there to tell her she didn't have permission to make out with Will? "I'm sorry but that's not the case. I'm not sure what you want to speak to me about. I'm just wrapping up though, so I can walk out with you."

Catherine's loud voice was already starting to bother other patrons, who poked their heads over their cubicles to frown, and Elizabeth didn't want to be part of causing a scene.

Once outside, they stepped off the main walkway onto a grassy patch by the front cathedral-style windows of the historic, church-shaped library building.

"You are the girl who everyone is talking about, the girl it's rumored is trying to lure my great nephew, is that correct?" asked Mrs. Darcy.

295

Oh my god, Catherine Darcy *was* there to tell her she wasn't allowed to kiss Will! "I'm not sure what you mean."

"Don't toy with me. I know who you are! I know what you do. You're a *Bennet* and your family is responsible for almost ruining the marriage of Will's beloved parents, Frederick and Ladybird Darcy. You probably started the rumor about you and Will just to distress them."

Elizabeth was speechless. What in the world was this woman talking about? *I started a rumor about my non-existent relationship with Will so Will's family would come after me?*

"You know full well you are part of that coven of Bennet witches that conspired to destroy the peace and prosperity of my family. Ladybird has never fully recovered after your aunt threatened to drop off that bastard child at Pemberley. Your whole family harassed her day and night until she was barely able to remain in her own house."

Elizabeth was gobsmacked. She'd never heard about threats to drop off Richard with his father, and she didn't believe there was a harassment campaign. How would her mother and aunt even be able to access guarded Pemberley property? But there was a smidgen of doubt that set her back a step.

"*Your* mother threatened to expose Fredrick, a respectable man, for having fallen victim to your aunt's orchestrated seduction. She demanded money from him. Yes, your mother, Janet Bennet is her name. She likes to be called *Mrs.*

296

though she has never kept a husband."

"Excuse me but I'm not going to just stand here and let you insult me and my family any longer." Elizabeth's words were fierce but inside she was shaken.

"Wait, I'm not finished. Do you think Ladybird Darcy would ever allow her son to consort with a Bennet trollop like you?"

She had a flashback to Will's expression when he returned Lydia after drag racing. His aunt didn't look like him, but she had the same expression of disgust on her face he had shown while glancing around at Longbourn.

"I'm sorry but we're done," said Elizabeth firmly.

"Not yet. You may not be able to relate to such a thing but Will has character; he feels guilty about that bastard child and he wants to make up with your family by flattering you with his attention. But do not think you seriously have a chance with him. Every young woman in this town would bend over backwards to have him. Why in the world would he ever choose you?"

"I'm sure it's his decision whom he dates, not mine, not yours, not his mother's either unfortunately." Elizabeth felt a touch disoriented, like she needed to catch her breath.

"Obstinate, headstrong girl! His esteemed parents have more social clout in one pinky than your entire trailer park and will never allow you to set foot at Pemberley. If you succeed in drawing him in or even getting a bastard by him, you'll be condemning your child and yourself to a life without family or friends. Your kind will never be received by anyone in his family. No one will even mention your name."

Elizabeth was astonished to feel her eyes tearing up. Even if this nonsense were all true, which it most likely wasn't, was she really going to cry because she was told she could never have a relationship with Will Darcy?

"Goodbye," Elizabeth said, shaky as she started to move away.

"And your dealings with my pastor, Reverend Collins!" Catherine Darcy called after her. "I know you lost him to your friend Charlotte. They both laugh at your attempts to get my nephew. If you continue to go after Will, you will end up alone and miserable and scorned."

Elizabeth turned and glared, "We have nothing else to say to each other, Mrs. Darcy. Please leave me alone!"

As Elizabeth started to move away again, Catherine Darcy followed on her heels. "Wait, I'm not finished with you," she hollered, almost running after Elizabeth and moving remarkably fast for an elderly person. "You may be successful in the short term, but you can never overcome the fact that my nephew would not do anything that would detract from his legacy. His children will not be of a Bennet, I promise you. Our family will never be polluted by the likes of you."

Elizabeth swung around, stepping in the imposing

woman's direction. "Do you realize you're standing in front of a public building talking about whether Will Darcy is going to have children with me? This will tend to increase the rumors that have been so upsetting to you."

"So those rumors are false? You admit it?" asked Mrs. Darcy.

"I'm not going to tell you about my personal life."

"Do you or don't you admit to trying to entrap him?"

"What? Of course not."

"Good, you must promise to stop having anything to do with him immediately! There's no reason to prolong this another moment. His parents are beside themselves. I will speak to them to reassure them that you have seen reason and further steps need not be taken."

Elizabeth snapped. "I will promise no such thing. Ever."

"I've waited. I put it off, hoping I wouldn't have to do it, but you leave me no choice."

Elizabeth felt nauseated, astounded that such a woman had her keyed up.

"Are you aware that I work closely with the Derby Town Council as a representative on the school board? Do you think for one moment that news of the X-rated photos of you hasn't spread all over town? Believe me, you will be losing your position at West Derby Elementary as soon as those photos come out. There is no way anyone on the school board will vote in favor of a girl who might infect the minds of vulnerable school children with pornography."

"There are no pornographic photos of me. That's a lie," said Elizabeth, straining her diaphragm for enough breath to keep talking. How had she been drawn into directly addressing Catherine's accusations as though she needed to defend herself?

"Is that so? I believe there are many townsfolk on DerbyCentral.org who say otherwise. I've heard there are pictures of you and Mr. Wickham George, a disreputable man who has been receiving the charity of my nephew Fredrick but is a disgrace to his own family. Rest assured; I will speak to Will's parents about this matter. They too have members of the school board who are loyal to them."

Elizabeth's shoulders were high and tense, every nerve in her body on high alert. "I'm an excellent teacher and Principal Elliot will tell you so. Also, I am single and an adult. So whatever photos anyone posts online are irrelevant to my character as it pertains to teaching children."

"Ha! I knew it! Miss Bennet, you still don't seem to understand whom you're dealing with. I can guarantee you that I will use my sway to get you fired from your job for cause, for inappropriate, unprofessional conduct. I run the school board for all intents and purposes. I am a named benefactor of the school music program and a personal friend of the director of music. I'm not a musician myself, but I have always been admired for my incredible natural taste in music that would put your abilities to shame."

Elizabeth barked a laugh in the midst of her panic attack. She was dealing with a preposterous woman making outlandish statements. Yet, she realized that Catherine Darcy was in fact a very influential person in town and could get her way. This wasn't an idle threat; losing her job was now a bona fide possibility.

"Yes, you see now, don't you? You're about to burst into tears." Catherine Darcy was a Disneyfied villain now. "If you go against my wishes and continue to be seen with my great nephew, you will become a pariah like your aunt, huddled up in a tiny house stuffed to the gills with tables and chairs, prostituting yourself for a piece of real oak furniture. Your aunt hardly got any money from Fredrick for herself, all was set aside for the bastard boy's use only and he's off partying with it. Getting pregnant by a Darcy did not pay off as she planned. You likewise will get nothing from Will, and you will remain white trash as you've always been."

With this, Catherine Darcy stormed off. Done with her. Elizabeth collapsed onto a bench.

She considered calling Will Darcy and demanding he tell his aunt to butt out of her life. *Your aunt Catherine wants me to promise not to get it on with you, but that shouldn't be a firing offense at my job.* If Will heard about the conversation outside the library and got annoyed and told his aunt to stay out of his private affairs, what were the chances such a woman would be reasonable and do as her nephew wanted?

Could his aunt Catherine's warnings about Bennet sluts trying to get knocked up by him freak him out? He'd previously told Elizabeth he had reason to be cautious around Bennets and that he'd "seen things." Add to that the Lydia business.

Elizabeth once again thought of asking Will for a loan to buy the photograph of her and Wickham.

Yet dignity and self-respect wouldn't allow her to turn to Will Darcy for that kind of help. She'd spent the past year telling herself she was an independent, successful person. Now she must hold her head high and act like one. She could not hide. She could not raise a white flag in defeat.

On the phone with Blue Russian, she negotiated the price down again, getting him to agree to $2800 so she could pay $200 to a Las Vegas attorney, who took pity on them and offered to lower his fee and help them produce a legal document stating that Elizabeth Bennet owned the rights to Lydia's video. The photo of Elizabeth was not a part of the deal.

Elizabeth paid for a plane ticket in Lydia's name that could be used on any flight home and also paid for vaccinations that were required before Lydia could work at the research facility in Antarctica.

Wickham and Lydia were evasive when Jane asked them how they were paying for their plane tickets to the South Pole and Wickham's gambling debts. And mysteriously the subject was dropped.

Elizabeth spent almost all of her savings but felt she'd done the right thing. At Longbourn, she waited for word from their lawyer that he'd made the exchange at the agreed to location in the lobby of a big casino on the strip.

It was possible she'd lose her job because she didn't use her savings to pay for the photo of herself instead of Lydia's video. But it was the only choice, notwithstanding the fact she'd lose her income and ability to help Lydia again in the future.

Doing the selfish thing and using her limited resources to buy her photo with Wickham instead of the video would just be a way of paying to get herself out of having done something stupid and reckless. She had carelessly allowed a risqué photo of herself to be taken after she'd been drinking. She had hooked up with a guy she barely knew after being warned about him. She needed to face the fact she was the kind of person who did just this sort of thing. She had to accept responsibility, accept the consequences of her action. It was painful but necessary.

By not spending her savings to save herself she had enough to save Lydia, and although her sister was foolish and thoughtless, she was too young to be lost. Elizabeth got many second chances after the mistakes she made at seventeen. A college admitted her after her bad grades early on in high school, and she was able to excel because of this opportunity. She got away from her abusive boyfriend without permanent physical damage because Mrs. Bennet and Mrs. Bennet's boyfriend at the time protected her from her angry ex whom they feared might go berserk and kill her. She had been afforded the opportunity to move on, regain self-confidence and prosper.

Lydia must have second chances too, especially if the cost to Elizabeth was only a few thousand saved from the decent salary she'd made teaching for one year.

It was hard to think she might be fired from her job, the best thing in her life besides Jane. She broke down imagining her students being told "Miss Elizabeth isn't coming back." They and their parents would think so many awful things about her when word got out.

Looking for another position in a neighboring county must be thought of. Maybe she could work with less impressionable older students, or maybe she could work at a private music school like she had been doing all summer. Her commute would be longer, but she'd still be using her teaching degree.

Elizabeth deleted Will's number, labeled 'Darcy' despite his objections, from her phone to prevent herself from acting on an unnerving yet persistent impulse to call him to try to mitigate the existence of the racy photo of her with his archenemy. She couldn't apologize for being defiled by Wickham's penis. She wouldn't ask Darcy for help. She wouldn't ask him to intervene on her behalf with his aunt. She had to survive on her own devices. Anything else was degrading to the person she wanted to be.

Locked in her mother's bedroom, Elizabeth fell face first on the springy bed and sobbed over the idea of never again seeing Will Darcy on terms like those she experienced at Pemberley. What a thing to give up. The romance of that night. The aching desire she felt for him. The way he'd spoken to her with something close to adoration. Those things he said to her, saying he became more attracted to her after getting to know her.

She wiped her face, opened her pixelated laptop computer, and posted the photo of her and Wickham anonymously on DerbyCentral.org.

When she checked back later that evening, she found the photo had not only been shared seven times, but someone mentioned it had been posted previously elsewhere on the site. Under Beach Ball photos, not surprisingly.

Elizabeth checked and found an overlooked posting from weeks earlier containing the exact same up-skirt picture of her and Wickham. With sore eyes, she searched desperately for Lydia's video but didn't find it. Thank god.

It was a bittersweet day when Lydia's phone was

confirmed to have been returned, back in their possession by way of their charitable Las Vegas attorney whom Jane got on the phone to thank profusely. He ended his call with Jane by saying he hoped to meet her someday.

The check to the pornographer was a special cashier's check, that acted like a bearer bond, but they were surprised to have to wait for confirmation that it had been cashed. They didn't want to bother their underpaid lawyer, but after several days past with no verification from the bank, Jane finally called the attorney.

He said it was unusual that the blackmailer had not cashed the check but not to worry yet. Maybe Blue Russian was making plans to avoid tracing or to launder the money through a shell company. "Give him a week and if it's not cashed by then, we'll worry," their attorney told Jane.

#

Lydia was calling five times a day now, talking mostly of how wonderful her future husband was. She had no regrets, was totally unrepentant. Lydia thanked Elizabeth for spending her savings but clearly believed she deserved the gift from her comparatively rich sister.

For Lydia, there was never enough praise of Wickham. He was the best man who ever breathed. Best at everything. He caught the biggest fish ever seen, was the best looking man on the planet, was smartest, cleverest and wiliest by far. He even ran faster than any man in town when thugs he owed money to showed up at his door.

Elizabeth spoke to Lydia only a few minutes, not wanting to tell her what she really thought and got an earful instead of giving one: "Isn't my fiancé wonderful? Don't you wish you could've got him, Lizzy? But he chose me. Poor Lizzy. I'm about to be a married woman and you don't even have a boyfriend."

Mrs. Bennet was hardly less effusive. She praised Elizabeth's generosity then praised Wickham even more for taking such wonderful care of her dear Lydia by feasting with her on crab legs at the hotel buffet.

Elizabeth would never underestimate her mom or Lydia again. Their attitude toward romantic relationships was beyond belief. She'd always known something was very wrong with her mom's ideas about men and women, but she could not have predicted her mom congratulating Lydia on the achievement of being engaged to be married before Jane.

That being said, Elizabeth could only blush in response. It's not like she'd ever done better than her mother or Lydia with her own attempts at getting a guy.

#

At 8pm on Wednesday, August 28, there was still light out at the 67th Annual End of Summer Street Fair. The fair took place at Derby town square located at the corner of Ocean Drive and Market Street.

Organized to help local businesses wrap up the summer with plenty of sales on Derby Yacht Club T-shirts and printed floral wrap dresses, folks mostly ambled around buying taffy and ice cream.

Jane and Elizabeth were out, wandering aimlessly, not buying anything except a piece of fudge to share and unsuccessfully trying to cheer each other up by performing the Bechdel test and avoiding the subject of men.

They were happy about their sudden luck in buying Lydia's video, and her and Wickham successfully making their flight to the South Pole for their work at the research center's commissary. There was no more talk of Wickham's gambling debts or requests for help from Lydia, and Elizabeth and Jane were surprised at how well things were looking on that front.

They talked about apartments and cars. Elizabeth had been saving up for both but would have to start over. Who knows how long she'd be stuck at home and on a bike. Worse than that, by next month she might be jobless.

Everything had happened so fast. A few days after Elizabeth's run in with Catherine Darcy, a letter arrived from the board of education saying there would be a hearing about her "inappropriate conduct." It was scheduled to take place at the September school board meeting right before the start of school.

After this, Elizabeth sprung into action and lined up a temporary position as a waitress at the pub near Longbourn. If she lost her job, she wouldn't be without income until she found another teaching position.

All she needed was to make sure she got some good recommendations. Her boss for summer music lessons said she had a way with teenagers and it was hard to find instructors for that age group, so he was one reference. Principal Elliot would be another, hopefully.

Bingley had called Jane the night before, asking how Lydia was doing with oblique, polite questions that never involved the words porn or sex tape. They had a pleasant conversation, but nothing was said of him returning to Derby anytime soon. Jane hadn't had the nerve to ask him. He was excited about his travels and had a lot to say about his love of Italian food.

"Miss Elizabeth!" a pair of little girls screamed.

Elizabeth woke up from her distracted daze. "Oh my gosh!"

Claire and Olivia from her band at school grabbed both her arms and swung her this way and that as Jane laughed, looking proud.

The girls' parents were with them. A cool looking couple in their early forties greeted her with almost as much enthusiasm as their daughters.

"They still talk about you all the time and can't wait for 5th grade band to start," said the mom.

"We're amazed how you were able to keep them both in

line," said the dad, before looking at his wife and laughing. "At the beginning of the year we were worried a new teacher right out of college might have trouble with this rambunctious pair."

Elizabeth smiled and chatted with the girls about practicing and taking care of their instruments, but her thoughts wandered to how soon she might not have the job teaching these kids.

Had their parents got a whiff of the photo of her and Wickham that was all over local social media?

Jane was complimented on her sparkly eye makeup by Olivia and Claire's mom, who like a lot of women seemed a little wary of talking to Jane until she realized she wasn't stuck-up.

Jane had just recently started a job at the cosmetics counter at a big department store and, despite things with Bingley being up in the air, was feeling better about herself after depositing her first paycheck.

As Elizabeth said goodbye to her students and their parents, she looked around and saw Will Darcy on the opposite side of the square by a children's clothing shop.

He was as handsome, well-groomed and forbidding as ever, standing with three men and two women his age.

Elizabeth didn't recognize any of them and was dying to identify the females. "Do you know them?" she asked Jane, who followed her gaze to Darcy.

"No, I've never seen them before at the club," Jane replied

anxiously. Her thoughts clearly jumping to Bingley and the many evenings they'd spent together at the yacht club.

Elizabeth tried to catch Will's eye, but he kept looking past her to a display of camera drones with flashing lights.

Finally, after she bounced a bit, their eyes met and she wanted to shout "yay!" but she kept her arms at her sides and didn't wave frantically as she wanted.

The back of her neck tingled with excitement as she recalled pressing her lips against his open mouth at Pemberley. But in an instant, his eyes lowered, and he looked away.

He'd seen her. She was sure he'd seen her. Their eyes had met.

Olivia ran up to Elizabeth with a flower in her hand.

"Oh, thank you, it's beautiful," said Elizabeth, bending over to the girl's level as she took the gift and talked to her about her plans for swimming lessons the last week of summer break.

Elizabeth hoped Will would take the opportunity to make his way over to where she stood with Jane. The thought made her smile widely as she thanked Olivia again and got her to promise to be careful crossing the street.

When Elizabeth stood up, she looked in Will's direction, but he was gone. "Jane, where did he go?"

"Oh, I didn't see. Sorry."

Elizabeth turned in circles, looking everywhere.

But he wasn't there.

He had seen her. Yet he had walked away without coming to speak to her.

She couldn't hear what Jane was saying. Her ears weren't working.

All was lost.

He was done with her.

An up-skirt shot of her with Wickham was in the public domain and of course Darcy had seen it. She blushed all over at what she had done. It wasn't just stupid, it was vile. Rubbing Wickham and getting him off when she only met him earlier that same day. A total womanizer who was probably at that moment screwing her barely legal sister.

Elizabeth wanted to throw up and probably would have if she'd eaten dinner.

Jane suggested pizza.

"Can we just go home?" Elizabeth whimpered.

"Yes, of course," said Jane, looking miserable and not just out of empathy for Elizabeth. Jane was unhappy in her own right because she had expected to run into someone who knew Bingley, someone who'd say they'd spoken to him and had some update about him. Any mention of Bingley would have been nice.

Jane was so in love she took a pregnancy test when she was only one day late because she couldn't stand the idea of a birth-control failure ruining any hope of Bingley ever trusting her again. Elizabeth grieved to think how desperate Jane was to not do anything to displease Bingley. There was nothing like the vulnerability of being a poor, fragile woman.

They walked in the direction of Longbourn but didn't talk. Passing the bus stop along the way, they didn't try to catch the bus but kept walking in silence.

Tears trickled down Elizabeth's face. Oh, the perverseness of realizing that now that she was over her dislike and really liked him, Will was no longer interested in her.

Such a loss ... to her ... to him too.

He suited her and she made up for his deficit of liveliness.

He was the sort of person she needed. Intelligent, upright, honest, not enamored with the sound of his own voice. Confident enough to handle her irreverence without taking offense, even when it was squarely directed at him. Nothing could touch him; he had real strength. He had told her he was drawn to her, yet she didn't flatter or kowtow to try to impress him. She didn't massage his ego, but he still evaluated her fairly.

Darcy was prosperous not just because he was born to money but because he made responsible choices and was not getting into ridiculous binds because of his looney family. He was an entrepreneur, and anyone could see the success of his business just by driving by one of his coastal developments.

His family threw parties that didn't serve dishes with the main ingredients of white bread and ketchup. They appreciated the arts and supported local musicians. The beauty they

---

surrounded themselves with showed good taste. Will was an informed person, not a gossip and fluent in English you learned from reading books.

Most important of all, he was willing to acknowledge his faults and change.

Elizabeth couldn't afford most of Darcy's pastimes but she would have enjoyed riding along. With her teacher's salary, she could afford to do a little traveling with him. Maybe NYC for a Broadway show or Cape Hatteras for snorkeling. She'd always wanted to try jet skis. She would be a great travel companion, low maintenance, low expectations. She wouldn't complain about having no AC or subpar service.

Will wasn't a typical spoiled rich kid. He was concerned about those close to him, protective and generous toward his friends and family — think of how he treated Bingley and Jane on his yacht. He knew his father wasn't perfect but he honored him. He took on more than his share in caring for his sister, even when she got herself into serious binds. He enjoyed his wealth and privilege but didn't flaunt it or screech around corners in fast cars.

And he was so genetically blessed, with beautiful soft grey eyes and lust-inducing sculpted facial features. His slow hands on her body were pure pleasure.

Why hadn't she seen the appeal of him much earlier ... before she made her one summer hook up the worst possible choice imaginable?

He'd been improving in her estimation since the apology letter. His reserve and his stoic deadpans were not off-putting anymore; they were attractive. And, those things he wrote about her in his letter and his texts.

But now, he was horrified by her family's growing association with Wickham. Disgusted by her hook up with him the night of the Beach Ball. Clearly he no longer wanted to hear her witty retorts. He didn't want to smile at the things she said anymore.

Everyone in Derby was learning about Lydia and Wickham, with Lydia telling all her friends that she was going to marry him, at the same time a photo of Elizabeth making out with him was posted everywhere. Her family was the Wickham harem according to some anonymous user on DerbyCentral.org: "Soon the Bennet girls will save time and have group sex with Wickham George."

Elizabeth had never directly answered Will's question about whether she had sex with Wickham, so he must think she did. And she wouldn't debase herself by pleading her case to him as "it was only a hand job."

His aunt Catherine must have told him about how she was in trouble with the school board and was in danger of losing her job. "Miss Elizabeth Bennet posed for a dirty picture and violated the code of conduct," he'd have been told by Catherine Darcy or someone else. God, that sounded awful.

Her desperate mind told her she should have gone to speak with him as soon as she learned about the photo. Or she ought not have finished her chat with Olivia but walked right over to him. She should have pursued him, tried to explain herself to him.

No, there was no way out from under this.

Will didn't even want to say hello to her. He saw her and left.

She was connected with what Will tried to avoid. Indecency. People leaching off his family. Disloyalty.

Was she ever really an option for Will Darcy? Not much of one but maybe.

Not anymore.

Chapter Twelve

The trailer's front door creaked as Elizabeth walked out wearing black pants and a cream-colored summer sweater. The smell of old fruit from the garbage cans irritated her nose. Strands of hair from the messy bun at the back of her head tickled her cheek.

She mounted her Vespa, carefully avoiding smearing grease on her clothes, as a delivery truck pulled up.

A woman with "executive couriers" sewn on her shirt got out and handed her a large envelope. It was stamped "Same Day Delivery. September 3, 2019."

Elizabeth felt the sun peeking out from behind a cloud.

After signing her name by the X on the screen of a small

tablet, she stammered, "Thank you so much."

Not wanting to be late for her meeting, she immediately ripped open the mailer. Her neighbors across the street stared as the brown delivery truck did a three-point turn in the dirt lane.

Inside the envelope she found a short cover letter from her boss, Principal Elliot, telling her to give the enclosed letter of recommendation to the school board members at their meeting, which was to begin in an hour.

He'd responded to her request and sent a recommendation. She'd called his office last week asking for the favor. This sure was cutting it close. Thank goodness he chose to contact her by same day mail.

... Miss Bennet is such a promising educator, we have drawn up a multi-year contract especially for her and have the full support of the parent-teacher organization in doing so ... our school's burgeoning music program would be devastated by her dismissal.

Trying to catch her breath, she hopped back onto her bike with a little wobble and turned the key to a smattering of rumbling. Her eyes watered as she followed the skid marks leading to the main road, then made her way to the office of the superintendent of schools across town.

A smiling middle-aged man in leopard-print glasses greeted her at the door to the offices, "Hello, Miss Bennet, we're glad you made it. I'm the assistant superintendent of schools."

"Oh, hello, it's nice to meet you. I have a letter to give you." Elizabeth handed him the letter from Principal Elliot. "I wasn't sure it would arrive in time. I mean, it was just delivered this morning."

Pulling his glasses down the bridge of his nose to examine the folded stationary, he said, "Yes, it's a fine statement on your behalf. I believe we most likely will discuss the issue at the end of the meeting. One of our town council representatives, Catherine Darcy, initially asked to speak on the subject, but she may have sent someone in her stead."

Elizabeth stopped breathing. "I was hoping I might be able to speak to the board too."

"If you must, but I believe it would be most effective to let this letter speak for itself. The board was sent a copy also." His eyebrows arched behind his glasses. "Otherwise, the least said on the subject, the better, don't you think?" he said with a slight cringe.

She nodded, hopeful yet terrified, then found a seat in the back of a large meeting room as the chairwoman for the board of education called the meeting to order.

Catherine Darcy was nowhere in sight, but Elizabeth waited and waited for someone to say something about that wretched photo of her with Wickham. Everyone she ever knew had commented about it on DerbyCentral.org, so why not let some school board members she'd never seen before have their

319

turn.

During the final minutes of the meeting, the assistant superintendent in leopard glasses got up to speak. "I've been putting this off in case Catherine Darcy decided to appear today as originally planned, but it seems she has indeed changed her mind and declined. Is that correct?" He looked to the chairwoman running the meeting.

She nodded back at him.

"Well, I will make a brief statement for the record if I might." He cleared his throat. "The office of the superintendent of schools has decided to retire the matter of a first-year music teacher's unfortunate photograph with her date at the Beach Ball. A letter from the principal of West Derby is admitted to the record." He waved a copy of the letter in the air.

"Does Miss Elizabeth Bennet have anything to add?" He turned to Elizabeth.

"Uh, not really, except ..." She thought of the prepared statement she'd memorized and decided to recite just the last sentence of it. "I just wanted to say that *sharing my love of instrumental music with the clever students of my hometown's school district is exhilarating fun and a great privilege.*"

The chairwoman looked pleased. "Okay, then if there's no other new business, this meeting is adjourned."

That was it.

People started filing out of the room.

Elizabeth jumped up and went over to thank her new best friend. "Do you know why Catherine Darcy cancelled her appearance today?" she asked the assistant superintendent.

"No, I don't," he replied, smiling but all business unlike his glasses. "But the matter is dropped. And, in the future, please take care, Miss Bennet."

"You bet," Elizabeth exclaimed. "Thanks again."

His grin was paternal and seemed truly kind.

Out in the parking lot, she looked up at the sun, blowing kisses to the wind and thanking God, then she noticed Cornel Darcy exiting the building and nearly fell over her bike.

He hit her with his come-on grin that was understandably effective with women.

She smiled back at him, totally baffled. "What in the world are you doing here?" She couldn't manage a proper greeting.

"I don't know. I had to make sure some important letter was delivered by 9am or the world would end. And then I had no choice but to sit in for my grandmother at the Board of Ed meeting ... as if I could sit through that crap. I went upstairs to chat up this girl I know."

Elizabeth gasped. "Cornel! *Who* sent you? *Who* has you checking on letter deliveries?"

"Hm, come to think of it, I don't think I'm supposed to say anything about that... uh, to you or to anyone, actually. Sorry. Please don't ask."

No, it couldn't be. "Did Will have anything to do with this?"

"Do with what?" he asked, a terrible liar — a family trait?

"Your being here. And your grandma not coming to the meeting to disparage me to the board as she threatened."

"Oh, yeah, sorry about that. She's a bit extreme sometimes. Just ignore her. That's what I do most of the time. Shit, I definitely wasn't supposed to say anything about this to you. My mistake. Forget about it, okay?"

Elizabeth's face collapsed. "Your grandmother spoke to me about ... Will ... at the library ... just the other day."

"Right. Sorry about that," he grimaced.

"You know?" Elizabeth exclaimed, staggered.

"What do you think she did immediately after speaking to you?"

She paused to think. "I don't want to imagine. Did it involve calling me a lot of horrible names?"

He laughed. "Yes, she went to visit Will at his office and I was so unlucky as to be there with him *and* his father at the time. We were supposed to go out for a three martini lunch. God, I ran out of that place faster than a fox at a hunt."

Could it be? Could Will have gotten involved in saving her job, intervened on her behalf with his aunt and made sure the letter of recommendation from her boss arrived.

Who could have stopped Catherine Darcy from showing

up? Only the heir, the pride of the family, could have driven her from her purpose.

As Elizabeth rolled over the facts and probabilities in her head, she *was* ready to have Will's children as his aunt had foretold in horror.

Yet Will hadn't even acknowledged her at the town square the other day. He'd seen her, their eyes met, and yet he left without coming to talk to her. He hadn't waited a few minutes for her to be done chatting with her students and immediately left the area after she spotted him.

Maybe he sent Cornel to make sure the letter got to the board because he didn't want to do it himself. He didn't want her to thank him directly. He didn't want her to know he got involved on her behalf. Cornel had been told not to speak with her.

Will Darcy is not trying to win me.

#

She rushed over to see Jane at the cosmetic counter of Fords Department Store and waited patiently until it was time for her sister's fifteen-minute break, then broke down behind a perfume display.

"Please, you have to help me stay strong, Jane. I don't want to lose my resolve now, not after all that's happened. I can't chase after him, beg him to have me. I can't lower myself, act like some chick desperately going after him."

"Of course not," said Jane, squeezing her in what could certainly be marketed as an inappropriate girl-on-girl embrace if someone took a snapshot and posted it online — much like her outdoor make out session with Will Darcy could have produced an unfortunate photo.

"Oh, I want to do what you've been doing and not complain but it's so hard," said Elizabeth. "I keep thinking that I could easily go prostrate myself to him, get him to be with me, to take me to some hotel and fuck me despite all the Wickham stuff. God, I'm so weak. Just the thought of what I'm giving up, the possibility of something like good sex for once in my life, any real passion in my life. When we were together at Pemberley it was so intense, so amazing."

Jane looked like she was about to cry, although Elizabeth was pretty sure she wasn't just thinking of Darcy but his best friend, whom Jane used to have a lot of sex with.

"You would not believe how he kissed me, and it was all him! I did *not* jump his bones, I swear." Elizabeth wiped her eyes with a scratchy tissue from the makeover table. "And now I'm just going to let him walk away without a peep. Because if I run crying to him I'll lose my self-respect. And he would never think of someone begging him to take her as worthy — he has the ego everyone says he has. Ever since my dad died, I've been trying not to become the woman who'd settle for a guy who looked down at her, treat her like she was lucky to be with him. I can't throw myself at Will."

"But, Lizzy, you forget that he might—"

"No, stop, please don't raise my hopes. I'm trying to stand firm. I need your help. I have to accept this."

#

Their Las Vegas lawyer called the next day and asked to video conference.

Elizabeth was now sure he liked Jane, but instead of flirting with her sister, he immediately got down to business.

"I just learned your check has been voided and will not be cashed. BlueRussian@cheapemail.com has seen the error of his ways and is worried that the young woman in the video, Lydia Bennet, was underage at the time it was taken, so the footage is illegal and worthless, thus he cannot accept payment for it," said their lawyer, a five o'clock shadow showing off his handsome dark brown skin.

Elizabeth and Jane just kept shaking their heads and wondering if it was all a dream as they heated up leftover spaghetti and sat down to watch *Dirty Dancing*. They got a call from Lydia bragging about how all the guys at the research station were in love with her.

#

Friday was Jane's birthday, and Elizabeth bought $10 gourmet cupcakes to eat at the beach. But by the time they were both off work, it was too windy, so they headed to the mini golf course by the boardwalk which had picnic tables set up by the 18th hole.

Past summers they'd spent a lot of time in epic mini golf battles. This summer Jane had been with Bingley most of the time, and they hadn't played together even once, so they decided to play a quick round for old time's sake before eating their cupcakes.

It seemed they'd have the course to themselves, but a group of high school boys wearing prep school jerseys showed up just as they started.

The boys wanted to rush through the course and quickly became ticked off waiting for Elizabeth's carefully lined-up shots.

Shrugging, Elizabeth gave up on strategy and worked to get her ball into the hole quickly, even if it took a rapid succession of lousy putts.

When Jane got into trouble in the water trap by the plaster Grand Canyon on hole #4, the guys started yelling, "Foxhounds suck!"

"Do they think we're in high school?" whispered Elizabeth.

Derby High School, with its foxhound mascot, was her and Jane's alma mater, and it had a cross-town rivalry with the all-boys prep school west of Rosings Park.

Elizabeth and Jane decided to skip ahead, nudging their

balls into the hole in order to allow the impatient boys to rush onto green #9 the minute they were done with #8.

Leaning on her golf club like it was a crutch, Elizabeth glanced over at the picnic table where she'd left the box with two cupcakes.

The golf game was getting dull. Maybe they should go eat.

Then she saw Bingley climbing over the white picket fence that enclosed the golf course.

"Bingley!" she yelled impotently.

He had the exact same grin on his face as before, although they hadn't seen him in four weeks.

"Hey!" he called, waving with his right hand, a bottle with a poofy lavender ribbon tied around it in his left hand.

Elizabeth couldn't look away if she wanted to. She just stared, mouth open, her eyes fixed on him.

He approached her looking rather chipper.

"Your mom said you two were eating cake by the ocean," he said, smiling widely. "And then I saw your scooter." He pointed to her parking spot along the fence.

As he turned to Jane, who was behind Elizabeth on the green, his smile flickered with worry for a moment, then he gave a little shrug and sprinted right up to her and got in her face, whispering something Elizabeth couldn't hear, before stroking her cheek with his free hand and giving her a loose hug with his bottle-laden one.

Jane looked faint. She was motionless, hadn't moved an inch since Bingley appeared as far as Elizabeth could tell. "I can't believe you're here," Jane finally said.

"Surprise! I got in late last night." Bingley laughed with his charming boyish grin. "Then I stopped by Longbourn earlier today to find out where you'd be tonight for your birthday."

"You flew all the way back from Rome?" Jane asked.

"Yes," he said, flushing a bit, but still sounding unabashed about any implied extravagance in flying across the Atlantic to deliver a birthday greeting. "Have I really been away so long? ... You're looking at me like I'm a ghost."

Jane's eyes were watering and she bowed her head, not seeming able to meet Bingley's happy eyes in kind.

He reached for her, pulling her into another, tighter hug.

Jane let her head rest on his chest.

Elizabeth turned away, swinging her club through the air aimlessly.

She decided to skip ahead a few holes and walked over to put her ball on the starting mat for #13. Then she alternated between hitting her and Jane's balls like she was really into the game and determined to make some good putts. But of course she actually was trying to give Jane and Bingley a little privacy.

When Elizabeth looked over at the two, blinking because she could hardly believe what she was seeing, Bingley was kissing Jane although Jane barely responded, looking rather passive.

His lips read "Happy Birthday" as he held up the gift of champagne, which he kept hold of, not handing it over so Jane would have to lug it around.

As Elizabeth started hole #14, Jane and Bingley walked across the golf course landscaping, closer to where Elizabeth stood holding her club.

Elizabeth couldn't make out all of what Bingley said but she strained to hear, taking shot after shot, puttering around with her red and blue golf balls.

"... I can't believe the progress at Netherfield... I was so worried that when I wasn't here to oversee, nothing would get done. Will's been a great help..."

"... what you've been through with Lydia!...It's heartbreaking...and it's all worked out now? ... That's not perfect by any stretch of the imagination but it's amazing that..."

"You like the people you work with? ...I like your new eye liner ... The job is fun for you? ... "

" ... I know you're still so unhappy I went away, but I feel like I've had a chance to get some perspective."

Elizabeth watched as they stepped onto the golf course, blocking part of the green. They were getting into the big issues right quick. Bingley stood so close to Jane his clothes brushed against her. He and Jane were smiling but not as jovial as they used to be together. There was unresolved tension.

Jane's mouth was moving but she wasn't speaking loud enough for Elizabeth to hear.

"Yes, of course I met lots of people in Rome," said Bingley, "as many as I could, I wanted to spend time with locals, but I haven't been seeing anyone. I spend a lot of time alone in the shower." He laughed at Jane's blush. "...I told you I didn't consider it to be a break up, I just needed time to think some things over ...

"...I had a visit from my mom and she was telling me I wasn't being realistic if I thought you were going to share things that were so monumentally upsetting to you, just like I wouldn't be sharing my humiliation at varsity lacrosse..."

He had been talking about Jane to his parents! Elizabeth remembered Jane saying that he and his parents were even closer than Darcy and his. *He's discussing what to do about Jane with his parents!*

"...I never accused you of anything, but I don't like the way I've seen women around here go after Will with dollar signs in their eyes, willing to do anything for a piece of him and I worry that you're so insecure about all the same stuff..."

"I try to be honest," Jane said louder, plaintively.

"I want that but maybe it's not as easy as I hoped."

The prep school boys on the course behind Elizabeth started yelling something at Jane and Bingley.

Bingley never looked intimidating in general, but he gave

them a glance that said *you don't want to start something with me.* Bingley held himself like he was used to having his way, telling people who worked for him what to do.

Jane took up her golf club to rejoin the game with Elizabeth but didn't hit her ball more than once. Instead, she watched Bingley as he told Elizabeth about his plans to stay at Netherfield that night and unpack some crates he'd shipped to the house.

"And how are *you*?" Bingley asked Elizabeth boisterously, putting his arm around her and kissing the side of her head. "Now you have to tell me what's been going on with *you.*"

"We have cupcakes," she replied stupidly.

"Do you have cups?" asked Bingley, laughing enthusiastically as he raised the green bottle in his hands and gave her a knowing smile. "I'm not supposed to say anything but if you look at this bottle of vintage French Champagne that no one has ever heard of you might be able to guess who picked it out." He held it out for Elizabeth to examine the label.

She felt pain, not pleasure upon realizing the thoughtfulness of the gift. "Oh, that was nice of him," Elizabeth mumbled, wanting to hide her sadness that Will wanted her to celebrate her sister's birthday in style but did not want to be around her. "He didn't want to deliver it himself?"

"He's had a lot of business to attend to lately."

Elizabeth nodded, glad they both so easily understood

who was being spoken of.

Jane suggested they take a break from the game to eat the birthday cupcakes.

Bingley was agreeable. As always.

After Elizabeth cut the giant specimens into quarters with a plastic knife, she handed out slices and they all three sampled the creamy icing that crunched like crème brûlée and massively overpowered the light, fluffy cake underneath.

"You two like this?" Bingley laughed, setting down his portion. "It's too sweet."

Elizabeth laughed, ate her own piece, then eyed the leftovers, wanting to gobble them too.

Jane was polite with Bingley as the three of them chatted, but she was not acting as emotional as she must be feeling inside. She was wary. Bingley had dashed her hopes but not so much so that he turned her off. Her cheeks were beginning to take on a glow for the first time in weeks.

The champagne was much subtler on the palette than the baked goods, and they sipped it leisurely, enjoying the crisp fruity bubbliness as Bingley described a run-down hotel in Collevecchio where he purchased a fireplace mantel for Netherfield.

When Jane and Bingley started eyeballing each other wordlessly, Elizabeth got up to hit a golf ball around the 17th green. Playacting zealous love of mini golf would be a new skill added to her resume.

She was ready to call it a night and go home to practice her oboe and never wanted to hit a golf ball again unless she was allowed to use full force and send it flying over a fence.

Then she heard Bingley shout, "Hey, we've been expecting you! You're late."

Turning, Elizabeth saw Will Darcy approaching the picnic area where Jane and Bingley still sat. He wore dark blue jeans and a dull black tee shirt, the most casually dressed she'd ever seen him.

Stopping opposite Jane, he spoke to her, seemingly wishing her happy birthday.

Elizabeth spun around and set up for a difficult shot on hole #18. Her ball was orange now. She must have swiped someone else's ball by accident.

Footsteps told her Will was walking up behind her but she assiduously stuck to practice swinging for the long putt she was about to attempt.

He stopped behind her, quiet, then gently wrapped his arms around her from behind. His warm hands covered hers as he guided her swing, tapping the ball and sending it slowly along the uneven green until it dropped into the hole, out of sight. She was big stuff at mini golf but he'd clearly been playing on real courses.

Elizabeth chuckled to herself, Darcy's bare arms causing

her goose bumps, but she continued to passively snub him.

He leaned in, breathing into her hair like he was smelling aerated wine.

She glanced back with an expression saying she was not overly excited to see him. "I'd been expecting you to call me, or text me, for two weeks now and had all but given up."

His smile was affectionate, unrestrained, not like the normal Darcy quasi smile.

Inside she swooned but for his eyes she shook her head and shrugged.

"Sorry about that," he said softly, gripping her hips like he was picking out the best puppy in a litter.

She leaned back, propping herself against him, allowing for no chance of falling out of his embrace.

He took her club from her and chucked it off to the side. The entire front of his body, including a lot of heated denim over rigid bone and muscle, pressed against her back side.

The Will Darcy she stumbled into at Netherfield, as well as the formally-dressed Will Darcy she kissed at Pemberley, would be out of place at a mini golf course, but this smiling, pine-soap-smelling Will Darcy merely dwarfed every object of interest on the golf course with his presence. A windmill, a waterfall, the Eiffel Tower, and Godzilla.

Oh god, she didn't want to have to think of it, but he couldn't be the only guy in town who hadn't seen the photo of her and Wickham. Yet as she glanced back at him he didn't look like he'd been vomiting recently.

Fuck it, this was her chance. He'd come for her. He'd sought her out. It might be called too eager, but she spun around and lunged at him.

Bingley laughed from his seat a good ten yards away.

Darcy was surprisingly even keeled, and didn't stumble back, nor look shocked, just took her into his arms like it was wholly expected.

She panted against his shoulder, telling herself not to loosen her grip even if it got awkwardly long before she was able to speak.

He lifted her off the ground an inch and turned her away from Jane and Bingley's view with the slightest sway.

She laughed at being held in the air, feeling a burning determination. She had to say something about the school board meeting.

His expression was calm anticipation.

Clinging to him so he wouldn't be able to pull away, she spoke into his neck, "I don't know exactly what you did, Darcy, but I have to thank you for helping me with the school board. I could tell from something Cornel said to me that you played a part in keeping your aunt from testifying against me."

He leaned his head back, moving only enough to look at her face, not pulling away, just shifting, and whispered, "I wish ...

Cornel wasn't supposed to say anything to you."

"No, don't blame your cousin. I pulled it out of him."

Darcy nodded as he extended his arms, allowing her to gain her footing.

He took her hand and led her away from the 18th hole to a mini Mount Everest with a cement bench cut out of it.

His sculpted face was suddenly grave. "My aunt should not have been threatening you because of your connection with me," he said, taking both her hands as they stood face to face. "That was entirely inappropriate."

Her face burned, loving that he just said they had a "connection" when a minute ago she would not have acknowledged a connection between her and Will Darcy under FBI interrogation.

She had to focus every bit of energy in her body on not crying or, worse, starting to apologize about the Wickham photo.

"You shouldn't stop me from thanking you," she warbled, pulling herself a little closer to him, not able to meet his eyes fully but glancing up at him every third word. "Whatever you did, rush delivering that letter from my boss, or tying your aunt up in the basement Tuesday morning, I'm indebted."

"No," he answered firmly, not smiling at her joke. "I do *not* want you to feel obligated to me in any way!" He looked at her like she'd threatened to smash one of his family's priceless heirlooms.

"What do you mean 'obligated'?" she smiled gently with wide eyes, trying to soften him. "I'm just saying I appreciate that you used your influence over your aunt."

He nodded, shifting his weight from one leg to the other as they stood next to 15-foot-tall Mount Everest.

"Maybe you yourself should have felt *obligated* to text me after the jazz party," she quipped.

His original soft, smiling mug reappeared.

It was so hard for her to not mention him turning away from her at the street fair nine days ago.

"I heard you looked into a house at Oak Creek," he said, changing the subject.

"How do you know that?" she asked, a light salt and sugar aroma coming from the candy shop on the Boardwalk.

"I've been a part of that development from the start, but that's not how I know you were there. Bingley was visiting with your mother this morning and got her to promise not to tip off your sister that he was back."

"Oh," said Elizabeth. "What a perfectly reasonable explanation, and I was hoping to have some snooping to hold over you."

He smirked twisting his full lips. "Bingley also told me your mom refers to you as *my silly little Lizzy.*"

She laughed, raising her chin. "She's never been able to figure me out, but I'm still going to let her use my credit score to rent the place at Oak Creek. Although, it's not like I have the down payment to *buy* a house. We're looking into renting."

He nodded, seeming sincerely encouraging. "Which house did you look at? There are five different floor plans. If there was a large tree in the front yard as your mother described, you probably looked at the one on the corner of Oak Ridge Road."

"Yeah, that's it. If it works out, you can help us carry boxes because you'll know your way around the place," she said, imagining him with a French Horn in his arms.

He nodded. "Do you get the master bedroom if your name is on the lease?"

"Even better; Mom and Jane are upstairs, and I'm in the basement apartment by myself."

"That's right. With a separate entrance, correct? Not many of the houses have basement apartments. Will this be the first time you've had your own space?"

"Yes, it will be the first time I've lived anywhere other than Longbourn, even for college. I'm ecstatic." Her cheek muscles quivered as she smiled harder than she's smiled since she was ten years old celebrating her birthday with both her mom and dad for the first and only time.

He stared at her, his eyes turning pensive, and it seemed he wasn't in a rush to fill up the void with talking.

He looked her over, checking out the shorty romper she wore. It was a sort of loose-fitting shorts and halter top combo made from dark fabric covered in spring flowers.

His eyes caught on the skin-colored bra that peaked out from under the top, and she was reminded of the two of them in that corner bedroom at Pemberley discussing women's undergarments.

Could anything ever again be as sexy as the way he touched her that night? Yet, even now, she wasn't completely comfortable about the idea of having sex with him. Will was so good looking. She'd never dated someone she found so attractive. Not that she dated anyone unattractive but nothing like Will Darcy.

His body was just about perfect. Shaped and tall. She stared wantonly. She lusted for him in a way she had only done with rock stars before.

"How surprised were you to see Bingley today?" he asked, breaking the silence. "I mean, we don't have to talk about Bingley and Jane per se, but I wanted to know how surprised _you_ were since you were here too when he showed up."

"Uh, huh, you don't want to talk about Bingley and Jane but you helped him choose a birthday gift for her, Darcy?"

"Call me Will."

"No, I believe I can only ever call you Darcy. Or BillyBob if you insist."

His full lips twisted in a benevolent sneer. "I'm not giving up, Elizabeth, and a battle of wills between us could get intense."

His hands rose to the sides of her top, just below her underarms where the elastic of her bra was visible. A bold choice of location for a caress but he was super gentle as he touched her skin.

She laughed, looking down at the thin cotton of her blousy top and seeing his hands on her in a way the high school principal would call unbefitting a young person.

"We're two very obstinate people," she said breathily. "But I still think I'll win."

"Can I persuade you not to call me BillyBob by offering to help you fill out your rental agreement?" he asked, lowering his hands to her hips and pulling her toward him.

She smiled. "Well maybe a quick proofread would be helpful." She thought about having him look over her application to rent the house, which at first seemed like a good idea but then seemed like a terrible one.

He looked like he wanted to kiss her but there was so much they needed to discuss. Actually, he looked like he wanted to take her clothes off, and this was far too tempting considering the alternative was discussing all that had happened, including her Wickham pic.

Her voice croaked a little as she began to speak, "I ... I was about half as surprised to see Bingley today as I was to see you after you turned away from me at the street fair last week."

He squinted, looking self-aware but not particularly remorseful. "Yes, I was not ready to speak to you then."

"Huh? Why?" Suddenly it occurred to her. The photo. It had been spread all over DerbyCentral.org before the street fair. He'd walked away from her that day because he'd just seen it and was profoundly grossed out. Her heart raced as she panicked, preparing to defend herself, even as she told herself not to be defensive but frank and honest.

"Someone who thought less of you would have had a much easier time talking to you that day."

"Really?" Agony mixed with euphoria.

He looked away, like he didn't want to say it, then nodded, "Yes." Taking her hand in his, he held it motionless. "But tell me more about what you thought of Bingley's return."

Her mouth watered, wanting to kiss him. "Do you know how long he's back for?" She'd done the hug thing already and was now feeling bereft by the lack of embrace. She could wrap her arms around his neck again and kiss him in the process. But what if he responded too ardently and she wasn't able to stop herself from jumping him. She felt hyper, like her feelings could bubble over at any moment, at the slightest provocation.

"I don't know exactly how long he's back for," said Darcy, sounding calm, "but he says he's going to finish Netherfield and have his parents here for Christmas. I'm not so sure about that timetable, but ... we'll see."

"I think Jane is happy to see him but scared that whatever she did before to send him off will happen again." She blurted it out, giving her thoughts away without consideration of who she was talking to.

His brows creased.

Elizabeth felt Jane's haplessness in her own chest.

"I don't think he believes your sister is involved in anything untoward. He never thought that, Elizabeth. He was getting rubbed raw by the whole dynamic around here, so much attention from people because of Jane, including premature talk of marriage and babies, and then everyone telling him fantastical stories about your family that he dismissed out of hand until some of it was verified. He'd have preferred Jane be the messenger."

She smiled at his apt description of events. "Verified for him by *you*?"

"He got a lot of filler, which was enough to get him asking me for details and then asking me about trusting Jane. I advised him to make sure she was feeling the same for him that he felt for her. That's the worst of what I did."

Elizabeth nodded, trying to take on a philosophic view of Darcy's interference. "But Bingley can't just walk back up to her and act like nothing happened."

"Oh, no, he knows he did something significant. He knows he has much to reestablish. If he was worried about trusting your sister before, now she's not trusting him and he understands that."

"What have you said to him ... about Jane ... recently?" she asked with a sniffle in her voice.

"Don't worry, Elizabeth. I said nothing to get in the way. In fact, I said I may have been wrong in my estimation of your sister's attachment to him given her reaction to his leaving, which I think surprised even Bingley. He said she told him she couldn't continue to talk to him over the phone if he wanted to be away from her. And she followed through on that."

"She was too sad to keep rehashing things on the phone; she was not making an ultimatum," said Elizabeth.

"I get that. What I'm saying is that she wasn't acting like someone calculating the best way to preserve his fidelity but someone who was struggling to keep herself well, which he found telling. There was no doubt she was truly feeling the separation. Maybe he needed to see what the relationship meant to her."

"I'm glad you call it a relationship. But the idea of testing Jane is abhorrent to me."

"When did I not call it a relationship?" He pulled at her arm, bringing her closer, holding her as he looked down at her. "The whole idea of testing her was not ideal but it came out of his believing he was in danger of losing trust over her holding out on him."

"I know you and Bingley aren't consulting me, but I don't see Jane as misrepresenting anything about our family; I see her as trying to interpret everyone in the most positive light."

He nodded. "Elizabeth, I *am* consulting you right now." He smiled, widening his eyes in a question, *aren't I?*

"Maybe it's a flaw for her to be so optimistic about people," said Elizabeth. "But it's sincere coming from her. If I said my mom is so happy Bingley enjoyed his Italian adventure, it would be a complete lie, but Jane sees everyone and everything with rose colored glasses and she would truly mean it if she said that."

He looked at her thoughtfully. "But she can't take it to the point of being knowingly blind about certain conduct, such as your aunt's."

"Come to think of it, Darcy" She stiffened. "*You* must be threatened by the same dangers as Bingley." She was avoiding agreeing with him about Jane. "What sort of tests do you employ to ferret out untrustworthy women?"

He actually had the nerve to laugh in her face with a knowing grin.

She gave him a fierce look.

"Frankly, I don't have any tests," he said. "But I do have a very effective, useful knack for quickly pissing off anyone who's feigning partiality for me." He laughed at himself, like he was happy for being too annoying for schmoozers to successfully ensnare.

She nodded, smiling yet desperate to hear him say more

about *her*, about her as a woman he might not fully trust. She felt her eyes brimming and tried to smack this down with a dose of reality. He hadn't even apologized for ignoring her at the street fair and she was eagerly anticipating sex with him.

"Would you like to go out to dinner sometime?" He waited a moment. "Not tonight but when you're free. I know you have to start teaching next week when school starts." His face froze in a placid, hopeful yet *anxious* expression.

"Eh," her jaw went boneless a few seconds. "Sure ... although I haven't really eaten tonight, unless you count those cupcakes Jane likes and I eat too much of."

He smiled, looking thrilled. "Yes, I saw the mutilated cupcakes."

From the look of combined relief and joy on his face she could tell he'd been worried that she might turn him down.

Then the thought of Wickham reared its pretty-boy head. Oh, god, did Darcy somehow not know about the photo? She had to mention it and find out the full story. She couldn't pretend it wasn't out there.

"I guess you might wonder how the situation with Lydia turned out." Her breath hitched as she felt pure terror. "She's moved away."

Even if there was zero chance she'd ever sleep with Will Darcy, she would never again be hooking up with some guy she just met because it was not worth this excruciating embarrassment.

"I heard," he answered curtly.

Elizabeth blushed. What exactly had he heard? It surely wasn't flattering to her or her family. How bad was it? "At least they're gone from the area for a while ... I guess. To be honest, I don't think I want to see my sister for a while. She's been doing some things the last couple weeks that I didn't realize she was capable of."

He nodded, tight lipped.

Elizabeth was very excited by the idea that they had a dinner date but his reaction to her allusion to Wickham terrified her. He must know. And this meant she was destined to have the most horrible conversation with him about how her date with Wickham was memorialized for all eternity in a photo. He would confess his reluctance to date her because of this. Then after discussing the events of that night a few more times, they'd have a whopper of an argument and never speak to each other again.

She shook her head, suddenly dejected. She was so appreciative when he asked her out but the Wickham thing stood in the way of any real hope for them.

"I'm sorry," he said softly.

She couldn't look at him, only whispered back, needing him to say more, "Sorry?"

"He's a villain."

She nodded, still not looking. "I can't imagine what you

346

think about ..." She flicked her eyes up a him for a split second.

"My father has made me swear not to hurt him," said Darcy.

She chuckled, feeling such regret. "Is he the reason why we didn't talk when I saw you at the street fair?"

He looked into her eyes, not allowing her to look away, even though it was so uncomfortable.

"I...uh..." she stuttered.

"I'm sorry you crossed paths with a child predator," said Darcy.

She furrowed her brow. "Oh, right." He was thinking of Lydia, not her. "Seventeen-year-olds are underage."

He breathed hard, looking furious.

"I can't bring myself to ask if you thought anything about ... *me* being as lame as my sister?"

He broke eye contact, looking to the boardwalk in the distance.

Now she'd done it.

He did not want to answer her question. He knew about the photo. She'd been deluding herself to think there was a possibility he hadn't seen it. He was conscientiously avoiding mention of it. To spare her feelings. To prevent a premature detonation.

"Where do you like to go out to eat?" he asked when he finally returned to her, his eyes softened to a beautiful kindness she could get lost in.

Then she saw something else in his expression that was hard to label. A hint at some sort of awkward sensation he was experiencing but didn't want her to notice.

"Darcy, tell me the truth, did you ... do you know anything else about ... are you not telling me something ... ?" She started hyperventilating.

He looked guilty. He was hopeless at being deceptive.

She screamed, "No! Oh my god. You didn't."

He winced.

She stepped toward him, striking her fist against his chest and bursting into tears. "No!"

He looked so self-conscious she knew she was correct.

"You didn't!" She jabbed her finger into his rib, realizing she was drawing Bingley and Jane's attention, as well as anyone else in the vicinity.

"What did you do, Darcy? Did you do something? Did you get involved in Lydia's horrible ordeal? Oh my god, no! Oh my god, you're killing me. How could you?"

He looked worried but not confused.

"You did something?" Her heart was leaden and dead. "The cancelled check?"

"I don't want you to worry about ..."

"Shut up, Darcy! What did you do?" She play hit him again and again until she just sagged against him in defeat, tears pouring down her cheeks. "Did you buy off that porno dude? How did you find that asshole?"

"I didn't need to find *him.*"

This was a complete and full confession. He meant he only needed to find Wickham to get to the blackmailer.

"Oh, my god! Darcy, why? Why would you get involved in something that must be so completely and utterly repulsive to you? Why would you do that? Jane and I were taking care of it! We are the ones who should be cleaning up Lydia's messes."

"I had hoped that I would be able to prevent you from learning anything about—"

"What are you doing, Darcy? What the hell are you doing to me? What makes you think you can be a fucking hero?" She was trying for angry but only got to overemotional.

"Like I said before, I don't want you to feel obligated to me in any way."

"My ... my family ... *is* obligated to you if you convinced that porno guy to give up the video blackmail scheme."

"Elizabeth, your family owes me nothing. Seriously. As much as I respect Jane, and your mother, I thought only of you."

She felt herself lose consciousness for an instant and had to lean back against Mount Everest's snowy cap. She had so much she needed to say; she could not faint. "It was Wickham all along who was trying to extort us as Jane and I suspected? You know I told them I didn't care about that stupid photo of me and

I certainly wasn't going to buy it from them." Her degradation washed over her again.

"He went after you because he thought you had money and he wanted to hurt me, as always," Darcy said with feeling, no sedate languor.

"I ... I can't even imagine what you must have thought ... of me, not just Lydia."

He shook his head. "I hate that he hurt you."

Was that it? But she needed him to say more. "That's not enough. You're not telling me everything. I know you're not."

"It's all worse than you can imagine, Elizabeth. You can't even think like him. I spent a week getting him to confess all his debts, making him agree to get a real job at that commissary where they are now. He just wanted me to pay him off no strings attached."

"You went to Las Vegas to see him?" she spit out the words, shocked again, more aghast, as if that was even possible.

"I spoke to him and Lydia a number of times. I tried to convince her to leave him and come home but when I realized that was impossible for her I told him he was going to jail if he didn't cancel that check you gave him and hand over every copy of that video. She was under 18 when they made it."

"That's true. You're right. We never even made a big deal about that because she's 18 now."

"His friend, the degenerate going by the name Blue

Russian, didn't want five to ten years in federal prison and he caved right away. Wickham wanted all his debts paid, which I realized had to be done, but he also wanted a windfall. It was a lot of trouble bringing him back to reality. Lydia was not around when he was saying stuff about how I was going to have to pay for your sister's reputation or you and your family would be shattered. Lydia does not want to know the truth about him; she won't believe what you try to tell her. She seemed very keen on the job at the research facility and eventually Wickham got that I wasn't giving him anything without him leaving Derby for good."

"I can't even begin to repay you ... or to thank you properly for going through the torture of negotiating with and bribing someone you hate so much."

He nodded, looking sickened as she would expect discussing such a topic but also so sad she wanted to comfort him. The worse part was not the money she owed him.

"I don't want you to talk about repaying me, but I do hope you don't mind my telling you the whole truth now that the jig is up. There was one more thing. All my interactions with Wickham were strained by his hourly references to the photo he had of you, which was already at various places on the internet before he or his friend put it on Derby's online page. I can't begin to tell you what it was like for me to have him use that against me over and over again."

She felt so much pain but also an unexpected feeling of

hope that she could overcome this. He hated that photo so much, but he'd come for her. "What in the world are you doing standing here with me? I wouldn't if I were you. I've already wimped out and didn't contact you because I was scared about that photo."

"I know he's a monster, Elizabeth. I know he tricked you into taking the picture and I know you can't go back and undo it."

"I did not have sex with him if that's what he told you," she said, her cheeks scalding. "Not that it matters one way or the other. It's atrocious either way. I trusted this guy I knew for ten hours. But we didn't get beyond third base."

"Uh, you, uh, don't have to tell me about that, but, um, I am glad to hear that," he slurred and jumbled his words then took several deep breaths. "I knew he was lying about a lot of what he said, that he was saying whatever jumped into his head if he thought it might injure me. But I couldn't pretend I didn't care. Just like when I saw you at the street fair, Elizabeth, I couldn't pretend I didn't care about you and just come over and shoot the breeze with you and Jane. I was dealing with Wickham at the time and worried I might say the wrong thing to you when we spoke, which I knew we would do eventually."

"Oh god, it hurt so much because I wanted to talk with you so bad that day. I was afraid of losing my job and Jane was getting really depressed and everyone was saying creepy stuff about me online."

"I certainly wasn't there for you. This ghastly business

has so many negative repercussions. I can barely speak of it without wanting to hit something. But I was concerned about ... When I saw you at the street fair, I wasn't sure what to say because I had been hoping you'd agree to go out with me but feared that if I asked you the wrong way, you might slam me like before."

"Wow, that's what you thought? I think you may have misjudged what my feelings are now."

"When you shut me down in my car on the ride home from Rosings Pool ... I needed to be told those things, Elizabeth. It was god awful for my feelings but I needed that. Not a gentle nudge but a sledgehammer."

"Darcy ... Will. I thought your offer was equivalent to calling me a worthless slut. I took it really bad. Like I was nothing, just a loser who went with anyone who showed the slightest interest. Maybe it was my own insecurities but you brought them *all* out of me at once. I was ready for the nunnery."

"Wait, it was not just your insecurities about your background or undeserving guys you've dated. I was to blame. You didn't do anything wrong that day. I did. You don't have the same regrets I do. I was insulting; I'd been unfairly belittling you from the time I met you, unconsciously at times but still. I kept telling myself not to like you because it was beneath me. I was self-important, insensitive, and clueless. You showed me I had behaved insufferably and wasn't worthy of you, and it was the most impactful criticism I've ever received."

"Oh, Will, it could get worse for you next week when everyone you see in Derby asks you if you got any further with me than Wickham did in that photograph."

He actually smiled a little, much better than she hoped for given her crass and depressing allusion. "The only thing that could drive me to meet with Wickham to talk about his sex tape for five days straight was the idea that he was going to irreparably injure *your* happiness, which mattered more to me than punching the person who hurt my sister in the face."

He paused, looking at her. "What I said I wanted from you when we left Rosings together is not what I want now. I want much more than that."

"Oh my god." She shuddered. "Don't stop talking."

"You sure?" he smiled, eyebrows arched.

"Yes, I can take it. Say everything."

"Elizabeth, I confess that I do hate the idea of people in Derby talking about you and Wickham, but you and I together would cause a lot of talk all on its own. I just want a chance with you. Not that it's going to be easy, but I don't want to make decisions based on how things look, like my dad did in his treatment of your cousin Richard. I want to do what's right for you and me, despite my parents' evil protégé who's worse than your aunt Phyllis ever was — unlike your aunt, Wickham targets vulnerable people who don't have the resources to handle him;

he thought you and Jane were pushovers and he could take all your money."

He inhaled with a rough, throaty sound. "I'm not thrilled people I have business with can look at a photo of you with Wickham. I've already had to respond to questions about it. And of course I don't want to become the butt of jokes, well ... with one exception, I'm okay with *you* making fun of me."

"Right. I'm special," she mumbled, her lips pursed as she sniffled, feeling humbled by his words.

He nodded with a boyish grin. "You making fun of me has changed my life. I look at things, at what's important in life, differently. I admire you. What you do for your sisters. Your work. Your intelligence. Your sense of humor. Your optimism despite so much, and even how you treat your mother when she's ... you know .... I was thinking about her earlier this afternoon when news about the new house for her came to me. She loves you and Jane and that's what really matters. She's taken care of you on her own all these years. She's been there for you."

"You and my mom have just about as much in common as me and *your mom*," she said.

"Certainly, that's true, I don't see all sunshine and daffodils. I recognize there are a lot of controversies on the horizon."

"You mean if we got together?" she asked breathlessly.

"Do you want to try that? Or am I asking too much too soon?"

"Of course I do. Of course I want to try. My change of heart is pretty obvious at this point. I mean, I've been crying and screaming at you. What else could that mean?"

His head tilted back, his generous lips pressed into a thin line. "Maybe it seemed like I backed away after we were at Pemberley together, but from the moment I left you that night I was planning what to do about Wickham and Lydia. I know I said some things earlier that night, when we were walking on the beach, that might have made it sound like Wickham is my Achilles heel, but that was ego talking. *You* are my weakness. You make me vulnerable. I don't want to ruin a chance with someone as important to me as you because I feel association with Wickham is an indignity."

"You're trying to kill me, Darcy. You want me to keel over, right?"

He squeezed her as his arms crossed at her lower back and kissed her very gently, with only the slightest touch of his lips.

Her weepy emotions and stinging cheeks loved his softness.

"I think we should go somewhere," she said, pressing her hips against his and wanting the feeling of being on his lap again like at Pemberley. "I think I need to just chill a bit ..." She looked at the dug-out Mt. Everest bench behind her but it didn't look comfortable enough for cuddling.

He nodded. "Maybe we should go back to my place? I'll make you some dinner."

Chapter Thirteen

The car stopped at the end of a crushed seashell lane winding through the woods. The modern ranch was greenish grey, almost hidden in the trees and so small and low to the ground compared to Pemberley House.

Inside was simple and modern with floor-to-ceiling glass for half the wall and wood paneling on the other half. The home was probably on the dark side even during midday sun.

Near the entryway was a sleek kitchen island topped with five brass burners. Two stools sat at the island with room for more. The fridge had clear glass doors and the square sink was set in front of a big square window with a lonely-looking tray of succulents on its sill and a view of the woods.

The focal point of the open floor plan was a giant fire place with a dark suede couch set in front of it. No TV. Two black-and-white dogs were sleeping on the modular sofa until Darcy ordered them to get down.

Darcy grabbed stuff out of the fridge, such as a brick of fancy Dutch cheese, which he set directly on the counter. Then he went to find some bread to slice and put in the oven to toast. No toaster. As soon as the bread was in the oven getting crisp, he opened a bottle of wine and sat down like he was ready for dinner to start. So bachelor.

Feeling somehow at home, she smiled as he jumped up to get some fruit he had in the bottom drawer of the fridge after remembering someone had given him plums.

Back and forth he went, like a mama bird feeding its baby.

She happily sat awaiting his ministrations as he handed her things to try like a pecan and pomegranate crisp.

Slipping outside through a slider door as big as half a wall, he picked some mint for a leftover pea salad then set out a plate and cloth napkin for each of them.

The way he waited on her was so sweet, and every little jam or pâté they sampled was nicer than most of her prepared meals.

To eat and look at him while relaxing in the easy

minimalist décor was a balm.

Oh my god, she thought, were they going to his bedroom after this? It was so much for one day.

When he snapped at his dogs to stop begging for food, know-it-all Darcy returned, but she understood him now. He was serious and could be severe, but he was truly kind.

Shire, the smaller dog, was friendly and nuzzled Elizabeth's leg. Felix seemed jealous of the attention Elizabeth was getting from his master. He expected food to be handed to *him*, not some girl.

Elizabeth wanted to make Darcy laugh, not just smile, and tried to think of a funny story to amuse him with. Maybe she could interest him in a blow job by telling some tale about the one raunchy party she attended in college.

Darcy got up and walked to a cabinet to pull down two bowls. On the way back to his seat he leaned over to kiss her.

The kiss was over too quick.

He sat down, taking a sip of wine then leaned over and grab the leg of her stool, pulling it across the hardwood floor with a scratching sound.

She looked at him wide-eyed and he leaned in for another kiss.

She felt shots of spiky anticipation in her abdomen as he molded his lips to her mouth with barely there smacking sounds. She knew she could get pleasure from sex but also knew that for her there was pain too. Did he understand this after what she'd already told him?

He broke off the kiss, pulling back. His face told another story; he didn't want to stop.

"I want to ask you some questions," he said.

"You can ask me anything." She took a deep breath, shifting to get comfortable in her seat. They both seemed to be finished eating after polishing off small servings of homemade peach yogurt. "If there's something I don't want to talk about, I'll just say so."

"I don't want to upset you or be intrusive but I feel like I need to ask about that guy who you said got violent with you?"

She closed her eyes. "Right."

"But if you don't—"

"No, it's okay." She looked at him, seeing remnants of the warm smile she loved, and felt braver. "To keep to the shorter version, basically, I lost my dad to a drug overdose, accidental I believe although he was kind of a depressive personality, and I was angry at him for being so reckless and abandoning me or at least not making the effort to stay alive for my sake.

"I got high on attention from men, so although I was only a teenager, I snuck into bars and met this twenty-something guy who was a chain smoker and just wanted to have sex with me, which I was okay with until he slapped me across the face. We were arguing about something — I can't remember what, probably whether I was going to go buy him cigarettes — and he hit me and then I just froze and then the next five minutes were unbearable. I got out of there and never spoke to him again because my mom and her boyfriend at the time threatened to blow his brains out with a shotgun."

"What happened during the five minutes?" He exhaled loudly through his nose.

"Very painful sex," she said dully.

"Did you ... ever talk to the police?" His clenched jaw seemed to make it hard for him to speak.

"I did not. Didn't talk to him either; I just lay there. I was temporarily mute."

He exhaled loudly, and slowly.

"I'd make it into a much better story if I wrote it out for a movie screenplay," she said. "There would be swords involved, pistol whipping, stuff like that."

He almost smiled. "It's not a good story as is."

"No. But now I get to hear your story," she chirped, trying to sound upbeat. "What's your number?"

"Do we have to move on so quickly?" he asked plaintively.

"That's all there is to tell, really. Except I've had discomfort during sex since that day, so that's the lasting effect. I have trouble relaxing and trusting anyone enough to let them in, so to speak, so intercourse can be difficult, at least at first."

He looked like he was angry.

She wanted to tell him to cut it out. She was allowed to be angry about it but having him angry was only a burden.

"That was six years ago?" he asked, keeping his voice low and gentle.

"Yes."

"He's around thirty now and lives in town?" he asked.

"Yeah, sure, you want to bulldoze his block?" she chuckled. "I never go there."

He smiled. "That's not a bad idea."

"No, I don't want to talk about him or his address. He's just a creepy loser."

"How can anything be so fascinating and yet so heart wrenching? I mean, fascinating in that your body is so connected to your emotions as you describe."

She shrugged. "Because you haven't put me to sleep with the story of *your* sexual history ... Go for it. What's your number?"

"My number?"

"Yes," she answered. "My number is six which includes my first serious high school boyfriend, aka *the jock,* the violent loser I just mentioned, two guys I met in college, and 2 one-night stands that were kinda drunken and not terrible but not great. I almost had sex twice this summer but didn't get past petting or hand jobs or whatever you want to call it. You?"

"Uh, it's interesting that you mention casual flings," he

said, stretching his left shoulder then resting his elbow on the stone countertop, "because I definitely have had more of a problem with that than you. I'm not a six."

She beamed at him wantonly. "*Do tell...*"

He laughed, bursting into a smile, which was a relief after her depressing story. "Do you want to sit by the fire?" he asked, standing up.

She followed him over to the couch, and he reached across the floating fireplace mantle for a button that caused the tiny embers in the fireplace to burn brighter. She heard snapping like with a roaring fire and smelled wood burning. This was a mystery because it seemed like an automatic fireplace. Maybe it was an automatic starter but wood burning; there was definitely smoke and a chimney.

Will sat next to her, his legs touching hers as they turned to look at each other.

"I don't have any stories nearly as, uh, interesting as yours," he said, "but in the past five or six years, since college, I've probably ... had some sort of casual sex over a dozen times."

She widened her eyes for his benefit. "*Really...?*"

"Just back in June, at the beginning of the summer, I was telling myself now that I'm back in Derby, I have to stop fooling around. I'm not proud of my track record. I think it's a sign of being shallow."

"Just wanting to get laid? You mentioned that while we

were walking on the beach here. Remember?" She looked in the direction of the ocean, which had been only just visible in the low light when they had arrived earlier that evening. "I'm totally onto you. We both have that problem, but I'm the one who has to stop myself because I already have a reputation as a slut and you don't have any such reputation that I know of."

He shook his head solemnly. "You've had a lot of unfair crap thrust upon you. I am not going to be any part of that. I promise you. I disavow all of that Bennet girl nonsense."

She nodded, not wanting to ask how much he used to buy into it before he disavowed it. "And what about longer relationships?" she asked. "Tell me about those."

"I would say Anne, whom you met, would be a longer relationship, even if it was only a few months. We've known each other forever. The de Bourghs are family friends, which is why I'm so careful *not* to raise expectations with her ... or with Caroline Townsend. I avoid committing to anything with women because I don't want to feel *obligated* to keep things going. I wouldn't get to ten if I counted all the relationships I've had that lasted more than four months."

"Tell me about them! I'm not ashamed to be nosey. Which ones were exclusive?" she rushed out.

"Living in France, I ... oh Jesus, this is going to be telling. Confessional even. I'm probably giving away too much about myself, but I'll do it." He arched his neck, looking at the dull white wood ceiling.

She stared. Everything about him was erotically tinged now. The way his neck muscles moved. The five o'clock shadow on his face. The way his crewneck stretched across his torso. The casual slump of his arm against his side. She felt everything in her ovaries.

"Earlier this year I met a graduate student at the Sorbonne in Paris who was brilliant, well-traveled, and not ready for anything serious, but that only ended because I had to return home in June for business with my father. Also in France, I met a sort of earthy chef living in a small town near Colmar, who was remarkably serene despite her hectic lifestyle; it was impressive actually. There was also another Anne, a redhead; she and I were together for almost a year; she was always making plans with friends and hosting dinner parties that went on for hours; she could start a conversation with anybody she met, but she also had a husband whom she was separated from. My girlfriend from high school, who now lives in California, was my first long-term relationship. That lasted more than a year. I wish I had something more interesting to tell you, but there's not much else. There might be more than five relationships if you count dating in college but that's not worth getting into."

She wagged her head. "No, that all sounds interesting. Sounds great actually. I want to move to France."

He smiled, stretching his arm along the back of the sofa.

He reached for her hair and twisted strands of her shoulder-length brown locks around his fingers.

"You have to tell me all your stories of sexual dysfunction too," she whispered, leaning her head on the sofa cushion. "That'll make me feel better."

He chuckled. "Perhaps I should be happy to be boring."

"No, that's not good enough. I need more. What about how lame you were with your first girlfriend and how you disappointed her in bed? Come on! I don't believe you impressed your first. You were having sex with the same person for over a year while in high school? What is that? I don't believe that."

He laughed again, and shook his head self-deprecatingly, like his anecdotes were tedious despite her eagerness. "No, I did not have sex with a girl in high school for over a year. We were not serious until we'd been dating quite a while, but it wasn't a disaster. It was good. Very good. Maybe I'm square. I like missionary sex, and I don't really have any complaints about relationships in terms of sex. When we break up it's always a problem with my temperament, personality differences, my doing something insensitive like, uh, my high school girlfriend broke up with me when I left a party without her; she was there with her friends and I was tired of them and just left. Oh, and my worst fault is, according to women I've dated, being quote/unquote emotionally unavailable."

"That's some real shade, Darcy. Who said that?"

"I'm trying to be more considerate in my old age, but I haven't always been invested in dating as I ought. Maybe in the past two years I've been genuinely interested in trying to keep a girlfriend long-term. Before it wasn't something I cared a lot about. I wanted sexual relationships, but I felt lackluster about other parts of dating."

"That is amazing," she stumbled. "I can't even ... All the sex you've had was good? For her too?"

He put his hand to his forehead and rubbed it. "I believe so."

"This is bad. I'm going to call you unemotional soon just out of spite."

"Please don't," he smiled. "It triggers me."

She laughed although she knew he wasn't being totally facetious. "So you like vanilla sex. You're old fashioned?"

"I don't dislike anything; it's just that I have a strong preference for what I'm told is basic."

"Oh," she blushed. "Could that be ... romantic? A preference for a face-to-face embrace is romantic maybe?"

"Yes, I agree."

"Who's complaining?" she asked.

"I hear a lot that suggests to me my straight male contemporaries have far more complicated turn-ons."

"They watch porn and say they want to try anal sex," said Elizabeth dryly.

"Exactly."

"Yeah, that's pervasive." She was suddenly thoughtful, feeling almost shy. They were definitely going to end up in his bed.

"I thought a lot about what you said to me before about having problems with, uh, clamming up during sex." He twisted his lips. "And I did an internet search."

She jumped up onto her knees, making the dogs bark as she got in his face. "No way!"

He pulled her to him, as he halfway reclined on the sofa cushions. "I didn't need to, actually. It just said it's nervousness. You knew that already. And I bought sexual lubricant. I have it in my closet. Unopened."

She felt light-headed and bent into a contorted position like she was passing out on him. "That was probably a smart purchase because I definitely want to try something." She wiggled around on top of him, adjusting her position until he grabbed her butt over the thin fabric of her romper and held her against his hip. He was definitely turned on.

He touched her cheek with one hand and the back of her head with the other and pulled her lips to his, looking drunk.

The kiss was more freewheeling than before, all over the place as she felt his breath on her cheeks and nose and eyelids, the faintest trail of saliva around her mouth.

"Did you read anything else online?" she whispered

breathlessly, thinking of how she's been suffering through disappointing experiences while Darcy was off having fun with his French girls.

"Really obvious stuff," he answered. "Go slow. Don't rush."

"Like you normally rush with your French girlfriends. Get it over so you can fall asleep."

He shook his head no, confidently, not blushing as far as she could tell. "No, I don't actually."

Darcy spent a while trying to get the dogs settled by the fireplace before walking her down a short hallway to his bedroom with a giant glass wall facing the ocean, although the view was completely black now.

His bedroom had a huge platform bed with low side tables and a lot of empty floor space. No dressers. Just a wooden Shaker-style chair. Rich people interior design?

He pointed out to her the opened door to a dungeonous bathroom.

Her eyelids lowered, she walked into the bath and the lights went on automatically, illuminating grey marble floors, an oversized shower, an alcove with soaking tub sunk into the floor like a small indoor swimming pool, and a separate toilet room with a bidet and bronze fixtures.

She washed up at the trough-like sink with waterfall

faucet, not wanting to spend time staring at herself in the mirror for fear it would make her self-conscious.

As she walked back out, she noticed the master closet didn't have a door, just a panel wall that acted like a screen. It was one of those huge walk-in deals you see on TV. She could see Darcy standing by a tufted bench with tons of walking space all around him. Clothing hanging along an entire wall in the back. Tall, dark cabinets next to him.

It looked like he'd taken off his shoes, and his jeans were sagging so maybe he removed his belt. As she watched, he took something small out of a chest of drawers set up in the middle of the room.

She went to the bed and sat down, feeling the silkiness of the comforter made of some fancy sateen cotton.

She kicked off her sandals, and her feet sunk into a black lambskin rug.

He walked out of the closet and came toward her with something in his hand.

She turned and flung herself onto the bed, scooting over until her head was on the far-side pillow.

After setting down what he was holding on the nightstand with a tap and a thud, he lay down parallel to her, his arm reaching across her body.

His hand touched her cheek.

She reached for him, combing her fingers through his hair

and kissing him like it was just a common everyday activity.

He leaned farther over her, hovering, face to face, not rushing to peck at her, just slowly moving his lips against hers.

She tilted her head, joining her lips to his at different angles, feeling how overly endowed he was compared to her tiny insignificant lips.

"Are you nervous?" he asked.

"Is that a joke? Yes, I'm nervous. Aren't you?"

"Usually around you, yes, but not now." He relaxed against her side, their bodies touching from head to feet although she was on her back while he was lying on his side.

Bending his knee, his bare foot prodded her ankle with its boney joints.

His hand found the bare skin on her neck, and he traced the top of her outfit with a feathery touch, finding all her exposed skin with a deliberate slowness that didn't stop or limp along or get in a rut by repeatedly touching one place.

"Do you want to undress?" he asked.

"*You* get naked. I have flaws," she said, feeling a touch of fear in the pit of her stomach.

He jerked up at her words, grabbing her under the arms, pressing his mouth to her right ear. "Stop it," he huffed.

"Great, glad to see it's so easy to summon bossy-ass Will Darcy when needed."

He chuckled like he didn't have a care in the world.

Unforced, unfeigned laughter that was better than the opening chords of an opera.

Sitting up, he pulled off his shirt tossing it on the floor like he wasn't an anal retentive neat freak as the state of his home suggested.

She looked at his pampered skin, trying to find a blemish.

He examined the top of her outfit, searching for fasteners and things holding it in place like that night at Pemberley when he took her dress off.

Working at a tie on her shoulder, he got stuck trying to undo a knot and picked at it. "The shoulder ties are looped together?"

She nodded, reaching to help him as she stared at his upper chest, which was smooth and defined unlike the ripples of his abs. He was nothing like a pumped-up gym goer but his muscles moving under his skin were defined and Grecian.

He slid her top over to one side, out of the way, so he could access her bra. After running his hand over its seams and lace, he spotted the closure in front and pulled it open.

She stretched out tall so her stomach was not sticking out and finished pulling down the ties of her romper.

He carefully pushed aside the entire cup of her push up bra and examined the marks left by its underwire, lightly caressing her as her legs quivered.

She thought of how there was nothing he didn't see; her

body was fully lit by the lamp on the table just next to them.

He didn't meet her eyes more than an instant before looking back at her chest, drawing circles, nudging her up and to the side, kneading her.

She closed her eyes, giving into it fully, hoping she wouldn't inadvertently gasp.

Tilting back her head, she felt her neck cooled by air from a vent above, and he licked the skin around her nipple, making her chest heave and her vocal cords hum a low note.

She wanted his mouth on hers but he was all about sucking on her, mouthfuls of her breast, then her areole until she was aching for him inside her like an enormous slut — her hips didn't exactly gyrate but hopped a bit with adrenaline.

When he pinched her nipple with his finger and teeth she was about to tell him to stop when she realized her pelvic muscles were spasming like an orgasm.

There was no way he was going to move quickly to intercourse as her racing thoughts wanted. She needed to communicate. "I don't think I'm supposed to come yet."

He finally looked up.

"Just do something limply and half assed, okay?" she said.

He smiled then got up and unbuttoned his pants.

As he started to take off his boxers, she looked down at her half-removed romper and decided to pull it off the rest of the way, removing the shorts.

The happy-looking reddish skin on her chest made her think of all the blushing she did around him. But her sore nipples longed for him to suck on them again, which was crazy considering how she wanted him to stop a minute ago.

Naked, he climbed back on the bed beside her.

All she was wearing was low rise underwear. She lay back waiting for him to take over again.

He propped his hands on either side of her head, hovering over her, most of his body above her but not touching her. He leaned in and kissed her.

She raised herself to meet his mouth, opening to him, and feeling his tongue against her teeth, then her lips.

She was so anxious. She wanted to get this over with quick, but she told herself to chill as he moved in and out of her mouth, causing little zaps of pleasure.

Her hips shifted in an automatic reaction, and he responded to this immediately, lowering himself onto her with full body contact except for his left leg on the bed which he used to prevent himself from putting his full weight on her.

She felt everything, his erection, his warm smooth skin everywhere and the stubble on his face, the only place he shaved.

It was far more relaxing to focus on his prickly facial hair than anything else, but feeling his penis against her thigh was such a distraction.

His body smelled fresh and soapy and she breathed it in.

As he kissed the hair line by her ear, she thought of the discomfort she'd experienced in the past.

He pulled back a little and rested on his side next to her.

She bit her lip as bad memories flooded over her, and she tensed up.

Still skin to skin all the way down, his hands became so gentle, just fingertips as he stared at her face and caressed the side of her neck and shoulder.

She tried to give him a what-are-you-looking-at look, but it was probably just silly.

She half lowered her eyelids, practicing square breathing.

He reached for the nightstand to unwrap the lubricant and open a box of condoms.

How is that going to slide into me pleasurably? she pondered as she openly looked down at him. In general, she really wasn't intimidated by male anatomy, but when it was on the cusp of invading her, she got attentive to details and specifics.

He flipped open the bottle of clear liquid and squeezed some onto his pointer and middle fingers.

"This is going to take some will power," she whispered into his neck, feeling her muscles clenching.

"I'm almost positive I googled something about this once," he said, his face saying he was making a joke. Of course all the women he'd met before had enjoyed being fingered.

The skin inside her vagina could only tolerate so much before she was done for the day, like a paper snowflake that broke apart when touched too much. "I think I might want to just skip straight ahead to that," she said, trying to mirror his smile as she motioned toward the apex of his legs. "No fingers."

"How about both?"

She panicked. This was going to hurt. Did he genuinely understand?

He sat up and reached over to pull down her underwear with his left hand and right thumb.

"I'm not sure what makes you think I'm going to like that," she motioned at his lubed up fingers, "but I have to be honest, I'm probably going to end up hitting you."

Her vulva was so exposed and defenseless as she gazed down at herself.

"Why don't you grab me and if I hurt you, you can inflict the same amount of pain on me?"

"Oh, really, with fingernails too?" she asked.

"I'm willing to risk it."

"I gotta say, I'm feeling rather hungry again... and thirsty too."

He just smiled in her face, unconcerned by her apprehension.

He reached between her legs and she felt a little petting with his ring finger and pinky which felt nice. She arched her back.

She had short pubic hair, and he was touching it then moving onto her bare inner thigh, her lower belly and then back again.

There was nothing possible to object to in it, just a little ticklishness so she opened her legs, feeling only a little slutty as she got the creases and depths of her inner thigh caressed.

Then one slimy finger ran along the middle of her labia where she was so sensitive and gun shy, parting her skin.

His knuckles nudged her thighs farther open and then he returned with slick fingers tracing the curves and layers followed by an indirect touch on her clitoris.

All the while his face was tucked in by her neck looking down at her body.

She tried not to think of his probably painful erection.

She was doing nothing for him, not offering any sort of release, but instead of trying to start something she found herself meditating, focusing on his light touch between her legs, trusting his gentleness to continue.

He leaned over to kiss her mouth and she told herself not to overreact, just be passive, and he did a slow tongue thing that went on and on while his hand was now wet from her body, not just the lubricant.

She'd felt wet since at the mini golf course but now he was in it. Fingering her maybe an inch while his penis was prodding her thigh nearby.

She had to save the rest of her tolerance for intercourse. She should say something.

But before she opened her mouth, he climbed over her and opened her legs, resting his penis along her labia.

"Are you on anything?" he asked.

"No, nothing," she breathed, realizing she was short of breath, her chest rising and straining.

His right hand ran along her body, cradling her breast for a moment, then running a finger up to her chin. She smelled herself on him.

He was not rushed at all, his breathing steady, but she felt like she was hyperventilating.

Reflexively, she thrust her hips upward against his erection, and his penis throbbed against her opening. Due to his locked arms, he did not crush her chest or abdomen.

He got up on his knees and grabbed the condom he brought out earlier and opened the packet.

She wondered if he was ready for her reaction to his penis trying to push inside her. If *she* was ready for her reaction.

He put on the condom and then squeezed out more lubricant. Again he brushed his fingers against her inner labia and then he moved his hand to apply the slippery lubricant to himself.

It might have been a good time to start looking at his

attractive face and body, but she saw nothing as he sealed his lips against hers and reached under her knee, lifting her leg.

She brought her other leg up as well, reckless about how wide open she was to him.

He didn't really lower himself onto her so much as wrap his arms around her. One arm slid under her lower back and pulled her up to him. His other arm reached behind her neck, his forearm bracing his body against the firm mattress.

His left hand slid from her back to her butt where he squeezed her and nudged her hips to a sharper angle.

She got lost with his maneuverings as his mouth was sucking her lips until they stung, then he bit her.

She nipped him right back, and he pushed into her about an inch, holding her in place with both his arms, one on her butt and one by her shoulder.

She felt herself spasm and relax a bit, then her muscles clamped on him uncomfortably. "Don't move," she warned.

"I can so feel it, exactly as you described," he smiled, breathing into her mouth a whiff of wine mixed with a hint of lip balm.

Although she was not hurting, she worried about him trying to move in and out of her.

His penis felt too big and his grip on her so tight. He had her in a body lock. Her legs were opened wide like he could thrust into her and she'd be in agony if he went at it full force.

"Please don't move," she repeated, feeling her eyes tear up. She was trying to stop herself from yelling at him to loosen his grip or just completely fucking let go of her.

She had her red line ready to enforce if he crossed it.

"Push against me," he said.

"No thanks," she said, sniffling.

"Just a tiny bit."

"I meant what I said," she insisted. "You can't move."

"I won't move. I promise," he replied.

"Let me close my legs a little," she said, pushing at his chest which immediately gave way to her touch.

"You can trust me. I won't move." His words were great but he was panting like he was going to nail her to the bed any moment.

She leaned her head back so his mouth was against her throat and felt the sharpness of his teeth on her skin. She hated her body for spastically wanting to throw him off of her.

She tried squeezing her legs around him, but for her bravery she got a nice jab, not painful enough to make her want to stop but the discomfort and fullness were as anticipated.

She whispered, "Don't do an inch by inch thing, just go in as much as you want and then totally stop moving. Don't pull out."

Before she finished the last word, he seamlessly pressed into her, taking her breath away but the stinging friction was definitely helped by the slippery lubricant.

He stopped and did not pull out of her. Just dove in and waited.

Her insides already felt scorched and tender. There was going to be so much pain if he went at it.

"Just go ahead," she moaned. "I can't relax but I certainly would be even more unhappy to back out now."

"I'm fine with not moving," he said, stroking her hair with one hand and her lower back with the other. "Are you okay?"

"For now, yes." He was wrapped around her like a claw game but it wasn't actually bad; she felt amazingly secure. Just dandy. However if he pulled out of her and plunged back in repeatedly, which guys were apt to do, she'd be yelping.

He kissed her neck, resting on her pelvis, so full inside her.

"I'm about to tell you to just hurt me," she murmured.

"I doubt that will work but you could try me," he answered, seeming very focused on nibbling her shoulder bone.

She breathed deep. "No, I don't think I will. Not yet."

He was tasting her skin and ignoring his desire to thrust; she was sure of it.

She was hating life.

"When you say just hurt you, you mean ... move?" he asked calmly.

"Yes, just have sex like normal non-defective people."

He laughed. "You don't feel defective. You feel warm and tight. The skin on your neck however, does feel a bit cold and frightened."

"If I told you to just get it over with, would you?" she asked.

"Again, probably not," he said.

"You're not 100% certain."

"I can't be unless you actually try me."

"I hate myself. I'm pathetic."

"No," he whispered. "I'd say you're flexible and noisy."

"Stop making excuses for me."

He squeezed her butt, leaning into her a bit.

As if she needed more penetration. Wasn't he already fully inside her?

She pushed him back, but when she stopped pushing, he slid into her again, without asking.

She frowned at him, their eyes locked.

It felt almost confrontational. He was like a gun, cocked and ready to shoot, and she was taunting him.

He ran his long, no longer sticky fingers along her scalp as his penis adjusted its angle a bit.

He paused to stretch his shoulders, then rocked against her as she arched her back to accommodate him.

"What are you doing?" she smiled at him, so close his face was an unfocused blur of guilty grinning. "Didn't I make it clear this is going to be your first lousy sexual experience? Now get on board."

"How about moving just a little bit?" he said softly, a bit of a laugh in his voice and his dick buried deep inside her.

She was about to shake her head no, exasperated with her body. Instead, she reached for him, shifted her hips back and then pushed forward slightly.

He followed her lead and repeated this short motion once, twice and again until she was breathing raggedly, her legs twitching.

He pushed up onto his hands, pulling halfway out of her and immediately dove back in all the way.

She yelped at the scratchy pain and gave him her most pathetic look but decided not to say stop.

He maintained eye contact and did the halfway out and in thing three more times until she let out the longest angriest moan. Not exactly screaming but loud.

Had she screamed before? He said she was noisy. No, she only hummed loudly before. Please, please.

"Is that the best you got?" she asked sadistically, ready for a lot of pain.

He did not smile or respond with thrusts, just studied her in a way that somehow made her feel closer to him than she'd ever felt before.

He was trying to gauge her reactions; with so much focus,

he was trying to determine what to do to make this work for her. He was not even factoring in his own pleasure. He was definitely not enjoying this much so far.

She reached for his cheeks and kissed him on his lips and eyelids, forcing him to close them.

He took the opportunity to start a sort of rhythm for the first time. Sounding like he was whistling with clenched teeth, his movement stopped and started like there was a hindrance, something causing a hitch.

She gritted her teeth, telling herself it wasn't so bad. No worse than a sunburn. But who wanted sex to be an irritation?

With a loud inhale, he pulled back and froze, checking her face, which she was sure wasn't totally encouraging.

Lowering his lips to her mouth, he opened her with his tongue and, with a jerk, thrust his hips against her, not holding back, plunging in again and again. She squealed into his mouth, shocked, but at the same time excruciatingly turned on by his show of courage. Such a butch move after the way she'd been acting.

He gave it to her, screwing her, not letting up or slowing down, his arm muscles straining, so tightly wound as she held onto him. Her vagina contracted around him as he worked her muscles like he might massage the tightness out of them, probably savoring some intense squeezing.

"Do you like it?" she huffed, breathing out with every one

of his successive thrusts, her insides so overstimulated like they'd already been fucked long and hard.

His mouth moved to her ear. "So much. You?" he answered breathily.

Her pelvic muscles twitched and she nodded, "yes," looking into his eyes like they were having some great meeting of the minds as he thrust against her pelvis and thigh, pressing her into his bed.

As he rolled his body against her, she could feel him everywhere. The hair on his chest scratched her nipples, his toenails nicked her ankle, and his knees felt as hard as a rock. She felt his rough shaved face on her upper chest when he tucked his head for a moment of inertia. He didn't fuck with a slow languid groove like his sedate drawl.

A buildup took hold of her as her muscles relented, lessening their grip on his dick.

"Wait," she gasped. She was finally opening up to him and wanted him to feel the difference. "Wait a sec."

But it didn't need to be said. He reacted to her loosening with deep, even thrusts that went all the way in and out, making her gasp like a wanton whore.

She wasn't exactly sure how she was communicating what she needed, but he continued with long strokes running against her clitoris followed by contrasting shallow ones.

He was in control. She was losing control as her arms and

legs moved around him frenziedly, adjusting her hips constantly to get pleasure from him. She traced the muscles on his back and arms, so sexy as they flexed. She bounced on the bed, her breasts jiggling.

He held her at an angle and continued giving her evenly-paced firm strokes again and again in the exact same location and with the exact same force.

She started coming, her eyes watering as her mouth opened against his neck, tasting salty skin, and she felt clenching and relaxing of the same torturous muscles that had tried to slow him to a halt for what felt like an eternity.

Peaks of pleasure culminated in her fully clamming up again. "Don't pull out! Don't move!" She had him and wasn't letting go.

He collapsed on top of her, still hard and fully inside her as she felt him ejaculate in three gushes.

She went lifeless and felt every single muscle in her body unclenching in a way she wasn't sure she'd ever felt before. A perfect state of jellyness.

Her legs fell open as if she were ready to be fucked again, and in truth she wanted another orgasm, which she could not possibly survive because her skin was raw from being stroked by him in a condom for almost half an hour.

When he rolled over onto the bed beside her, she reached between her legs, her fingers prodding her own skin, but she was not in the condition she thought she was. She sat up and saw no redness or marks.

An hour later they were in his shower with multiple shower heads coming from different directions and enough room for six people.

She felt no pain or stinging after effects. All lightness and bliss.

They laughed as they washed each other, and he got to see how she was actually very attracted to him despite her body's earlier reluctance as she went down on him while water sprayed her head to toe.

"I saved you a trip to that hotel you like," she rasped, flicking him with her tongue.

He couldn't stop smiling. Who was this guy?

#

The next morning Elizabeth woke to a black and white snout in her face. The dog tried to lick her but she weaved out of the way, falling out of bed.

She found an unopened box of muesli in the kitchen cabinet and poured two bowls.

Out the window by the fireplace was a view of Pemberley Beach in the distance and Pemberley House off to the right. She just stared for a while.

Later, on the couch with Will, she was ready to pliantly

give him another blow job if he asked her. The gentlest sex kitten in the world if he rubbed her the right way. But, no, she knew they were going to end up in his bed after the walk on the beach he promised. She was going to be learning to love his penis inside her vagina, not her mouth. Old fashioned lovemaking with modern athleticism was his decided preference and aptitude, and she was going to be a convert for him.

"I can't take condoms," he mumbled, his mouth inches from her ear. "They're horrible for your sensitive skin. What about an IUD?"

"Oh, sure," she said, pulling down a borrowed white tee to cover her underpants. "That's like a thousand bucks, right? No problem."

Derby Public Schools did not have a health insurance plan that covered birth control because it didn't want to promote slutty behavior in its female employees. Unslutty behavior like giving birth and using Viagra was covered.

"If we didn't have to use condoms, it would be so different in terms of the friction that you're very sensitive to."

"Brilliant insight, Darcy," she agreed, only somewhat facetiously. "I wish I had thought of it."

"If you don't start calling me Will, I'm going to hold you upside down by your ankles and--"

"Okay, okay," she laughed, cutting him off. "I don't want to hear what you'll do to me."

He wrapped his arms around her waist, pulling her tightly against him. "You once told me I could never pay for anything for you, but you need to compromise on that." He looked like a rumpled god, his hair messy and his sunken cheeks darkened with stubble. "For the most part, I understand and I totally respect your attitude and don't want to infringe on your principled decisions, but there have to be a few exceptions." He sounded like an arrogant shit but an arrogant shit she wanted to have sex with again.

"Uh, I don't know; we'll see," she said noncommittally.

"Elizabeth, you have to come around on some of these things because, believe me, there are items I cannot compromise on."

She felt her pulse quicken. "What in the world does that mean?"

"My home, my family, my land. It's not negotiable. I can travel and visit other places, but I could never live anywhere other than Pemberley. I have my grandfather's and great grandfather's legacy that I must live up to."

"As opposed to people like me who have no family and no heritage of any importance?" she asked sarcastically.

"You are the most talented and beautiful young professional in this town with the most sparkling personality to boot. I want to be associated with you in everything you do, in all your dealings with people, including your students and your family. But I have certain things I need from you and they're non-negotiable."

"Non-negotiable?" She was so shocked by his tone she didn't feel annoyance.

"It means we have to talk about this, and you have to be open minded." His full lips taunted her as he spoke, bragging of how much time he'd spent kissing her last night. Their plumpness reminding her of how much effort he put into helping her ease her way into sex and enjoy it.

No. She wanted him but this was too much. She sat up, got in his face. "Wait, stop right there. What, according to you, is non-negotiable? Because that sounds like total bullshit."

"Some people have religion or something else they can't compromise on. Maybe the number of kids they want or their political affiliation. I'm negotiable on all that. But if you were with me long term, you need to know now what you'd be up against in terms of my pride."

"Uh," she was speechless.

"I don't want you to change anything about yourself. Not your clothes or the way every other word out of your mouth is a synonym for slut. I never want you to feel like you need to be transformed in any way. But I care about you being safe and well cared for and I can't compromise on that. You must give me your dangerous ex's name and address. Also, carrying instruments on a bike is going to be a problem right away."

"Well, I'll probably get a car eventually, but that's not your concern, Will."

"Uh, the thing is I can't let that slide." He exhaled loudly. "You have to borrow a safe vehicle from me for now."

"You're out of your mind."

"You have to compromise on issues of safety, Elizabeth."

"How about I compromise on my safe word ... Instead of 'Go fuck yourself,' I'll choose 'Fuck you'?"

She got a stiff chuckle out of him which she relished.

"Elizabeth. Please. Can you agree to what I've asked so far?" he begged.

"I don't know. I'm feeling confused now."

"I have access to things, easy access to things, like a boring, safe car and you can benefit from this without any inconvenience to anyone," he said.

"What else is there? I want to hear your entire list of non-negotiables. Then I'm going to write one of my own that's twice as long."

"There is something else. One of the most important things. I would never, under any circumstances, ever be willing to marry you ..."

Her heart stopped beating, leaving a painful dullness in her chest.

"...Unless you took my name," he added.

Her heart started pounding again at a livable pace.

"If we stay together, you would have to come to grips with the idea of being 'Elizabeth Darcy.' I know it would be difficult for you in some ways, but I'm not willing to compromise on continuing my family name."

She couldn't speak or even open her mouth. She felt tears at the corner of her eye and hid her face against the side of his chest, trying for composure.

He patted her, waiting quietly, his breathing deep and even.

When she finally spoke, it was without anger. "When you dump me, or uh when we break up, all I'll have is what I've earned for myself, my independence, and my infamous name. You want me to say I'll give these up?"

"Elizabeth, you are way too powerful to be dependent on anyone. You don't *need* anyone. Nothing controls you."

"Not a single thing you just said is true," she said softly.

He shook his head, taking this as a joke. "I'm predicting the opposite of a breakup. I'm planning for what I want, which is this woman who calls my yacht a little boat and has some very intimate insecurities and an unflinching sense of humor. I'm telling you where I stand because I'm determined to make this work. The way we are together is amazing. It's what I want. I didn't always realize this, but I now know you are what I want."

"Oh my god," she sniffled with a half-smile. "But ... your parents might not think much of me."

"It won't be easy, but they'll have to come around and treat you well because I won't give in. It's not something *you* have to worry about. I'm responsible for dealing with them. And I've already factored their reaction to you into everything I've said."

"Yeah, well, my mother is just wild about your arrogant ass," she said with a smirk.

"I think she'll like me better after I give you a car."

She punched his upper arm, feeling a knot in her stomach and laughing at the truth of his words. "Oh my god, this is going to be so much drama. You and me, I mean."

The End

Made in United States
North Haven, CT
14 October 2024

58897603R00215